AMANTE

THE DOMINANT LOVE DUET BOOK 2

EVELYN MONTGOMERY

INTRODUCTION

This book contains passages in Italian. For quick reference, the translation has been added in italics either before and/or after the Italian phrase.

This book also includes dark subject matter, violence, language and light BDSM. Reader discretion is advised.

"Cheeks blushed & pussy wet."
-Leonardo Moretti

To the Leonardo's of the world
& all the dark romance lovers
who can't stop dreaming about them.

LEONARDO

6 MONTHS LATER

"I told you, Kid," I hear Nitti hiss at the new guy, a soldier not much older than I was when I joined the family. "You answer to Leonardo now. *Capire?* He's the new *capo di tutti capi.* There are no other bosses above him. Remember that!"

The prick slightly glares in my direction before heading back out the door he came through a few minutes before and I can't help but let out a laugh. He has a lot to learn, but good thing he has a patient teacher. I've knocked bigger attitudes off of lesser men and enjoyed fucking doing it. Matteo comes to mind, Big Jim too, and I'm taken back to a time when everything I thought I knew in life changed in an instant.

I lean back in my seat at my desk in the office of my new larger-than-life house and sigh. I've won and lost more than I thought I ever would since then, and if you would have told me what I was going up against, I may have never agreed to take on the job I did. Especially when I consider all that was at stake, and all that I lost.

Nitti walks to the bar across the room and pours both me and him two fingers of one of my finest scotches. I watch in silence, the memories of those days still playing with my mind like they have every day since Luigi finally met his demise. I know they will continue to for the rest of my life. I'll always be haunted. He took something from me I can never get back, and for that, even death was too great a reward for him.

I can't say I know what I did was right. But I did what I had to, and will continue to, despite what I thought before and regardless of if others agreed; in hindsight, all that we found out after the Lombardi Family was taken down I wasn't wrong about a single thing - except one. A fate I will never escape, not even in my grave. But, it paved the way for a new heir to take his rightful place.

Me.

Leonardo Moretti.

I'd rather rot in hell before taking my father's name. Lombardi dies with him and his rotten son Angelo. I don't even want to so much as hear the name ever again, a fact many that surround me know well.

The only thing I wasn't expecting when all was said and done was Nitti stepping down soon after and giving me his blessing for taking full control of our operation. Something that hasn't been done since Sofia's father ruled, Lorenzo De Luca, and something I wasn't expecting - not ever.

"That new guy is going to give you two a run for your money, I guarantee that," Sofia says, walking into the room as if she knew I was thinking about her, her father, *the family*, and what it all means to me now. With our fronts finally united, my family and the Nittis, I feel the power I always knew was my own and know without a doubt, with the men I have backing me, nothing can harm those I love most now.

Nitti makes his way across the room and hands me my drink. "Nothing our boy here, *Amico*, can't handle," he says, as I take my glass and cheers him. I give him a challenging look for calling me by the nickname I hate before raising my eyebrows in agreement, smiling, and taking a sip of the 20-year-old scotch.

A knock sounds at the door and instinctively we all turn to look. "Boss," the new kid says. "It's time."

Raising my glass, I take down the contents in one gulp and set the empty tumbler on a nearby table. Not sure if I am ready to face what I am about to, a takeover that still threatens to kill every last one of my nerves, I know only one thing matters in the outcome - finally getting what I fucking deserve and have wanted my whole damn life. I button my suit's jacket as I exit the room and quickly make my way towards the back of the house. Sunlight shines in from outside and I take a moment to stop and look in a passing mirror to make sure I "look the part."

"Don't worry," Nitti says, as he strides up beside me. "The only way out of this, is walking straight through," he chuckles, and I feel myself roll my eyes and my stomach begin to get sick with anxiety. "One way or another, it all stops now. Time to end something that never should have started in the first place. Agreed?"

I give him a tight nod in the mirror as he walks away before I look back into my own eyes. Nervous. Sweating. Slightly fucking more afraid than I have ever been before, I turn to the doors leading outside and see Nitti and Sofia standing beside them.

"You ready, Leo?" Nitti asks, making me slightly irritated and I don't give a shit if he does notice. I throw my shoulders back and pull down on my suit jacket, making myself look confident when I am anything but. Not taking my silence as an answer, Nitti continues. "Just by the looks of you, something tells me you're about to take on the biggest fucking job you've ever agreed to. I want to know your head is in the game." I look past him, through the glass doors, to the garden in back, and feel the tension leave as something I needed to see suddenly comes into view. "If you do this," Nitti says in a low stern voice. "There can be no turning back. There can be no doubt. You are all in. *Siamo chiari?*"

Yes, *we're clear!* In fact, it's finally all clear, more than it ever has been in my whole damn life, and I don't waste a minute longer as I confess the only truth I have ever known to be real.

"I made a promise to a girl a long time ago," I insist, keeping my eyes trained on the object outside as Nitti and Sofia reach out and grab a door handle each. "I don't break my promises, Nitti. The only oath that will ever matter most in my life, I gave to your daughter when we were kids."

The doors open and my breath catches as I look out into the distance, tears burn the back of my eyes as I stare out across the yard and all I needed, all I've ever wanted, finally comes into perfect view.

"I was 'all in' the moment I laid eyes on her," I whisper, as she turns and her white dress catches the light as I watch my bride, my life, my whole fucking world smile back at me. Maria Nitti.

I take a step outside and watch as her own eyes well up in tears. She walks toward me and I know she was right. Keeping her with me, near me, will always ensure her safety. The only mistake I ever made was letting Luigi in between us when he almost took her life a few months back. A mistake that won't happen again as soon as I make her my wife, unite our families, and finally put an end to the feud that has gone on way too long.

"I love your daughter," I whisper. "And I'll die doing what I *have to do*, to protect her, always."

PROLOGUE
LEONARDO

24 HOURS LATER

I KEEL OVER in pain and spit blood out at his shoe. My head throbs. My wrists burn from the zip ties. My side stings from the piercing cut inflicted by one of the men to my right. But my heart bleeds, fucking aches as his next words echo through my ears.

"We'll kill her anyway, Amico, with or without your help. So tell me, where is Maria Nitti and maybe we'll find mercy and end your life quickly."

I look up and glare at the man in front of me. The man who not only stole what was supposed to be the best day of my life, but murdered my soon-to-be family, stopped me from claiming my bride, and now thinks I'll just hand her over, to what? Spare myself a little pain?

I died today. I'll die again every damn day until I can be sure that she's safe. That she'll always be safe from the monsters that seek vengeance in this dark life. The man before me stares down into my eyes impatiently, but all his endless promises, his threats, they're nothing compared to the hell I'm already forced to live.

"You'd have a better chance at trying to suck my dick than getting any information out of me, Alfonso Capone," I sneer, both of us knowing I'd slice him wide open if he or any other man ever fucking tried. "I'm all that's standing in between you and the control you want, take my fucking life, not hers, and maybe I won't have my men kill you after."

He smiles as he takes a step back and the two men that are holding me hostage tighten their grip on my biceps. He cocks his head to the side, and studies me for moments that seem to drag into endless agonizing minutes. Finally, he starts to laugh, an evil threatening laugh that does only one thing, make me want to rip his cold heart out with my bare fucking hands.

"Control?" he chuckles to himself as he takes another step backward. "Oh Leonardo, you have it all wrong."

He nods to his men and they pull me to standing, pushing me backward until my legs hit a chair in the center of the room and I'm forced to sit down.

"I already have all the control I fucking want."

He looks to the right with a stern glare and snaps his fingers. It takes a second, but a man appears out of the darkness and hands him some pliers. My nostrils flare as I watch him take a step closer, but that's all the reaction he'll get out of me.

I've been tortured before, by bigger men and in more

intimidating ways. Whatever he and his henchmen bring to the table is child's play compared to what I've endured. Let them bring their worst.

The only difference this time is, I've never had a bigger secret to keep than I do now.

Where Maria is.

That's a secret I know I will die before I ever tell any man. And one he's never getting out of me for a multitude of reasons.

"Nitti is dead," Alfonso whispers as he takes a step closer. "Luigi, too."

"I thought you didn't care about being the boss? Didn't care about the family. The job. What makes you suddenly so interested now," I grit out between clenched teeth as I watch the pliers in his hand glimmer in the light as he rotates them slowly between each of his palms. "You stepped down. Years ago. Why..."

"Is that what they told you?" he asks suddenly. "Is that what everyone thinks? I was forced to step down, Leonardo. I could never compete with Vincent. With Luigi. But now with them out of the picture, and a new *capo di tutti capi* who doesn't belong, didn't earn the right to the seat he's trying to take, suddenly it came to me. This is the perfect time to take my rightful place."

My eyes fill with anger, hatred, a venomous rage as he takes a quick step to my side and nods at his men. Vengeance fuels me for what he's done, what he's about to do, and I know I will get it. My revenge. Either in this life or in the damn grave. Alfonso Capone won't fucking stop me.

His men grab one of my hands and hold it still. I don't even fight them. I let them pull my wrist out to the side and then watch, eagerly awaiting what comes next so Alfonso knows I'm not fucking around. One of the bastards rolls up my sleeve as his cock-sucking friend next to me tightens his grip on my other arm. But my eyes stay locked on Capones. In the stillness before the suffering he intends to inflict, a sick grin spreads across my face. For a brief moment, I catch a glimpse of the doubt in his eyes. The fear that even if he gets rid of me he'll never rule the empire that he's trying so hard to steal.

I won't talk.

Never.

And there is nothing he can do to make me.

Eventually, Alfonso concedes. But not for my benefit. The bastard just doesn't even have the balls to do it himself. He hands the set of pliers to one of his men and my eyes widen slightly, but never leave his, as the man to my right uses the pliers to pull back my thumbnail slowly before ripping it off in one clean move.

I feel the searing pain. I can notice my finger bleeding by the warm liquid I feel running down the back of my wrist, but I don't fucking move. With my teeth clenched tight, I keep my eyes trained ahead, on Alfonso, so he fully understands who he's fucking dealing with.

"Go to fucking hell!" I hiss out before he gives his man the signal again and he rips another nail from my hand. I close my eyes, the pain phasing me just for a moment before I open them again and swallow down the bile that rises in my throat.

"If you refuse, if you don't tell us what we need to know, we'll find great joy in putting you in a very personal kind of hell you'd wish *would* end you, Leonardo. So it's best you talk now, before we have to keep each other here any longer."

He starts to walk away and I wince slightly from the pain but mask it well as he suddenly turns my way once he's crossed the room and I watch as the bastard smiles.

"I'm eager to take my place as head of this empire," he seethes. "And I'm sure you are just as eager to meet your Maria, in death inevitably, so why don't we save ourselves from all this bullshit and you tell us what you know."

I couldn't, even if I wanted to, and what's more, I never would.

Collin Fitzgerald and Giovanni, Luigi's old consigliere and Maria's mother's most trusted ally, took her once the shooting started. They followed my instructions to keep her hidden and not to answer to anyone, not even myself until they got word the coast was absolutely clear. Where she's being held, what kind of condition she's in, I don't fucking know, and it's killing me. Almost more than sitting here having to deal with these bastards when I know it's just a matter of time before my men get me out of here.

That is if the men in front of me don't get bored with the back and forth and kill me first.

Or worse, kill the men I have coming for me.

I cock my head to the side, my right hand beginning to shake from the pain, and glare at Alfonso. "I was raised in hell, brought up in darkness. There is nothing you can do that could make me tell you what you want to know. I will survive, Alfonso. And when I do, you better pray to whatever devil you pray to that I never find you, or your men, because I won't fucking kill you."

He glares at me. So much is being said without even uttering a word. Threats hang between us, but this is more than that. My warning is a fucking promise I don't intend to break.

"No," my whisper comes out with a heated breath through clenched teeth. "I'll make you pay. One body part at a time. Until you're a fucking shell of what you once were. And even then, not until you are just as useless to the rest of the world as you've always been to the mob."

He approaches quickly, reaching into his pocket and pulling a knife out from hiding. Flicking it open, he glares in my eyes as he stands over me so damn close I can feel his breath feather against my skin.

"Useless?" he hisses. "You want to know who's useless? Who will always be useless? A bastard son who has to ride on his bitches coattails to get anywhere in this life." His words cut deep, but not deep enough as I square off against him. "You think Maria will have any use for you once you're married? Once she fully realizes the power her family's name has? You're fooling yourself if you ever thought she'd actually let you rule once she knows just who and what she comes from."

I swallow hard because fuck if what he just said doesn't shake me a little. She is so much more powerful than me. Always has been. She proves it every day by being the one weakness that I'll always have. Always surrender to.

"The only thing Maria will do after you follow through on what you're threatening, Alfonso, is hiring a hit on you," I spit back in his face. "You're a dead man, regardless of if I live or die. So stop acting like you already rule the fucking world and go back to stepping down out of a life you aren't fit to run in the first place."

With a flick of his wrist, his knife slices through my thigh, and I muffle a scream as he tears it down vertically to my knee cap. Closing my eyes, I try to focus on her face. Her smile. Our love. I take a deep breath, pulling every bit I can from the memory before opening my eyes once again and staring straight into Alfonso's dark soul.

Pulling the knife from my leg, he leans in and says, "With you held captive and Maria forced to live in the shadows, I do rule the fucking world, Leonardo. Maybe you should get on your knees and suck my dick, Amico. Show some damn respect."

He takes a step back and I cringe from the pain, both in my thigh and my hand at my side. Thinking of Maria, of what we started, what we never got the chance to finish, I pull my shoulders back, force myself to look him in the eye, and harshly state, "I made a promise to a girl a long time ago," he rolls his eyes growing annoyed and motions to his man at my side who suddenly throws him a gun.

"And I'll die doing what I have to do."

He canisters a bullet. Then another. They click into place as the finality of my fate settles in my soul. I suck in a sharp breath as I watch him take aim.

"Protect her always," my voice shakes, "And never. Fucking. Stop."

I hear the click of the trigger seconds before the shot rings through my ears. I wait for the pain as I force my eyes shut and memories flash before them. Maria, myself, our child, the life we both wanted. Heartache settles in just as a sharp burning ache pierces my chest and darkness consumes me. My mind goes numb, my body falls to the floor, and I know I feel my heart stop beating.

PART I

CHAPTER 1

MARIA

"You go where they tell you to and don't fucking look for me, you understand?"

I can still hear the anger in his voice. The fear. The regret.

I can feel the tremble in his hands. The reluctance. His perfect control slipped as he forced himself to let go and I reluctantly held on tighter.

"No! Not without you!"

I look down at my palms as they shake uncontrollably remembering the last words I spoke to him. Walking the hallway of this vast mansion in darkness, I feel strangled, oppressed, pulled back into a hell I can't escape.

Blood. There was so much blood.

My eyes force themselves shut as I release a heavy sigh. Breathe Maria. You're not there anymore. You're safe. But Leo...

I shake the thought from my head. The one that crushes

me day and night since I've been torn from his side. The one that threatens to kill me if I let it, and I know it will if I ever find out it's true.

That he's gone. Forever. Dead. All because of me.

I won't let myself go there. I can't. Not yet. Not now. Not with so much at stake. Somehow knowing what we stand to lose ignites a spark in me and the tiniest bit of hope blossoms inside my chest. I hold onto it as I push one foot in front of the other and force myself to believe. To hold on. To not let go.

"Listen to me, Maria!"

My right hand comes up to my side as I hear his voice in my head and my body tightens remembering the pain I felt thereafter the bullet pierced my flesh. The fear I felt then still lingers as I find myself worrying again about what that bullet could have stolen from me, from us both, as I clutched him tighter and couldn't force myself to let go.

"Stay hidden. Trust no one but Collin and Giovanni!"

I feel myself tremble as my free hand reaches up and touches my lips the further I walk down the dark hallway. I can still feel his mouth pressed against mine in that final moment. Strong. Determined. Relentless. I can still taste him. Still breathe him in. It's the courage, the assurance, the absolution he released me of in that very moment that I've clung to over these past few weeks, praying for his return and not giving up any ounce of trust in him, *in us*, that we're going to be all right. We're going to make it through this. After all, we've already made it through so much.

"I love you, Maria. You will be a Moretti. But you need to

go. Now. Because I won't be able to live without you again. I swore to keep you safe. This is the only way I know how."

"They've got us cornered on all sides," my hands shake at the memory of hearing Collin's words in those final moments. "I found a way out through the back. But we have to go now. Before they get any closer."

My left-hand grabs at the fabric of my dress as the darkness and silence consume me, much like in those final moments we shared as I stride further down the cold hallway and into a future I can't bear to endure if I am forced to live it without him. In a moment of weakness, I clutch at my clothes like a madwoman, like a psychopath, a maniac, as I release a strangled, soft cry into the empty, hollow space around me. Just like I clung to him that day when I couldn't force myself to let go. When I couldn't bring myself to release him to a fate I knew he might not return from. I'm relentless in my release. Possessed even, as I try to tear the fear, the worry, the horrifying truth from my body and mind.

"Trust me, Maria," I remember his soft whisper as his breath feathered against my lips.

"Trust me!"

* * *

"Maria!"

Reluctantly pulled from my nightmare, the only solace I can find with my last memory of him, I fling around quickly at the mention of my name in the darkness. My eyes find Collin's in the dim light as it streams in through windows lining the hallway and the sun rises. My tired eyes focus behind him, on the ornate columns lined side by side through each stone window pane. Columns which remind me more of prison bars as the air begins to strangle me, my thoughts threaten to pull me under, and I force my gaze back on Collin to find him slowly emerging from the study.

He watches me carefully for a moment before shoving his hands in his pockets and looking towards the floor. I remain silent, feeling annoyance pull at my mind when I watch him take another step forward. He's oblivious to what I need most in a time like this.

I want to be alone. I need to be alone.

Much like I set out to be alone the first night I came to Italy.

Funny how your past catches up with your future until you can't make sense of anything at all anymore.

I don't know much about Collin. What I do, makes me uneasy. I remember him in brief encounters when I grew up in Las Vegas. But he keeps to the shadows, much like the man that I'm mourning. You would think I would see the resemblance and be put at ease, but something about the way Collin looks at me, something about the way he's constantly trying to study my every move makes me always very nervous in his presence.

"Shouldn't you be resting?" My ears hear his plea but my body refuses to give in as I watch him take a few steps closer. The way he's looking at me now makes that same chill rise up my spine and I shake it away, attempting to focus on what he's saying instead of the anxious way he makes me feel. "Your condition calls for you to think of more than just yourself, princess."

I glare at him in the darkness as he looks up and meets my eyes. I remain mute. Restrained. Closed off.

I never was one to let someone tell me what was best for me, except one man. A man I fear with each passing second might be gone from my life forever. But I can't let myself accept the fact that I might never get him back. Never get us back.

Breathe Maria, I whisper silently to myself as I close my eyes, forcing myself to remain strong. Trying to remember the strength, the relentless determination he made me promise, that I wouldn't give up hope. In the end, that's all Leonardo and I have ever had when we believed in each other enough.

Hope.

"Leonardo won't approve of you…"

My eyes flash open as I quickly stare at Collin with fury. With violent anger. All nerves and anxious feelings are now gone. "Then he can disapprove all he wants, himself, when he gets here, Collin." I grab on to that small amount of hope. The promise I made to Leonardo that I intend to keep. One that is quickly fleeting as I see the same doubtful look flash in his eyes. The same truth that we're all trying to deny. That he may not be coming back. The day we're hoping for may never arrive.

His gaze solemnly begins to downcast, but before it reaches the floor I blurt out, "but until then, I will do what I want, and not you, or Giovanni, or anyone else, will ever be able to stop me."

His stare jolts up to meet mine. His jaw ticks as he studies me and I can tell he's questioning how far he'd get away with pushing this. Pushing me. I'm just about to tell him how far I intend to *push* his requests, right up his ass if he forces the issue much further, but movement catches his eye behind me and I watch as his stance quickly softens.

"It never hurt a woman to stretch her legs and get a little exercise," I hear Daniella say as she steps into the hallway behind me. "Helps to clear her mind. Besides, between you and Giovanni, you're treating Maria more like a prisoner than the mafia queen she is."

I go to rebuttal as Daniella reaches my side. I'm not a queen, not like my mother. It's a title I fear I'll never be strong enough to claim. Especially if I'm forced to do so without Leonardo. And, it's the only fact that Collin and I seem to agree on, because he's relentless in calling me princess, and nothing more. A jab I know that's meant to put me in my place and remind me of how much I'm beneath the kind of power I truly need to rule the life that's been handed to me. As I glance up to meet Daniella's eyes, she shakes her head at my evident refusal of my position.

"Give her space to breathe, Collin," she quietly says. "Space to let go. Stress isn't good for her *condition* either. And suffocating her isn't helping." Turning to me, she brushes a strand of hair out of my eyes in a way that feels entirely too intimate before saying, "if you need to talk, Maria. I'm here for you. I hope you know that."

I shrug off her request and take a step back, focusing instead on the words she said before she made things a little too awkward for me. *My condition.*

I wish everyone would stop talking about me like I'm a

walking, time-ticking, obligation. A concern they'd most likely rather be rid of. The only *condition* I care about right now is the status and health of the one man that should be standing by my side. As my husband. And rightfully then, the only man allowed to talk about *my condition*.

My eyes fall to the floor as my right hand instinctively raises and holds my lower stomach.

It's funny. The last time he held me, I felt like one person. Even at almost four months pregnant, I was barely showing. Now, barely over a week later, tears well in my eyes as I take in the small bump that has now quickly formed in his short absence. Fear builds in my chest at the thought that he'll never see what I'm seeing, never feel what I'm feeling, as our baby continues to grow inside me. It's possible he'll never hold what I'll soon be holding.

A son.

Or a daughter.

Our child.

Our future.

A future that was torn from us far too soon when we had just finally really felt like we had started our life together. I should have never left his side. I should have stayed with him. My painful regrets clash together with my fearful future and I feel sick as it thrashes through my bloodstream.

"Daniella," Collin sternly whispers in the shadows. I look up as he regards her with irritation. His eyes flash to mine a moment later and that same anxious feeling climbs up my spine at the way he stares back into my eyes. "If Leonardo knew, when he finds out…"

"*If* he finds out, Collin," Daniella snaps. "Stop acting like her dictator, and treat her more like a friend."

"You don't understand, *mo anam cara*," Collin slightly hisses, as he refuses to back down, even to a woman he calls his *soul mate*. An Irish pet name I know Daniella loves. "He entrusted me with her. She's in my care. Her safety and the safety of their unborn child are my every concern right now, Daniella. She needs to listen or..."

Their voices meld together into an echo that pulses through my mind and proves to also be fiercely determined not to let go. I'm within, but also outside myself as I hear what they're saying but not one word seems to register. Their voices escalate. Their anger grows. My gaze once again finds the floor in front of me and I retreat into myself, into the horror that's filled my mind for almost the last two weeks. Then suddenly, I quickly pulled back at the words that leave Collin's mouth.

"Leonardo might be dead," Collin shouts. "It's time she starts thinking of more than just herself. It's time she puts the family first. Remembers her place."

Collin's voice breaks through my haze. His eyes instinctively meet mine, and it takes a moment for us both to fully register what he's just said in anger. His stare softens as if retreating and almost apologizing for the horror of what he's just proposed. But even the torture that awaits most men in hell is no match for a woman scorned.

Slap!

My palm stings as I take another step forward and it finally registers what I just did. I know Collin's ego can never be tarnished from a woman slapping him in the face, but my heart hurts as I realize I had no control and took my anger out on him. What he said is right, but I can't bear to admit it. I take in his silhouette, still looking to the side, his cheek slightly pink from my assault, and feel sorry for only a moment longer before the words he just uttered ring through my ears once again.

He grabs my wrist as it falls to my side, and my body flushes with a foreign feeling as his hand stays locked on my arm.

"Dead or alive, Collin," my voice comes out stern, raspy, aggressive even as I take a step towards him once again. "I know exactly who I am in this world, and I don't need you to remind me." He throws my wrist away, and it falls to my side. His eyes meet mine and an anxious feeling rises inside, but I ignore it the best I can.

What I don't add is that all I *do* need is the presence of a man who finally showed me my worth. My heart begins to bleed as I bite my lip and tears threaten to fall free. I need the man that finally showed me my strength. A strength I worry is fading each day he's not by my side.

"Regardless of Leonardo's fate," I continue, "you will never speak like that again. He's alive. He'll always be here. He's a part of my soul," I hear myself cry. "It's best you remember who you're dealing with for when he does return."

Collin's nostrils flare as he takes in my words. Any other woman and I wouldn't get away with the daggers I just threw in his direction. But he knows as well as I do the kind of man Leonardo is. Hell proves to be a beautiful heaven when considering the kind of fate anybody who wrongly crosses him inevitably meets.

Collin gives me a curt nod, eyes never wavering off mine, as he takes a step back and holds his silence. My breaths rise and fall quickly as he makes his retreat. I've never thought of myself as a strong woman. Never imagined I'd hold the position I do, and my heart breaks a little more knowing the pride I'd see shining back at me in Leonardos' eyes if he was here to witness this moment.

The gratification doesn't last long as I bow my head and take a step back, emotions once again getting the better of me.

"Excuse me," I whisper, not able to meet either of their eyes as I turn and quickly begin to make my way down the hallway. My feet quickly pick up their pace as I meet a turn and silently slip out of sight.

"She'll find her way, Collin," Daniella whispers.

"Perhaps," Collin whispers back with a sneer. "But she needs to find it fast. For Leonardo. For their child. For the family, Daniella."

My tears fall as I run down the corridor and find my room. With clammy hands, I quickly reach for the doorknob and fling myself into a haunted privacy that tortures me endlessly night and day. An isolation concealing my truth from the world. I fear I'll never be strong again. Not without him. And as much as I want to break free from the restraints I find in my seclusion, I also hate to admit I strangely find the strangling confines comforting. Drowning in it, I refuse to give up hope.

"I'm trying," my throat burns as it tightens around the words that break free from my heart in a whisper. "I made a promise to a boy," I cry harder. "A man who stole my heart a long time ago. A heart, a soul, I'll never get back if he dies. I swear, I'll die with him."

My feet give out as I clutch my sides and fall to the floor. My mind reeling with promises, murmured, whispered, groaned, thundered the last time he made me his and then promised me when the sun rose the next morning, we'd finally start our future.

CHAPTER 2

MARIA

TEN DAYS AGO

"And if you're a girl, Daddy is going to hire extra *membros* and *associados*. You'll have 10 pairs of eyes on you, every move you make, *bambina*. And that'll never change."

I giggle as Leonardo kisses my lower stomach and my hips instinctively turn into him. He grabs my sides and continues talking in whispers as I smile and run my fingers through his hair. His words are only for their ears, father, and child, and I'm completely and utterly fine with that knowing the man he is, and what's more, the father he's soon to become.

If his protection of me mirrors half the protection he'll give our children, they'll be more than cared for. The thought makes my heart swell as his fingers trace over my belly and he plants kisses along the curve of my hips.

"Something tells me, she'll hate you for that come the time she's 16, Leonardo."

His grip tightens on my hip as he ignores my comment and gently kisses a path up my stomach and across my chest. I sigh and my eyes flutter closed. He reaches my neck and licks his way to my ear before taking it between his teeth. My body instinctively shudders with arousal. His hand finds the apex of my thighs through my nightgown and he cups my sex sharply, harshly, before gently rubbing the edge of his palm slowly down my clit. A moan escapes my lips as he releases his bite on my ear and breathes into my neck causing goose-bumps to break out across my skin.

"She'll learn quickly that in this life, she listens to her father, Maria. Because he only wants what's best for her. Just like he'll always want only the best in the world for her mother."

Before I can respond, his face lifts quickly as his lips rush down hard against mine. His arms hold me tightly against his frame as he leans into me against the cool sheets. My mouth opens on instinct, submitting to what we both want. To give into our insatiable craving, the need, the obsession for our connection. His groan ignites a passion from the tips of my toes up to my head. It quickly spirals through my body as everything fades around us but the feeling of holding one another in our arms. His hips grind into my side on instinct, his length hard against my side as my body naturally pulls him in closer.

Our mouths, lazy with hunger, roam the curves of each other's lips. His hand raises my nightgown and he slowly runs his finger through my slit, finding me bare underneath and soaking wet already to his touch. His hum of approval matches the hiss that passes through my lips as my center dampens more and his mouth moves now with feverish greed against my own. My hips raise on instinct as he enters a finger inside me and slowly pulls it through my tightening walls. His touch always brings me to release quickly, but now, with the new surge of hormones running through my body, every touch, every caress, every stroke of his finger is enough to bring me to climax all too quickly. I always find myself instantly crashing over the edge, over and over again before I'm begging him to torture me some more, like only he can, in his dark and delicious ways.

"Don't think just because you're carrying my child I will take it easy on you, Maria," his breath feathers against my lips as he pulls back from our kiss. "Tell me, *mi Amore*," he grinds into my core and I whimper with need, "should I fuck you like a good girl, or a bad one?"

I grab onto him, needing more of the friction between my legs, but he's stronger than my hold and his body suddenly leaves mine. Before I can even open my eyes, he swiftly turns me over gently on the cool sheets. His right hand quickly finds my neck as he sternly holds me down against the bed. Moments later, I feel him gently straddle my hips. His long, thick erection slips up through the crack in my ass and I moan into the mattress, my head too clouded with impending ecstasy to think of anything else than the way he never fails to make my body, my soul, my mind feel. Claimed. His. Taken with a carnal need I'll never get enough of.

He does so in a way that never fails to leave me feeling cherished. Worthy. So loved.

He grips the hem of my nightgown and pulls it up to the center of my back, baring me to him completely. I intuitively raise my hips, needing what comes next. Wanting and needing him to touch me as my body hums with arousal.

"I haven't punished this fine ass in so long," he groans, as his palm lightly smacks my left cheek before he rubs away the light sting. My eyes close, and I let out a gasp of pleasure. "And I won't," he whispers, still holding me down with a strong grip on my neck as his hips back off my own. He runs a finger from the dimples at the base of my spine, down the center of my ass, until he finds my center wet, wanting, and then slowly slips a finger inside me. I gasp out as I attempt to push back against him, needing to have any part of him I can deeper inside me. "Not while your body cares for our child, Maria."

I hear a zipper and bite my lip in anticipation. My lower stomach clenching in a delicious longing as I wait to feel him inside me.

"But Maria," his words hiss against my ear as he lowers himself against me, the tip of his engorged crown breaching my entrance. "That doesn't mean I won't find new ways to bring you pleasure." He slips himself inside me halfway, and I hold back the cry of pure heaven the feeling gives me. His grip on my neck tightens just as I feel his hardness throb inside me. "And," he growls as he slams into my pussy harshly, burying himself to the hilt, and making me cry out as I fight back from falling over the edge. "It doesn't mean I won't punish you more after." He pulls out slowly and then even slower, pushes himself back inside my body. " I don't want you to hold back, mi Amore. If you don't let me hear, if you don't show me the pleasure only I'm capable of bringing to your beautiful body," he pulls back from my frame and grips my ass in his hand, "Then I'll find so much pleasure of taking it out on this fine ass later, Maria."

He keeps his grip tight on my neck, his length buried deep as I adjust to the feeling of him. I've felt him many times before, but never with such a frenzied need. Never with every nerve heightened to an almost unbearable high. Never so rock hard, so strong, so dense I can make out every curve, every ridge of his length inside me.

"Please," I hear myself cry as my body screams underneath him for him to move.

"Please, what?" he taunts me. I swear I can hear the smile in his voice, know it's spread across his handsome face as he torments me the way he likes. With what he's not yet giving me.

Just as I'm about to speak, he pulls his length slightly out of my slick opening, forcing a squeak from the back of my throat as I feel myself tighten and my lungs begin to pant. His palm smacks my ass gently, just like it did before. Enough to elicit a slight sting, but no more.

"Damn it, Maria," his voice growls. "Holding out on you is torture. The purest form of foreplay I've ever known. And fuck if it isn't going to make it painfully beautiful to give us both what we need after our child is born."

He leans forward once again, this time grabbing around to my front. I anticipate him and lift slightly on the mattress, allowing him to fondle my left breast. He palms it in his strong hand lightly, before tracing my nipple, working it into a tight bud, and then pinching down softly.

"I should fill you full of my hard cock and knock you up more often, mi Amore," he whispers in my ear. "Fuck you so much, you're always carrying my seed around in your wet pussy."

I gasp, but my breath catches in my throat and then quickly turns into a soft scream. He pinches down harder on my nipple just as his teeth take my ear in his mouth. His piercing bite matches the sting in my breast, both of them shooting a jolt straight to my sex.

"You still haven't answered me, Maria."

My eyes open, not understanding, forgetting for a moment, and then I smile.

God, I love him.

Always have. Always will.

Especially like this.

I feel his thickness grow inside me. Feel it throb with the need for release. I push my hips back, making him enter me further once again, and this time, a strangled moan forces itself from his lips.

"Please... Sir."

I feel the smile on his lips as he presses his face into the side of my neck and breathes me in. His hand releases its grip on my neck, but his fingers quickly find my hair as he wraps it around his fist.

"Good girl," he whispers as he slowly rises and fists my hair in his large palm. His free hand releases my nipple and travels south to my waist. He holds my hip possessively with a tight grip, slowly pulling out of my entrance until his tip is the only thing inside me.

He swirls his hips, coaxing moans, shrieks, gasps from

my lungs as his grip on my hair tightens along with the greedy restraint from his palm on my left side. His swollen crown rotates through my wet opening, caressing every aching inch of my sex, my body silently begging him to push further inside me as the beginning of my climax grows.

"This pussy was made for me to tease," he growls, as he thrusts forward and I scream. His grip tightens further around my hair until my head is almost pulled off the bed. I smile, the perfect mixture of pleasure and pain giving me what I've always wanted in life. What only *he's* capable of giving me. He pulls out and then slams inside me quickly again. And then again. His thrusts become animalistic as he forces his hips against me and my body pushes further into the mattress. I cry into the sheets. His relentless pounding increases with each yell that escapes my lips. His lax balls slap against my thighs, teasing, adding to my high, as I scream for him to never stop. But all too soon he's pulling out, releasing my hair, my hip, and gently flipping me over on my back.

I gasp for air as I look up at him in a haze and find his eyes glimmering with pride.

"So wet," I hear him say as he fingers my opening and my eyes roll back in pleasure. "So willing," he growls, as my knees fall out to the side and my body instinctively shows him I need more. "So beautifully responsive," he groans, as my wetness increases and I look to see his lips tilt in a slight grin right before my eyes focus on his face as it drops to my center. "So soft," he whispers, eyes never leaving mine, as he blows against my sex. "So tender," he murmurs, as his tongue flattens, his nostrils flare, and he slowly licks up my slit. His eyes never once leaving mine.

My eyes hood over with desire and match his own as his grin deepens and he licks up my slick heat once again. Slowly, his lips find my clit, and he sucks down lazily, staring into my gaze the entire time as my breathing quickens and I swear I'm about to climax.

He knows. He always does. And I feel him bite down lightly as two fingers dive into my heat. I cry out, but I never look away as he drives his fingers deeper, curving them perfectly and thrusting them over and over again deep inside me. His lips suck harder, and his eyes cloud over with determination.

From the look in his eyes, this is only the beginning of a long night of pleasure he intends to inflict on my needy body. He gives me a slight nod as he feasts on my center, an approval to let myself go. He holds my stare and my body convulses against him, around him, into him, as his free hand quickly holds my hip in place. I scream out in pleasurable pain, my body sure I can't take anymore, not able to look away from his captivating stare.

When my quaking lightly subsides, my breath still unsteady, my lungs still panting for air, he pulls his fingers free and rises off the bed. Slowly, he rejoins me, this time straddling my head from behind, as he braces his body over my own.

"Fuck if I can't get enough of this pussy," he groans, as his tongue meets my folds once again. I cry out just as the tip of his velvet skin brushes against my lips. I taste myself, his pre cum, and my body almost crashes over again from the aroma, the perfect mixture of him and me coating his hard cock.

"Suck me off, Maria," he growls between licks against my delicate flesh. "You're so fucking good at it. Wrap your tight, wet mouth around my dick, mi Amore."

I take him in my mouth as he forces his hips down against me and then feel myself gag as he hits the back of my throat. I moan in ecstasy as he simultaneously thunders a growl of pleasure just as he starts fucking my entrance with his thick tongue.

I need to feel the pain again of his cock choking me. I want to feel him thrust his thick, long, length back down my throat, and find myself getting off knowing I'm the one capable of giving him that amount of pleasure. I grab his hips and force him inside my mouth once more. The same pain ignites so much pleasure between my legs. I hear a louder growl from the man I love and swear I've never felt any higher than I do at this moment, with his tongue between my legs and my mouth wrapped tightly around his hard, thick, long, beautiful cock.

He pulls his hips back and my lips relentlessly try to suck him down. He pauses just before pulling out completely and lets me suck around his tip. My tongue swirls in circles and I know it takes all his self-control to not fiercely fuck my mouth like I can tell he still wants to right now. I hear him grunt, howl, hiss, as I swirl and suck his tip. My pussy is forgotten as his high builds.

"Fuck, you suck my dick like a damn queen, Maria."

He pulls back quickly as a loud pop sounds through the room from his length leaving my mouth. I go to rise, to protest, but he grabs me in his arms first and lays me against his chest. My legs straddle his hips on instinct as he rolls me on top of him. I rise off his chest just as my eyes find his and he positions himself at my entrance.

"My queen," he whispers as he tenderly brushes a stray strand of hair out of my eyes. "My everything."

His hips thrust up and I scream, the sensation too much as my body pulls back on instinct. He pulls me closer. Always. As my forehead falls against his own and we take a moment to just breathe each other in. Connected. Forever. More than anyone will ever know.

"Tomorrow," he groans, as my hips rotate and I look him in the eyes. "I make you, my wife."

His lips capture mine as he thrusts up inside me, muffling a moan from both of us as we quickly begin to chase our release.

His queen.

His everything.

His wife.

I wouldn't be any of those things if he wasn't my king first.

My master.

My dominant.

My everything.

A man I know I'll never be able to live without.

"FUCK, we thought we lost you there, Chief," a voice I haven't heard in years says to my right.

"There doesn't seem to be any internal damage. Lungs, heart, ribs, all check out fine," another voice says.

Sucking in a small breath, fire explodes in my chest before it catches in my throat, lodging itself there and threatening to destroy me. I start to wheeze before turning to my side and coughing up blood. Fucking pathetic.

"Shit, I tell you, this fucker has nine lives," the first voice repeats. I hack up what I know is probably a good portion of my right lung and spit out some more blood at his feet. "I bet he dies of lead poisoning from all the metal that's been left in his damn body long before a bullet ever calls him home."

"Don't be so sure of yourself, Ace," I manage, before the burning pain sears through my chest once again. I sit up a little straighter as the medic to the right of me changes the dressing on my wound. "Wouldn't want you to lose that bet."

Declan eyes me with mischief because we both know

there isn't a bet either of us has ever lost. A reason why we made a pact a long ass time ago to never bet against each other. Also, a reason why I dubbed the asshole with the nickname Ace decades before he earned the title. He's the only other man on the planet I've ever met that can cheat death as easily as I can. Call it luck. Call it fucking talent. Whatever the fuck it is, it's the exact reason why I called him for backup when my men failed me the day of my wedding.

"Where the fuck are we?" I hiss out a moment later. The makeshift couch I'm laying on is making the searing pain in my left side almost unbearable and something tells me we don't have time for fucking games, or bets. Just facts. Facts that will inevitably lead to Alfonso Capone's head on a stake in *Prata della Valle* for all to see if I had it my way after the way he cheated me out of the best day of my life. Facts that will get me back to Maria. To my child. The only *famiglia* anymore that will ever matter most to me.

"Burial Crypt," Declan says after a few moments have passed. "At La Chiesa di San Filippo Apostolo."

Fucking perfect.

My eyes roll back simultaneously with my head as I think of all the ways we're probably sitting fucking targets. Shit, I know Declan means well, but his line of work varies a little differently than mine. Typically, he's the good cop bringing the bad guy in. I met him when we were both new to the game before we ever picked sides. Back when we were just kids left for ruin on the streets of Rome.

My road in life was inevitably paved for me before we ever even met, although I didn't know it at the time.

Declan? Well, he fell in love with a beautiful Italian

woman who just so ended up being his partner in crime and then chose a purer form of justice over the adulterated hate fueling my veins. That doesn't mean we haven't gotten our hands dirty together over the years on a few jobs that flew under the radar. And that doesn't mean his ass is anything close to pure. The devil in him simmers under the surface. The dominance as well.

"I know what you're thinking," he huffs as I look up at the medic still tending to my wounds. "But we're covered here, Leo. Alfonso Capone is on the mainland..."

"So he's not fucking dead?" I shout, causing the poor bastard at my side, the medic, to flinch in fear as a low laugh falls from Declan's lips.

"Not exactly."

"What the fuck does that mean," I grit out as the physician eyes me timidly before making me sit up a little straighter to elevate my wound.

"By the time we got there, two of your men were dead and Alfonso and his group of associates were nowhere to be seen. We think they heard us coming. Either that or they were tipped off. A fact that would inevitably mean you have a rat in your operation."

"Wouldn't be the first time."

"Yes, but, it's the first time you have more to lose than gain. Am I right?"

I swallow over a lump forming in my throat and force the anxiety I suddenly feel down so as not to lose control.

"Maria?" I whisper.

"She's safe," he quickly reports. "Stateside."

What the fuck? I sit up a little straighter, ignoring the

commands from the medic to stay still and look Declan straight in the eye.

"What the hell did you just say?" I grit out as I force the poor schmuck still tending to my bullet wound away.

"She's safe," Declan repeats. "That's all you need to know."

"If we didn't have the history we do, Ace, you'd be a dead man for answering me like that."

"If we didn't have the history we do, Chief, you'd still be lying in your own demise, bleeding out and not collecting on a favor that I owe you, one that we both know is more than a decade overdue," he laughs again before rising from his seat and walking across the room.

I look down as the medic starts to address my other wounds, his eyes briefly catching mine and the fear that's in them doesn't escape me. Good. He should be afraid. The whole fucking world should be scared of the wrath I plan to unleash for what's happened. For what's still happening. A hell I thought I'd finally be free of.

"Want one of these?"

I look up and watch as Declan snaps open a briefcase. He produces two tumblers and a bottle of 15-year-old Pappy Van Winkle. I take a long inhale, breathe in a little deeper than before, and nod my head.

"Do you even have to fucking ask?"

He gives me a sly grin and pours us both two fingers.

"Tell me, what kind of woman finally got your ass to settle down?" taking a few strides to cross the room, he hands me my drink and then sits in a chair across from me.

I study the contents in the glass and think about Maria. I think about all the moments I'm missing now being away from her, of all the moments that will continue to be lost until it's safe for us to be together again. My back molars grind together in protest before I shoot back the entire contents of my glass in one large gulp. Looking up, Declan sees the tortured look in my eyes and hands me his glass with a sick, twisted grin.

"That's when you know it's the real fucking deal," he says, his hand still gripping the glass I'm trying to take from him. "When you can't breathe. Can't think. Can't fucking go on living if it means walking through another day without them."

I take his glass harshly and toss it back just as quickly. Gritting my teeth as the alcohol burns down the back of my throat, I look up at him and say, "I'll get through this a lot easier without your self-analyzing bullshit."

I hear him laugh as he stands and walks back across the room, but don't have the energy to tell him to fuck off any further. I don't have the fucking strength to deal with him anymore right now, and the realization makes me feel weak when I am never fucking weak. With a heavy sigh, I lean my head back against the couch and look up at the ceiling. *The real fucking deal.* Hell, Maria and I were born to be together. That kind of hold, that kind of power that brings two people together, hurts more than not being able to just breathe. In times like this, it kills you, slowly, as the time you should be united regrettably slips away. What finishes me off in the end, kills me inevitably even though I'm still somehow breathing, is the knowledge that I'll never be able to get the time back. It'll always be lost, like all the years she was lost to me before.

A lump forms in my throat. A fucking strangling feeling fills my chest and quickly begins rising into my neck. I need to get back to her. To them. My fucking queen and my unborn child. But not before there are no more fucking threats.

I hear Declan pour himself another drink and look up as he begins to walk back over with the bottle.

"How long am I stuck here?" I immediately ask. "The sooner I can put that piece of shit in the ground, the sooner I can get back to a life that was stolen from me. From us."

"Fuck, you've already been here close to ten days, Chief," Declan chuckles. "What's a few more?" He takes his seat and then leans forward and pours me a hearty portion of bourbon, almost filling the glass to the brim.

Ten fucking days? He can't be serious. Rage burns inside at the thought that I've already lost so much time. A madness builds. Strengthens. And fuck, I hold onto the insanity, knowing I'll need it to fight the battle that's standing before me.

"I don't have time to..."

"What? Lay low?" Declan mocks. "Because that's all you need to take the time to do right now, Leo."

"Fuck you, Dec," I seethe, just as the medic backs away, his job now done and I watch as he wastes no time as he retreats with haste back into the corner of the room. "Lay low? I've never heard such bullshit. Did you lay low when it came to you and Mags? Did you lay low when you reached out to me years ago and needed that last little bit of intel to make sure Mathew and Emma were safe? Who the fuck did you the favor of keeping eyes on them for seven fucking years, huh? Who the fuck..."

"Which is why I'm breaking protocol and sitting here now with you, Leo," Declan's tone is stern as he cuts me off. "Which is why I'm finally repaying my debt, in a big way, that's more than a decade past due."

I glare at him and hate the fact that he's right. What's more, I extremely resent the fact that I have no comeback. He used resources to get me away from Alfonso and his men that I know would get him fired. The FBI wouldn't overlook it as a minor indiscretion. Not when he's helping free a man that's been on their radar for years. They've just never had the evidence to bring me in. Thanks to a little help from my friends at the bureau. Present company included.

"But I'll tell you something that I've learned over the years," Declan continues, leaning forward and tapping his pointer finger against his temple, and fuck, I wish I had my Glock so I could blow his head clear off. "Something I wish I could have told my hot-headed self back when the entire world was stolen from me. Are you listening closely, Chief? Because I'm only going to say this once." I glare at him because we both know if I wasn't fucking immobile right now, I'd have his head in a vice and my fist repeatedly beating his ass. "There is power in the stillness. Perfection of skill, influence, control, dominance, in taking the time to lie low. Manage your emotions, Leo. Keep out of sight. Build in silence so they won't know where you're going to attack or what just fucking hit them."

"I always have control..."

"Not anymore you don't."

I look down and rotate the tumbler of bourbon from palm to palm as the bitterness I feel inside deepens. I take a moment to myself, rolling his comment around my brain, knowing he's right but hating to admit it. Looking back up as my defenses kick in I grumble, "What does that fucking mean?"

"The Leo I knew never lost a fight," Declan huffs, sitting back in his chair and flinging one arm over the back. "He never got taken captive. He never let anything cloud his judgment for one second. That's how he always won. Fuck, that's why I started calling you the Chief. Long before the title ever was bestowed on you by the mob. You lead, Leo. You rule. But not this time. This time was different."

"Bullshit."

"You're telling me you let them take you?"

"I did what I had to do. To protect what's mine."

"Then you just proved my point, Chief, and showed us all who really has the damn control."

Maria.

I bring my glass to my lips and take a long slow sip. She owns me. She always has. Always will. Ever since the first day she walked into my life and I handed her mine.

Maria.

I knew a long time ago she'd be the death of me.

Now, I'm fucking sure of it. Except there is a lot more to all this bullshit than Declan knows, and I'm not in the mood to debate the point of control any longer.

"How do you know she's safe?" I demand before taking a

large drink of bourbon. "How can I know she's with people that can be trusted?"

"Trust me," he grins. "There's no one else I have faith in more. Even if there once was a time she would've cut off my balls and fed them to me on a silver platter just to prove a sick fucking point."

"Life was easier when we were free men," I grin, getting lost for a moment in the irony of how we both started out. Fucking everything that walked our way and swearing we'd take a wife on our dying day.

Shaking my head, I bring my glass to my lips and take another drink, contemplating all he's said. I think about the freedom I've lost, and the control that long ago started slipping away the more I held onto a woman that will one day be the death of me.

"We were never really free?" Declan says quietly, reading my thoughts. "Because I'll tell you the truth, the only way to ever be free in life is to never fall in love."

I look up at him and give him a quick nod. He's right. Shooting back the rest of the bourbon in my glass, I hear him go on.

"When a man loves a woman, truly loves a woman, there is no other choice but for her to become his weakness."

CHAPTER 4

MARIA

"It's been almost three weeks, Maria. Eventually, you have to start facing facts."

"Fuck your facts, Giovanni," I hiss, looking up from my seat in the office and watching as my late mother's most trusted advisor flinches. I'm not a delicate flower, like some may think, but I don't usually go around cursing so freely either.

"The only fact I will face is the promise that Leo made. He will be coming back to me."

Giovanni gives me a contemplating glance, a sort of sad fatherly look that can only come from a man's heart that is breaking as much as mine. We've all been praying for the best these last few weeks, but even I have to admit I thought for sure he'd be back by my side by now. Or at least that we would have heard some word. Dead or alive.

"And what if he doesn't?"

My eyes close and I let out a heated breath at Giovanni's

words. Shaking my head, I bite my bottom lip and pray he doesn't continue.

"You have to prepare for everything, Maria," Giovanni whispers, making my blood pressure start to rise knowing I'm not making it out of this conversation until he obviously says what he feels like he needs to say.

"You are the heir to the Nitti name. The child you carry, if it is a boy, will be seen as the up-and-coming *capo di tutti capi*. A stronger boss, by blood, than any the *famiglia* has seen before. If Leo is not here to raise his son..."

"And what if it is a daughter?" I defensively blurt out as my eyes flash open.

He gives me a sly smile, as if to say men like Leonardo only breed boys, and then waits for me to continue.

"It could be a girl, Giovanni, and you saw how well that went over with my own father," I swallow over a lump suddenly lodged in my throat as pity fills Giovanni's eyes. "Well, boy or girl, they will have both parents present to raise them, and that's more than I can say for Leonardo or myself. Now if you'll excuse me."

I push off the desk in the main office, rising with building rage, and start to make my way towards the door. I'm so tired of everyone telling me to face facts when there is no fact yet to face. Leonardo is out there. I can feel him. He's a part of my soul, always has been, and always will be. If he was no longer breathing I'd die too. I can't give up hope. Not yet. I take a few steps toward the door, intent on putting this entire conversation behind me until Giovanni calls out.

"Maria, have you considered the fact that maybe Leonardo planned the attack?"

Stopping immediately, I take a deep breath and replay what Giovanni just said in my mind. He can't be serious. Letting the breath out slowly, I debate a few questions of my own before turning around to meet his stare.

How could he even suggest that? Why would he think Leonardo would want to kill my family? Why would he think the man I love would ever put me, or our child, in danger? Then again, it's not the first time I would have been played at the hands of Leonardo Moretti. But it would be the first time he would have made a move like that without good intentions for the outcome. Without the reassurance of my safety in the end.

I still haven't turned around when Giovanni continues. "Leonardo was once denied reign to Luigi Lombardi's empire because of blood. If he did plan this attack..."

"He'd risk killing me before our child was ever born, Giovanni," I snap as I turn quick on my heels and stare him down. "Why would he do that? What would he stand to gain then? He was already handed the title by my father. He'd only..."

"Be destroying all obstacles and ensure he'd be keeping his title," he blurts out harshly. "These are facts you need to consider, Maria. These are the things a queen who runs an empire like you needs to look at if you're going to be successful in running the family business."

"My husband runs the family business."

"And your husband is not here, Maria," Giovanni snaps making my heart hurt and my blood run cold from the God-awful truth I can't deny in his statement. "He hasn't been in over three weeks. Business is falling through the cracks.

People are starting to notice. Starting to talk. If he doesn't show his face soon we can't keep up the facade that you two are safe after the attack and somewhere on your honeymoon. All of this and more are just more facts you're not facing."

"I know all of this and the more you're hinting at, Giovanni," I shout as my voice betrays me and starts to shake. "So much more it kills me inside. But you don't understand the nightmares, the terror, the stress and anxiety that lies awake with me in our bed at night. The bed I should be sharing with my husband. I know what people are saying. I know the horror that might lie ahead for me. What I don't know is how to process it. How to handle it. How to walk through life without him."

"You have to find a way, *il mio bambina*," he attempts to console me. "You have to try."

"I can't," I whisper, as tears begin to fall from my eyes. "I won't. Moving forward means accepting he's no longer here. It means the hope, the faith that he'll come back to me alive, starts to die."

Giovanni softly studies me as I begin to fall apart. I grab my stomach, feeling sick and torn. Part of me believes I can do what he's asking me to do and still believe Leonardo will find his way back to me. Another part of me is restless, relentless in the belief that if I start to live without Leo now, I'll be living without him for eternity.

"Only the strong survive, Maria," Giovanni finally whispers. "Especially in our way of life."

A small sob escapes my lips as I cover my mouth and force myself to try and keep it together. Leo was my strength. Except all he gave me seems lost now that he's gone. I find myself once again that shy, timid, somewhat helpless girl I felt like when I first embarked off to Italy for answers not too long ago. In all the madness, all the secrets, Leo made me realize my strength. And it's something that's faded and diminished quickly in our time apart.

"Stop treating her like a damn victim and then maybe she'll see she's already surviving, *consigliere*."

The voice comes out of nowhere and I whip around quickly in its direction. A woman stands in the doorway. One I've never seen before. She studies me briefly before lifting her eyes and glaring at Giovanni. Taking off her long black gloves in a strong yet elegant manner, my eyes flash behind her when I see the house butler, Jerry, scurrying through the office door.

"She just barged in, Sir," he stammers, addressing Giovanni and not me. "I tried to stop her, but..."

"She's already got clearance," Collin beams, pushing through the doorway behind him and striding pridefully across the room. He glances at me once, and the look we exchange sends the same chill I'm accustomed to when he's around down my spine. "Not that she'd bloody need it. Probably couldn't find the likes of her written down on any of your fancy lists."

He drops himself angrily onto the couch and throws his feet up on the coffee table. His eyes find mine, and I swear I see concern written in them for a moment as he regards the tears in my eyes, but if so he masks it beautifully a moment later as his jaw sets and irritation for my weakness fills them a moment later. Brushing the wetness off my cheeks, I stand up a little straighter and turn back to face the woman behind me.

"Mafia princess," Collin taunts from his position on the couch. "Meet the Ice Queen."

The woman in front of me smiles wickedly before handing her gloves off to the butler. She takes off her coat next with the same elegant diligence in which she handled the gloves, and then tosses them at the man beside her when she's done. My eyes widen, because sure, I thought she'd probably be dressed to the nines under the mink that was keeping her warm a second ago, but I wasn't expecting her to be packing and strapped with a holster around her back and left pant leg.

"Does she have clearance to carry those weapons?" Giovanni demands behind me. His voice attempts to sound threatening but it shakes with the same nervousness that I feel inside.

Collin just laughs as he leans back and props his hands behind his head. "Does she look like she'd ask for clearance?"

"Who are you?" I blurt out, my defenses finally finding their way to my conscious as I take a heated step in her direction. "And what do you want?"

"Who I am, isn't important. Neither is what I want." I glare at her suspiciously as I take another step forward and she continues. "Now, what I can offer you, that's the question you should really be asking yourself, Darling."

The way she says *Darling* is both demeaning and terrifying, making me want to find a place to hide and for some reason demand her respect at the same time. My family's under attack. My life, my child's life, Leo's life, all hang in the balance. The last thing I need right now is some woman I don't know walking in here thinking she owns the place when this is my home. My business. My future. I feel a scowl settle across my features as I take another step toward her in anger.

"There you go," she whispers, taking a step of her own to meet me in the middle of the room. "There's that fucking courage."

Collin's devilish laugh fills my ears before Giovanni demands, "Your name, *la femmina*. Don't make us ask again."

"Me?" she provokes, looking past me briefly at Giovanni and mocking him viciously before glancing back into my eyes. "Well, I'm the bitch your mother warned you about. The malicious tramp your father can't resist. The witch all good boys like to fuck in secret while their girl-friends whine and criticize my every fucking move in public." She glances back my way and gives me a devilish grin. "Because, let's face it, they're just never going to be good enough."

"Not like you, Mags," I hear Collin's low laugh ring out from across the room and it does nothing but just grate on my last nerve. Fire rushes through my veins at her words. There will be no fucking in secret here. I'd slit her throat myself for even trying, all she has to do is give me one damn reason.

"But don't worry," she smiles, obviously catching onto the madness building inside of me. "I've already got myself a king. I'm not here to steal yours, Darling. What I am here for, is to make you into a woman who's fit to rule beside the only man that's ever rivaled mine in life. The only other *il padrone* I'll ever show respect to after what he did for me. For *mi famiglia*."

I study her, unyielding at first, and then intrigued the next second at the facts she's presenting.

"I'm also here to bring you news," she says, taking a step around me and walking further into the room. I watch as she makes her way to the wet bar and helps herself to a drink. She takes her time, filling the glass with two ice cubes, slowly pouring the scotch into the tumbler, and then sipping slowly from it before turning back around.

"But first I need to know if we have ourselves a deal."

"What are you offering?" I ask quickly, needing to cut to the chase and hear whatever news it is that she brings with her. Especially if it's about Leonardo.

"I'm offering you a chance to see for yourself what you're made of," she suggests with a shrug, before turning and pouring more scotch into her glass. She brings it to her lips as she spins back around and takes a large sip, studying me over the rim the entire time. "No questions. No excuses," when I don't answer right away, she sets her glass down and stands her ground. "You do what I say when I say it."

"And if I say no?"

She shrugs, "Then good luck with that," she smiles, nodding her head over her shoulder in Giovanni's direction. He shifts on his feet annoyed.

"He was right," she says, stalking quickly back past me towards the door. "Only the strong survive, Darling. Where he's wrong, is it's like that in every fucking way of life. Not just yours."

She hastily grabs her coat and gloves from the butler still standing statuesque by the door with his mouth hanging wide open in shock. Can't say I blame him. I wasn't entirely prepared for the intrusion either. And Collin finding humor in the situation is just pissing me off more as his low chuckle finds its way across the room and into my ears once again.

Before I can stop myself, I ask, "And what if I say yes." She stops but she doesn't turn. "Tell me first. Your name. Your news. And don't make me fucking ask again, because I've been dealing with way too much bullshit these past few weeks and I'll be damned if you make me have to shift through too much more of yours before I have you thrown out on your ass."

Turning slowly, a wide smile spreads across her face as she slowly hands her things back to Jerry. She studies me for a moment, and I have to admit a few minutes ago the way she's looking at me now would've made my knees weak, my stomach sour, and my heartbeat wilder in fear. But not now. Right now I am so done with everyone's bullshit I don't care how many rounds she's packing on her slender body, I still think I could take her in a full-out brawl and win. In a quick turn of events, she brings her hands up in front of her and - starts to fucking clap?

What the hell?

Her hearty laugh is met with a low chuckle coming from Collin across the room. The only disapproval can be heard from Giovanni behind me as I hear him whisper under his breath that we don't know if she can be trusted.

But as the stranger walks back towards me, clapping for a victory I don't see in myself yet, I feel an odd sense of reassurance and confidence in whatever she has to say next. Whatever she has to offer.

I'll take it, just so I can continue to finally feel the confidence I'm starting to grab a hold of now. The courage, the assurance in what I believe to be true. And the strength I'm pulling from somewhere inside to stand my ground and not believe in anything else.

"Magnolia McClintock," she says, extending her hand. I take it a little timidly but ease up at the strong shake that greets me. Any woman who has strength like that is a woman I want on my side. "Maria Nitti," she continues with a smile I'm quickly starting to trust, "I'm happy to tell you, your fiancé Leonardo Moretti, is alive."

I gasp out and drop to my knees. Tears quickly fall from my eyes as I tenderly hug my stomach and can't help the smile, the happiness, the euphoric way it feels to finally hear someone tell me what I've been waiting three long weeks to hear.

"Now," she demands harshly causing me to take notice as I look up and see her raise her eyebrow at me with slight disdain. "Let that be the last time you fall to your knees unless it's for your fucking king."

CHAPTER 5
MARIA

THREE WEEKS AGO

My HANDS ROAM *down my breasts, flattening out on my stomach as I run my fingers across the Italian lace and then settle my palms on my hips. Looking up into the mirror, I smile at myself as my fingers raise and delicately hold the string of pearls wrapped around my neck. My face heats, my cheeks flush as I close my eyes and remember a time not too long ago I wore a different string of pearls and how my world was forever changed after that.*

Time pauses in this hectic day as I sit there with my eyes closed and run back through our love, from the very beginning to today. I don't know how long I've stood still like this, but I jolt when I hear a sudden noise behind me.

"You're an Angel in white, mi Amore," Leonardo whispers. My eyes flash open and I find his in the glass. "An angel I don't deserve."

Leaning against the door frame, hands in his pockets, his

eyes undress me in my wedding gown in such a way that it sends shivers up my spine.

"What are you doing?" I whisper as he pushes off the doorframe and quietly closes the door behind him. I turn around just in time to hear the lock click, and butterflies begin to dance in my lower stomach a moment later. "Don't you know, it's bad luck..."

"I don't believe in luck," he smiles, as he turns and starts to saunter towards me. "Only us. That's all the luck I'll ever need."

His eyes graze over my appearance and he takes his time memorizing me from the tip of my head to my toes as he walks across the room. His stare lingers on my breasts, my curves, Before raising and locking on my eyes. A heated look deepens in his stare. A lustful current is now running between us as he continues to come a step closer.

Reaching my side, he spins me around quickly. I gasp out as my eyes raise once again to capture his in the mirror.

"So elegant," he whispers, his hand raising and brushing lightly against the curve of my neck.

"So refined," he growls, as his hand fists the pearls. He pulls me back tighter towards him, the bulge in his pants growing and rubbing against my lower back.

"So fucking polished," I hear him groan as I arch my back with a carnal instinct and grind into him. My eyes close once again as his grip slips from the pearls to firmly holding my neck and he sternly holds me still in his arms.

I feel his hot breath on my ear, a moan slipping from his lips a second later as I force my ass back against his hardening length. His teeth graze against my earlobe and he bites down slowly.

"Seeing you like this," he whispers, as his left hand lowers and he fists the skirt of my dress in his palm. "Makes me need to fuck you dirty, Maria."

I let out a gasp as the skirt of my dress begins to rise higher. Opening my eyes, my arousal peeks as I stare at the man that has me in his arms. A man whose wanton stare is locked on my own as he places a tender kiss on my neck and raises my skirt to my waist.

He looks down and his grip tightens instinctively around my waist, holding me closer than he was before.

"Fuck me," he breathes out against my neck before his wide eyes raise in the mirror. I look down, my garter belt, and nothing else stares back at me in the glass. No panties. No barriers between me and the man I'm about to marry.

"Your bare pussy is drenched, Maria," he growls in my ear.

Slap!

I cry out as he spanks my sex and my head falls back against his shoulder. I feel his fingers a second later at my opening, a moan falling from my lips as he traces my velvet skin, the tip of his finger running lightly down the center of my sex.

He releases his hold on my dress, my hips, and I feel his fingers at the top of my spine a moment later. The top couple buttons of the back of my dress gently come undone. The zipper lowers slowly. I lift my eyes and hold his as his hands tenderly come up to my shoulders and he slides the white gown off my body. It pools at my feet leaving me standing before him in nothing but my garter belt and stockings.

"Spread your legs, Amore," he demands, and I do what he says instantly. His eyes never leave mine in the mirror. "Wider, Maria," his growl is harsh a moment later before I force my feet out as far as my balance will let me.

"Touch yourself," he demands.

My eyes widen in shock. This was not how I saw this playing out. But he holds my gaze, lifting an eyebrow in challenge.

"Don't make me repeat myself, Maria."

Swallowing over the slight embarrassment, my hands shake slightly as they raise to my center, and my eyes close on instinct. I feel a tight grip around my throat a moment later. A warning I'm not behaving myself and I shutter.

"Open your eyes, Maria, and watch how much it pleases me to see you play with yourself."

My breath comes out shallow as my eyes flutter open, but I keep my gaze downcast towards my feet. I hear Leo silently groan out behind me as he takes a step towards me, his front pressing up against my back.

"Eyes on mine then, Amore, until you're ready to see how I see you." Looking up, Leo smiles as his mouth settles next to my ear. "Good girl."

His hand comes out of nowhere and grabs mine, forcing my fingers to enter my wet sex and a gasp to escape my lips. His eyes lower as his hand leaves mine and I force my fingers through my folds.

"Up to your clit," he hisses before sucking in a breath and continuing to watch me pleasure myself in the mirror. I respond instantly, doing as he asks, my tender flesh throbbing as my climax builds. "Good girl, just like that," he breathes, his voice shaky, his chest rising and falling behind me fast.

His eyes meet mine, dark, slightly deranged, wanting something he won't let himself take and I can't understand why since he took me over and over again last night. His grip on my throat loosens as his hands fall to his sides and I look down to see them fisted in tight restraint. His knuckles are white, looking up, I see his jaw is clenched.

"Fist your tit in your palm," he growls out and I do what he says, pinching my nipple and letting out a light moan. "Hard. Harder, Maria."

I release a small scream as my fingers dip inside me, my eyes close momentarily and I do as he's demanding. Pulling out of my heat, I open my eyes as I circle my clit and watch him in the mirror. I swear he's about to break. Swear he's about to turn me around, pick me up in his arms and fuck me against the nearest wall. But he doesn't, and the curiosity I feel inside only heightens the experience. His eyes are on mine, watching as I pleasure myself in the mirror. My hands move quickly to bring my body to climax.

"Do you see that?" he rasps, taking another step towards my back, forcing me a step further towards the mirror as I feel his thick length press between my ass.

Finally, drunk on a high I've never experienced before, I look up at myself in the mirror. I see my mouth hanging open. My eyes clouded with lust. My perky nipples aching for his touch. My pussy is drenched as it runs down my upper thighs, thickly coating my legs as they start to tremble. I pinch my nipple again and let out another scream as I look further down my body and watch as my fingers slip in and out of my center.

My cum coating them. My nub is so tender, swollen with need as I pull my fingers out and circle, rub, anxiously caress myself needing a release.

"Fucking breathtaking," he breathes shakily in my ear.

And he's right. I've never seen myself like this. On the brink of a place only he can take me. I look back up in my eyes as my fingers work my center harder, faster, and swear I have never seen myself so high. High on what only he can give me.

I've never felt more alive.

"You need to cum, Amore?" he insists, and I moan as my climax approaches. "I wish I could taste you, feel you as you explode in my mouth."

"Why can't you?" I barely get out, as my thighs start to go weak and I know I'm seconds away from cuming.

"When you're my wife, Maria," he growls. "After I make you a Moretti."

I gasp as my climax hits and Leo's hand reaches out and grabs me around the waist, holding me up so I don't fall to the floor.

"I'll take you, like I've never taken you before, Maria," he groans. I let out a scream at his words as my world goes black and my eyes close.

"Look at me," he demands. And I do. I gasp, pant, and moan as I coax every last drop of my climax from deep inside myself and he watches it run down my hand.

"When you're bound to me forever, mi Amore, I'll take you higher than you've ever been before, but for now, there's so much more pleasure in waiting," he whispers in my ear just as I pull my hand away from my center.

He reaches around me and smacks my pussy, dipping his

finger in once as I let out one final gasp. His smile is contagious as he brings it to his lips and can't resist the urge to suck myself off of him.

"Get on your knees."

Anxiously I turn and do as he says. My eyes cast down. My smell perfumes the room around us. With the tip of his finger, he raises my gaze to his and slowly unzips his pants. Pulling himself free, I swallow hard before opening my mouth wide and anticipating him filling me. He strokes himself a few times and watches me as I grow needy.

"Those pearls," he says, a hint of mischief lingering in his eyes as my hand raises and locks around them. "Take them off."

Confusion laces my thoughts, but I do as he says and then wait for more instruction. His hand wraps out his tip, and I watch as he circles his crown a few times. When he pulls back down his shaft, precum spills over the tip and he wastes no time pressing it to my lips.

I lick it up like it's heroine. Like a junkie needing her fix. My eyes close, loving the taste of him on my tongue.

"Wrap those pearls around your fist, Maria, then jack me off with them."

I look up at him and see his jaw set tight as he watches my mouth close over his tip. I quickly do as he says, wrapping the pearls around the palm of my hand, my mouth wetting his cock before my hand wraps around his shaft. I watch as his head falls back a second later in complete ecstasy.

The sounds he makes spurs me on as I slowly pull his dick through the wetness, the pearls, as I suck on the tip of his cock.

"Damn," he hisses, as his head falls forward and his eyes

lock with my own. "Good girl," *he grates out through clenched teeth as he watches me with a fire in his eyes.* "That's such a good fucking girl."

I smile around his tip as my hand moves faster, my spit drips down his length and the pearls pull up and down his cock, rotating in my hand deliciously and making me aroused knowing the way they feel against his sensitive skin.

"You need more, don't you, Amore," *he growls and my eyes lift as he continues to fill my mouth, desperately pleading with his.* "Like me," *he sucks in a breath as I start to work faster.*

"Fuck it."

Hoisting me to my feet, he grabs under my thighs and lifts me in his arms.

"You were always destined to be mine, Maria. A piece of fucking paper doesn't change that."

Quickly, he thrusts up inside of me and I scream out. The pearls are still wrapped around his throbbing cock and now sliding in and out of my opening as he pulls out and thrusts back inside me again.

"Fuck, Maria," *he breathes, as he rocks me slowly back and forth on his length, his face coming to rest against my neck.* "You and pearls, mi Amore. It's always been a fucking lethal combination."

I smile as he sinks his mouth down over my neck and sucks down hard. Everything about Leo is lethal. The way he walks. The way he talks. The way he fucks. I'll never get enough.

He lifts me higher in his arms, pulling himself out from deep inside me, and holds me there, suspended in our love. I feel the pearls slip out of me before he pulls them from himself and discards them to the side.

"I can't fuck you like I need to and worry about those things breaking, mi Amore," he gives me a smile before planting a tender kiss on my lips.

"I don't think I'd mind, Sir," I purr as he takes my bottom lip in his and bites down gently.

"Hmm," I hear him groan as his tip slowly pushes back into my wetness. "But I do. Because when I make us both cum, I want no fucking barriers. Nothing between us as I claim you. Right before I make you my wife."

I moan out as he picks up the pace and starts to fuck me harder. "Your wife, God, Leo, I love the sound of that."

He pulls back and looks me in the eye. A sort of broken turmoil hidden in the back of his eyes.

"I've been married to you my whole life, Maria. Making it official changes nothing. You were destined to be mine the day you were fucking born. You'll always be mine. No matter what."

CHAPTER 6
LEONARDO

MARRIED TO HER.

Our families didn't need to be united for me to know I would always be wed to Maria.

She owns me, body and soul.

Just like I dominate her in every damn way I can. But she's the one who's always really in control. Of my life. Of my future. Of my heart.

"If we move now, I have it on good authority it might fuck things up royally, tip Alfonso off," Declan's low hushed voice explains across the table pulling me from my thoughts.

Fuck Alfonso. I've got that situation covered. Although Declan doesn't need to know that yet. Like before, there are things he doesn't know. No one knows. And for now, I'd like to keep it that way.

It's midnight, and this is the first time I've ventured out since the shooting. Ushered through the back of one of the only places I trust in Sicily, the owner more loyal to me through the years than my own men. I look around the restaurant thankful the place is deserted except for two guards that block both entrances.

"On the other hand," he continues. "I also have confirmation that not doing so might screw up your family's future the longer the rat sits in your operation."

"Any tip on who the fucker is?" I hiss out, taking a bite of steak and swallowing it down with a large gulp of whiskey. It's the first real meal I've had in weeks. Shit, maybe even close to a month. I should slow down, and savor the experience, but the topic of conversation and my unsated hunger make it impossible.

"Got some ideas," he suggests, his eyebrow raised as he sits back against the booth. I take another bite of steak before reaching across the table and filling my glass. The whiskey only fuels a fire, a vengeance that's long overdue as I impatiently wait for him to elaborate. I welcome the need for revenge as it builds in my veins. It fuels me in a way I haven't felt in years. A way I suddenly realize I've been missing for far too long.

"Care to share?" My tone is sarcastic as shit, and he laughs because even with the loaded question, I've known him long enough to understand he's got no plans to show his cards in this game before he's damn sure he's right.

"Taking you to Maria now could end your life," his low chuckle pisses me off as he reaches for the bottle of scotch and fills his glass almost to the brim. "If Alfonso has eyes on us, and I've been told he does, one wrong move, one careless step, and they'll be sending Maria your corpse in a body bag."

"You forget who you're talking to, Ace," a wicked smile plays across my lips as I sit back in my seat. "I've been called a lot of things over the years, Dec. But careless is not one of them."

"Or," he adds, cutting me off as he sets down his glass and throws his elbows back across the top of the booth. "Going back now could mean the rat goes further into hiding. It could mean they'll continue keeping to the shadows, until he, or she, can put you both six feet under."

"The rat deserves to die," I grit out, my mind tracing all the people that we kept close around us these last few months. The new hires, new family, and friends from Maria's life before Italy in Vegas, to Sofia and Vincent's side of the mob. "And die they fucking will. Now. Not eat at my table, take up space in my house, and get an opportunity to get their claws within an inch of Maria and my child."

"Even if going back now risks their lives, too?"

I glare at him as he picks up his glass and takes a drink of scotch. His question suddenly ignites a rush of anxiety as it spreads like wildfire through my veins. The pit of my stomach turns as I ponder his question and then ask one of my own. "What do you know?"

He shakes his head, debating whether or not to tell me, but in the end, only takes another long sip off his glass and keeps his eyes on mine. He stays silent. Unyielding in keeping his secret. Just like I'm keeping mine. And then...

"The rat's doing what rats do best, twisting and implanting lies to the ones you love most. The ones that could hurt you most."

But he doesn't elaborate. Something tells me I don't need him to. I read what he's trying to say. Loud and clear. Still, to move forward and make sure there are no mistakes this time, I need to know more. I need to know all that he knows.

"If things were reversed..."

"Like they were with Mathew and Emma," Declan snaps. Leaning forward, he sets his arms on the table and bends in, glaring at me with a building rage. "You sick fuck," his menacing voice draws out. "You got off on keeping me in the dark for years, only telling me what you wanted to."

"That was for your benefit..."

"The fuck it was!"

"It kept you from murdering innocent people in your quest for fucking vengeance, didn't it Dec?" My voice thunders through the room around us, echoing off the walls.

Out of the corner of my eye, I see the guard up front peek his head around the corner to make sure everything's all right. I turn and give him a heated glare. He immediately goes back to his post as I focus back on the man across from me.

This wouldn't be the first time Declan and I were close to killing each other. Shit, I know it won't be the last. He's as hot-headed as I am. It's a miracle we haven't shot each other yet.

"Maybe I'm doing the same, Chief," he hisses, leaning back and gesturing towards me as he picks up his glass. "Maybe I'm saving you from yourself. Ever think about that?"

My head falls back against the booth, my eyes close, and I hate to admit I'm fucking spent. From the way I need to get back to Maria, to the constant *need* to keep hiding, to the wounds that are still fucking healing and the war that's broken out around us.

"There's only one person who can save me from myself,"

I whisper, more to myself than Declan, but he hears and lets out a heavy sigh.

"Yeah, and what the fuck do you think I'm busting my balls doing? Trying to get you back to her, Chief."

My eyes open, I look over at him but keep my head rested back against the booth. We silently sit and study each other for a moment. So much is being said and yet neither of us even saying a word.

When I first met Dec, fuck, I never would've guessed either of us would be where we are right now. Pussy whipped. Loving every sick second of it. Only eager for one thing.

More.

"Shit did you ever think a woman would have our balls in such a tight fucking vice," he laughs, knowing exactly what I'm thinking and feeling just as lost as I am as to how we got here.

"With the amount of pussy we got back in the day, Ace, not a fucking chance."

"Fuck, in hindsight, right, Chief," he chuckles to himself. "Hard to not become a reformed man after getting a taste of grade-A ass."

"Prime pussy," I smile, taking a sip of whiskey and savoring the flavor as it rolls down the back of my throat, wishing it was Maria's cunt exploding against my tongue instead.

"Superior in every way," Declan whispers in agreement a moment later, caught up in his thoughts as he looks out across the restaurant. "The only kind of worldly voodoo magic that will ever change a man like us. Am I right?"

"Who's to say I've fucking changed?"

He eyes me curiously, a mischievous smirk spreading across his smug chin, before tossing back the rest of his scotch and refilling his drink. Fuck, maybe I have changed, and maybe this was always me. The hard exterior was just a shell until Maria came along and cracked it. I think about that for a moment, really letting it sink in, before tossing back the rest of my glass and shaking my head.

Fuck no, I'm not some fucking shell that needed cracking. But I will admit there will never be another woman for me besides Maria. I'll even go a step further and concede the fact that, in my past, I wish there were no other women except Maria. That's a certifiable fucking fact.

"I can't finish what was started like I need to, Dec," I finally let myself confess. "Not when she's thousands of miles away," I sit up straight as my anger gets the better of me and my fist comes down with a loud thud on the table a few seconds later. "Fuck, not when I don't even know where she's at!"

"That was your request, Leo. Remember? Keep her hidden, even from you. Not my doing, Chief. But she's being watched, well, rat or no rat. Try to rest in that."

"I can't rest," I choke out, my emotions getting the better of me, and startling both of us before I reign them in. Fuck, maybe I've had too much whiskey. Maybe the fucking shell is cracked. Controlling myself as best I can, I sit up a little straighter. "I won't rest," I continue, swallowing over a lump that's somehow lodged itself in my throat. "Not until I can get back to her side and do what I need to do. There has to be some way that won't kill us both?"

I study him a moment, willing with my glare for him to break and tell me what he knows, but he stays silent.

"Fuck, if I knew half of the shit you did instead of being kept in the fucking dark, I would've already figured out how to put all of this behind me and get back to Maria. Back to my fucking life!"

He rolls his eyes before raising his glass to his lips. It's not like me to lose my temper. I've also never been kept in the dark, not since my early days running the streets for Luigi. I make the rules. I enforce them. I don't sit like a fucking duck and have someone else tell me what to do.

"There might be," Declan shrugs, taking another sip of scotch. "A way."

I sit up taller and search his fucking eyes for any sign that what he's thinking might be too dangerous. Might not be worth the risk. He eyes me sternly, never wavering, never giving me any signal that it's a thought we're better off not acting on.

"When do we leave?" I ask a little too anxiously.

"It'll take a few days to make sure it'll work," he sighs, setting his glass down and leaning forward, his elbows propped once again on the table. "But, Leo, I just want you to make sure you're aware of the risks you're taking by moving when we're not certain..."

"I'm aware," I cut him off harshly. "Where are we going? Where's Maria?"

He sighs, looking around the empty restaurant as if we don't have the place all to ourselves. Finally glancing back my way when he's certain no one will hear, he whispers, "Chicago."

Fuck me.

"Seriously?"

He just nods and my mind goes blank.

Shit, looks like I'm going home.

I haven't been to Chicago in years. Haven't seen my house, met with my men, took charge of the operation there in almost a damn decade.

When I first made capo, Luigi sent me there to get me seasoned. But after a few years, hell, I figured I was there to build a life. And I did.

Big house. Large grounds. Servants. Fucking head butlers. I had it all. I got comfortable, which is never smart in my line of business. But with Luigi ruling Italy and his cock sucking son scheduled to take his place, I figured fuck it. I did the job I was there to do and started building a future for myself as well.

That is, until the day Luigi called me home, just a few months before I crossed paths once again with Maria, what I had built went up in figurative flames. Men who weren't fit to reign the streets of the city stepped in underneath me in my absence, and I haven't been back since.

"Chicago," I echo, questioning if I really heard him right and Declan just nods his head. "The way I left Chicago, Ace, I thought I was never going back."

"Fuck yeah, everyone else did too," he laughs. "Which is why it was the perfect place to hide her. Perfect place to build an army around her. Until the time was right."

"You telling me the time is right?"

"Could be, with a few little tweaks," he suggests, raising an eyebrow and taking a sip of scotch.

Chicago.

The word rolls around in my head as I think of all the shit I left behind. The world I wanted. The one I thought was mine - until it wasn't. Fuck. Walking back into that world is going to feel a whole lot like coming home and being sentenced to hell all at the same time.

CHAPTER 7

MARIA

"I CAME HERE to talk to the boss. Not a woman. I don't care if she is his fucking wife."

The sound of the man's nose cracking a second later rings through the room. Collin wipes the blood off his knuckles onto a handkerchief he pulls from his pocket before flinging it at the bastard who's hunched over cradling his face. My hand shakes as it rests on the arm of the chair I'm sitting in, but other than that, I show no other sign of the coward that's lying right underneath my surface.

"My husband is not available," I hiss out trying to seem larger than I feel inside and concealing a lie that could ruin our families if it ever got out. "In his absence, you'll address me, and next time, you'll show more respect if you stand any chance of getting what you came here for."

He eyes me with anger as he wipes his nose and then looks up to Collin for some assurance that I'm serious. He's searching for some sort of sign that Leo would trust me to handle the family business when he's not around. I can tell.

And he would. *Wouldn't he?*

The thought makes me second guess everything I thought Leo and I stood for. I raise my trembling hand to my face, brushing a strand of hair behind my ear before quickly slamming it back down to disguise the way it's shaking. I hear a tisk at my side and look up. Magnolia stares straight ahead. Her disapproval of my weakness is evident as I catch a small frown forming across her lips.

"State your name," my voice is demanding as I look back towards the man who's still trying to stop his nose from bleeding. "And tell me what you want. I'm getting fucking bored with the male chauvinistic dramatics."

"That's better," I hear Magnolia whisper under her breath. At first, her comment pisses me off more, and I take that fire and let it build in my soul. Looking up at her with a scowl she regards me knowingly and I see things a little differently as I thank her silently for the rage she's so easily planted inside me.

The man looks again at Collin and it only fuels another fire that I'm tired of brewing under my surface. I steal a glance Collin's way and feel a sort of indignation for the sense of power and position he holds here when this isn't his damn family. This isn't his world. And it's time he stops playing like it is.

He gives the man a head nod in my direction and I let out an exasperated sigh rolling my eyes.

"My pal Frankie knows who hired the hit on your wedding," the man stammers out a few moments later.

I sit behind the desk in the mansion's office and I'm immediately shocked to silence, hardly believing what I'm hearing, and desperately wanting the man to go on but not wanting to show that desperation to a soldier I don't know.

"He's been fucking this *moll*, Janet, for close to two months now, right," he continues, completely oblivious. "The other day, Frankie told me Janet started fucking this other guy, ya know. So Frankie got mad. Waited in his car for the prick and Janet to come out of her place, then made his hit," he shrugs, as if killing an innocent man for having sex with your girlfriend is a normal thing, "Grabbed Janet, took her back inside, started roughing her up a little."

Magnolia and I both lean forward in warning. The slimy soldier notices and takes a step back. His eyes trail from mine, to Collins, to Giovanni who is stationed on my other side, and then finally back to mine before he gets the hint to proceed with caution.

"Not bad," he explains, raising his hands as if to calm a fight that's brewing in front of him. "I swear, he only got in her face a little. Ya know. Maybe pushed her up against a few walls." I'm not buying it. He notices that I don't believe him and then shrugs again. "I mean, he didn't beat her. I didn't see any bruises, or blood or nothin'."

"Not that I'd take you, a man I just met, at his word," I hiss out harshly, "but get to the point where Janet tells your asshole of a friend Frankie who hired the hit on my family."

"I was getting there, Doll. I promise."

I roll my eyes and look up and catch Magnolia doing the same. *Doll?* Like we're all back in some 1930s Rat Pack movie. Hate to admit it, but that term grates on my last nerve. It's condescending. Demeaning. A pat on the head from a man who believes he's your superior, not your equal.

"Anys-ways," he begins to continue, "Janet and Frankie eventually work shit out, right? Like really work shit out. The pushing and fighting," he demonstrates as he talks, his arms flinging back and forth with his body, "Eventually, well, they start fucking, ya know."

He shrugs.

I roll my eyes because if this guy shrugs or says 'ya know' one more time I swear I'll shoot him before I ever learn who hired the hit. Mobsters, the lowest ones, are all the same. Uneducated sheep who follow around the shepherd because they're too dumb to ever think for themself.

"...And Janet gets all emotional," he says. "Saying shit like, 'I love you so much, Frankie. So much more than to ever hire someone to kill you.'"

I look at Magnolia and she studies me curiously before my eyes lift to my other side and catch Giovanni's. He gives me an all-knowing glare, one I quickly come to hate, and then settles his attention back on the man in front of us.

"So Frankie is like, what the fuck did this bitc...er, excuse me, Doll, just say? And he starts to get in her face again..."

"Sounds like these two need an anger management intervention," Giovanni whispers under his breath.

Our man shrugs once again and continues, "...He's like, 'explain Janet,'" theatrics ensuing as he leans over an imaginary person and yells in the center of the room, "'or I'll do you in, like your fuck buddy Joey.'"

Another shrug. Straightening up, he slowly looks back our way.

"And so then Janet explains, she's like, 'the hit on the Nitti family.'"

His eyebrows raise, and a smile spreads across his slimy face anticipating me to praise him for what he's just said. When I don't, he frowns and goes on.

"Frankie asked her what she was talking 'bout, ya know, and she told him that what happened was a hired hit. Not a fucking feud. Not gangsters just being fucking gangsters. Someone hired Alfonso Capone to take out the Nitti's. Your Mom and Pops. If they hit you too, it'd be considered a fucking bonus."

My knuckles turn white as I clutch the arm of the chair tighter and take in all of what he's just said. "Who?" I hear my shaky voice finally whisper.

"See, I asked Frankie the same question..."

"And did he tell you?"

"Yeah," he shrugs before laughing. "He definitely fucking told me."

"Then who the fuck is it?"

He stands silent. The tension in the room builds the longer he withholds information. Out of the corner of my eye, I see Collin take a step forward in warning, and even though I'm growing each day more and more to not like the Irish man, I'm thankful when the man in front of me starts babbling again so I don't lash out at him now in the presence of all around us and say something I might eventually regret.

"I need more protection on my street," the man baffles me saying a moment later. "I got kids, Mrs. Moretti."

My breath catches in my throat because it's the first time I've heard someone call me by that name. A name I don't really possess yet.

"Three of them. The oldest, Michael, he's been hanging

out with the wrong crowd, talking to the wrong groups of people, ya know. I don't need him fucked up on drugs and shit. I need him to stay in school and…"

"Mrs. Moretti doesn't need to be bothered with…"

"No, it's okay Collin," I hold up my hand, interrupting.

Collin catches my eye and I see his jaw tick. The same look he's been giving me since we arrived in Chicago flashes across his face making me grow slightly nervous. Remembering the hatred I'm starting to feel for him, I decide to hold onto that instead of the nerves as I look away and stare into the man's pleading eyes.

I didn't have the best childhood. From what I know, neither did Leo. I can give this man that much for his kids. Especially if he can tell me what he knows. Although, that quickly proposes another question. A bigger one.

"How do I know I can trust what you tell me?" I ask.

Another shrug.

"Do, or don't," he says as if he could care less. "But I wouldn't come asking for something for my children if what I was offering as collateral was a fucking lie."

I instinctively slide my hands over my stomach and feel the slap of his words. I wouldn't bet a lie against my own flesh and blood either. Then again, I'm new to this way of life. New to this town. What's to say this man really has children and isn't just entirely off his fucking nut.

"He checks out," Collin informs me, knowing what I've got to be thinking as I look up to meet his eyes. "Michael, 17. Sabrina, 12. Tony, 8. They live over by West Garfield Park."

I rest my eyes back on our friend and sigh. "I'll do what I can." He smiles, happy with himself after taking the information from his friend and using it to his advantage. "Now..."

"So Frankie told me not to come here, ya know," he cuts me off nervously. His whole demeanor suddenly changing. "Because, originally, I wanted to see the boss and this would've been a lot harder of a conversation for us to have." He laughs anxiously, but I'm not entirely sure what he's meaning, and what's so funny. "I'm not lying when I say, I'm kinda happy now that it was just you, Mrs. Moretti, because I've heard from the fellas, ya know, just how well your husband takes blackmail..."

What did he just say?

"...It would be a lot harder to get the protection I need for my family if I was a dead man," he laughs again, this time without the nerves. "I mean, I wouldn't blame a man for killing me coming to him with the information I have, not that I'm saying I believe it. That's for you to decide. It's just..."

"Stop fucking blabbering," I insist, "And tell me, straight out, what it is you're saying?"

He looks at me stunned, as if I'm an idiot and new to this. But *I am* entirely new to this way of life, and it's suddenly pissing me off even more that everyone else can see so too.

I stepped up over a month ago now and I've been running the family ever since. I wonder how long it'll take before the men in the operation stop treating me like a foreigner. Even still, I wonder how long it'll take before I'm accepted as one of them. Before I'm fit to be feared and treated with some damn respect as I walk among them. Then, I sit, wondering, waiting for whatever this cocksucker has to tell me.

An eerie feeling settles in the back of my mind already

knowing what he's about to say before he even says it. I know what he's about to say. I knew before they even brought him in to see me, but my heart doesn't want to hear it. I don't want to believe it.

"Mrs. Moretti," he continues, the nerves setting back in again in the sudden shake of his hands. "The man that hired the hit was your husband. Leonardo Moretti."

Before I can process what he's just said, my eyes raise and catch the strong intimidating frame of someone suddenly in the doorway. A second later they lock on a steel haunted glare of a man that's not a force to be fucked with. A man I feared I'd never see again. A man that I just learned may have hired the hit on my family. And a man that I also just learned may or may not want me dead as well.

Leo.

I don't believe it. It's a lie. Isn't it?

My heart sinks knowing this wouldn't be the first time we've danced this dance between us. But the confidence that's built inside me these last several weeks with him gone tells me I'm damn sure I'm going to make it the last.

CHAPTER 8

LEONARDO

"Shut the fuck up, Johnny, or Ace here's gonna find a way to make you disappear. *Comprendere.*"

It's not a question, and I don't wait for his answer as I take a step into the room and hold the eyes of Maria in her seat behind *my* desk. My dick hardens. My fucking breathing is labored as I try and control every carnal instinct inside me right now that's screaming, raging, telling me to stalk across the room, grab her out of my chair by her damn hair, and fuck her good and hard across *my* desk.

Fuck everyone in the room. Let them watch. And fuck the look of disdain she's giving me right now as I take another step towards her because I've never seen her look more fucking thrilling than I do *right now*.

In charge. In control. And hell if it doesn't make me love her, want her, need her more than I already fucking do in life.

"Mrs. Moretti is finished with business for the day, Johnny," my voice taunts, as my insides tighten and the name I've been waiting months to call her falls from my lips.

"Giovanni," I hiss, as my eyes raise and catch the stare of a man I got to admit, I'm starting not to trust. I casually unbutton my suit jacket, my right hand sliding into my pocket and wrapping around my knife as I take a few more steps towards Maria. "Show Johnny out."

Her eyes lock with mine, and I take my time walking toward her. Rolling the switchblade across my fingers. If Johnny here gives us any problem, hell if Giovanni or anyone else in the room refuses to do as I say, they'll be doing it risking their fucking life.

"I haven't seen my wife in quite some time," my voice is low and menacing. "And it's come to my attention, we have a little matter of business to attend to ourselves. The rest of you can show yourself out. *Ora, affrettatevi.*"

Giovanni steps down from his place next to Maria, as does Magnolia. They walk past me, whispering amongst themselves as they go, thankfully taking my words, the ones telling them *now*, and to *hurry*, seriously.

Collin follows, but not after a warning glance in my direction. Our families have always been aware of one another, and worked a couple of jobs together over the years against the Russians. I've grown to admire Collin for the brutal way he conducts business, but I can't say I entirely trust him.

Not after learning there's a rat in my operation. Everyone is under fucking surveillance. Starting now.

As they all leave, my stare never leaves Maria's. Even after I hear the click of the closing door, my eyes stay locked on her intense glare as my malicious grin deepens.

This is not the welcoming sight I thought I'd see. Not

when I laid awake week after week, closer to death than I'd ever care to admit, praying I'd be graced with one more day to see her beautiful face. I thought our reunion would have me staring in her eyes as she rode my fucking cock. As I made her scream from the purest form of beautiful pain I've ever given her, right before selfishly making her take more. Over and over again. Never stopping until we were both completely satisfied.

But as I slowly slip the knife through my fingers, I cautiously place my other hand in my other pocket, and come to a stop at the foot of the desk and diligently study her.

I'm fucking lost as I stare into her eyes.

I'm entirely too confused as I attempt to read what I've missed, what has changed, as it dances across her features.

But the longer I stand there silently looking at her, I realize it proves pointless to search her out as she continues to mask everything she's feeling inside except for the obvious displeasure she feels at seeing my face again.

My eyes slide down lower. My breath catches in my throat as I take in her swollen stomach.

Il mio bambino.

I hide my emotion as I feel my glare deepen and my eyes raise once more to her own.

I'll be damned if I speak first. She's sitting in my chair. Ruling over my kingdom. What's more, she's doing it with a fire in her eyes that deserves to be beaten out of her as I take her across my knee and remind her who's really in control.

Not just in this life, but over her fucking body. Her mind. Her pleasure and her pain.

All she has to do is keep fucking tempting me. Keep

looking at me as if I'm the devil and I'll find great pleasure in watching as she experiences a whole new level of hell.

"You have no right to call me by that name," she starts in a whisper, referring to the mention of her already being my wife. "We're not..."

"You have no right to sit in that chair," I cut her off, nodding towards my desk and watching as her eyes lower and she ponders her place. Not just in this house. But in life. "You have no right to rule a world you know nothing about, Maria."

Her eyes flash up and capture mine. Fuck, she has every right to reign in this world given her bloodline. What's more, my fucking blood mixes with her own as she carries our child in her womb. She has more rights than either of us.

But she doesn't hold the prestige, the rank, the power she needs to be influential and to make a difference. Not yet. But she will. Her uncertainty shows as her eyes slip once again and she rises out of the seat so quick to surrender.

We'll work on that too. The only surrendering she'll ever do again is on her knees in front of me as she's sucking my hard cock.

"Silly of me to think you'd be proud," she bites back as she makes her way around the desk and takes a step down from the landing. As she starts to walk towards the door, I turn and watch as she retreats and something deep inside me begins to hurt.

Fuck, we're far from done here.

"Silly of me to think you'd..."

"Come back?" I snap as I stare viciously at her back.

She stops, spins around quickly, and then levels me with

an icy glare. I smile after a moment when she refuses to respond and then glance towards the floor briefly as I take a step in her direction.

"*Mi Amore*," I sigh, "I thought you respected me." I look up as I take another step closer and watch her eyes widen in question. "I thought I could trust you, more than I found out I could trust your *famiglia*."

"So, it's true?" I cock my head to the side and bite my bottom lip, my cock hardening from just the nearness of her, from the earlier thought to make her submit on her knees in front of me like a good fucking wife should, as I wait for her to go on. "It's true, Leo. You killed them?"

Fire burns in her eyes as she steps into me. Our child stands between us, the only reason I'm not forcing her into submission right now. I watch as her spine straightens, her jaw sets tight, and the fire burns brighter than I've ever seen it blaze before in her eyes.

"I did what I had to do," I hiss back, stepping into her. "I'll always do what I have to do. For you, Maria. For our child."

"And that includes killing the people that brought me into this world?" Her voice trembles as tears fill her eyes. It takes everything I have in me not to break as she starts to fall apart in front of me. The first lesson in strength, is you stand tall on your own before you ever have people you know you can trust standing at your side.

"What happens in say five, ten, twenty years, Leonardo," she spits out as she takes a step back in anger. "When our child is older. When someone tells you I've been unfaithful?"

She points bitterly at her chest, pausing briefly to let her burn set in. And it does. It really fucking does. The thought of Maria ever being unfaithful stings as it worms its way around my heart.

I was prodding a snake earlier when I suggested I couldn't trust her. Up until this moment, I never thought of any other option *but* to trust her. She's the beginning and the end for me. Not trusting the woman I'm determined to make my wife is not an option.

She brings up a good point, though. What would I do? The burn in her eyes and the sickness I feel deep inside my gut clouds my better judgment. She turns her back on me once again and it has me reaching out to her in fury.

"Don't put your hands on me," she yells, spinning back around quickly to stare me in the eyes. She wrestles with her skirt while taking another step back and finally produces a small pistol from her side.

Interesting, Mrs. Moretti. Future, but fuck semantics. She's got me more than ready to fight as I square off against her, blood rushing through my veins, dick hard as fuck and a new sort of high fueling us, smoldering in both our eyes.

She looks me up and down as if I'm a threat. Then she looks at me like I'm a fucking stranger. As if I'm the damn plague. I stand there, stunned, realizing that hurts even more than drowning in a lifetime of thinking she'd ever be unfaithful.

"You did what you had to do?" she mocks.

I reach out and grab her wrist, taking a step into the pistol and holding it firmly against my chest.

"You want to kill me, Maria?" Her eyes flash and fill with

a need for violence, telling me yes. Our breathing quickens as she pushes the metal further into my chest.

"Then do it," I seethe, knowing she won't but getting off just the same on the intoxicating foreplay.

"This isn't the first time you set me up, bet against my life, in order to ensure a win, Leo."

My grip on her wrist tightens, my smile growing as I stare into her heated glare. "The only life I ever risk, Maria, is my own."

"Hmm," she smiles. "Doing what you have to do, right?"

"That's right."

"Well, then enjoy watching me do the same, Leo," she pulls her wrist away from my grasp, and I reluctantly let her go, "As I do what I have to do," she turns, quickly making her way towards the door. "Which is put me and *my* child first."

Something inside me snaps. Something I know I'll regret, but before I can tell myself I'll live to want repentance, I take two strides, grab her from behind and wrap my hand tightly around her throat.

"Leo," she breathlessly pleads.

But it isn't the pleading of a woman who wants me to make love to her. It isn't the begging or beseeching of a lover wanting me to please them the only way I know how. It's the anxious pleading of a woman who honestly believes the worst in me, and my heart hurts as my grip loosens and my hands fall to her stomach.

"*Our* child," I growl into her ear. "I would never, *ever*, hurt you, Maria, or *our* child. *Lo sono perso senza di te.*"

Her body softens, and her walls crumble slightly as she

hears the truth only she knows. I would be *lost without her*. I was once before. I made a promise to never be that way again.

"But," she whispers as a whimper escapes her lips. *"Mi Famiglia."*

"I'm the only family you need now," I hiss spinning her around and taking in her startled stare. "What I said before was wrong. I trust you, Maria. Like I thought you trusted me. The only thing that will ever matter to me more than anything else, more than anyone in *the family*, is you, and our *bambino, comprendere?* Nothing else matters now. No one else lives if they threaten to take what is mine."

"You're mine. Our child," I whisper, as my eyes lower and I take my hand and place it against her stomach, "is mine, Maria. I'll protect you both with my life. Always. I shouldn't have to tell you this, *mi Amore.* You should already understand..."

"Did they threaten you?"

My eyes raise instantly. My jaw tightens as it grinds in anger. "It's probably best we don't discuss it."

"If they threatened you, Leo, I'd try and understand. I'd try and forgive..."

"Forgive?" I snap, pulling her harshly into my chest as anger flares in both our eyes. "What I did needs no forgiveness from you, Maria. I don't need your mercy. I'll never need your blessing."

"So how I feel is disposable," she hisses back. "Indifferent? Inconsequential?"

"How you feel will not dictate my actions," I clarify, hoping she understands. "Sometimes, you won't understand,

and I won't waste my breath explaining it to you before I have to pull the fucking trigger."

"I won't live my life in a marriage that's a dictatorship, Leonardo."

"And I won't have my wife be a fucking weight on my shoulders, Maria," I yell, startling myself a little, but not her and she takes a step back and her glare deepens. "In this life," I continue a little calmer. "You either trust me, even when you don't understand or..."

"What?" she demands. "What? Our marriage isn't going to work?"

I wasn't going to say that, but I let it hang out there as an ultimatum anyway, hopeful that she'll take my side and cave.

"Sometimes," I grit out a moment later, "the things I might tell you could only hurt you. Could get you killed. I won't take that risk."

"I would," she insists instantly, her breathing coming quickly as she crosses her arms in front of her chest. "I always would. Do you want to know why Leo? Because I don't keep secrets from you. I never have. I don't want to have our life, our marriage, be full of secrets."

"Even if they're meant to protect you?"

"Yes," she shouts. "Even then."

"In life, you don't always get what you want."

"What is that supposed to mean?"

"It means, good luck with your temper tantrum, Princess," I take a step towards her, the beast in me finding sick satisfaction as she takes a step back in fear. "And you're not fucking leaving. Remember, Maria. You're mine. Always have been. Always will be. Fucking remember that."

"I'll do what I damn well please," she hisses, turning quickly on her heels and marching off towards the door.

"Not with my fucking child you won't."

She stops walking quickly. A dim reality pulling her back into our encroaching darkness. I'd never let her leave this house. And she damn sure isn't going to be let out of my protection so long as she's carrying my child.

She spins on her heels, a scorned look graces her features. "I'm our child's mother. I say…"

"The only one who has any say in this house, is me, Maria." Her eyes widen as I take a heated step in her direction. "You want to challenge that, go ahead," I tempt her with each calculated step I take. Each one is more heated than the other. "See how that works out for you. Just remember how it worked out for you before."

"I won't be held…"

"Hostage? Captive? Prisoner," I taunt, as I reach her side and brush a stray strand of hair behind her ear. Leaning in, I whisper, "My slave, Maria?"

She pushes me back but I'm always quicker than the brat that likes to reside under her surface. Grabbing her wrist and pulling her close behind me, I stalk off towards the exit. With a loud bang, I slam open the office doors and take in the startled expressions of the people still standing in the entryway.

Johnny is gone, but Giovanni looks slightly frightened as I pull a shouting Maria behind me and head for the stairs. Magnolia and Collin exchange a twisted smile before I catch the shake of Declan's head in the shadows. Daniella, I make note, is nowhere in sight.

"Let me go!" Maria yells, and I only tighten my grip on her wrist.

Quickly climbing the stairs and reaching the landing on the second floor, I haul her off towards the master bedroom and kick in the damn door. Her shouts have turned to screams as she digs her heels into the carpet and tries to prevent me from going any further into the room. But even her scratching claws couldn't stop me now. Turning and flinging her over my shoulder, I stalk across the room and as gently as I can toss her stubborn ass on the bed. She braces herself against the four-post frame and takes a deep breath. Seconds go by like hours as we stand off against one another.

"You can't keep me here against my will," she finally whispers once she's caught her breath.

With my head hung low and a devilish smile spreading across my face, my voice is low and threatening as I say, "watch me."

With that, I turn quickly, stalking out of the room and slamming the bedroom door behind me. She's quick to run for it, and I feel her pull back on the doorknob, yelling and calling me names I never thought I'd hear fall from her lips.

"Can I help you, Sir?" My old butler Jerry calls out as he rushes to my side with the key. I take it from him quickly and lock the door before Maria can get it open any wider.

"I want two men on these doors at all times," I demand, catching my breath and starting for the stairs. "No one comes in or out unless authorized by me. Including you," I hiss, looking at Magnolia as I reach the downstairs and seeing her smile widen "Declan, Collin, in my office."

"What about me, Leo..."

"Giovanni," I hiss, cutting him off and leveling him with a heated glare as I reach my office door. He's at the top of my surveillance list, and from the look I'm giving him now I'd say he finally fucking noticed. "I have good reason to believe you're the reason for my fucked-up homecoming. You're lucky you're still alive. You want to keep it that way. You keep your damn mouth shut, or next time you won't be so damn lucky."

CHAPTER 9

LEONARDO

"The Rossi family is asking for more protection on the upper north side, Boss," Collin informs me later that night, but my head is still fucked and focused on one thing. Maria. Which is an all too familiar complication, instead of my mind being wrapped around business as it should be.

"You want me to send a few guys from central up there until things cool off?"

"What's the damn problem?" I grit out, sitting up straighter in my chair and attempting to focus. We've been in my office since I locked Maria in our room, eight hours ago. To say I'm fucking spent from the briefing I'm getting upon my arrival, as well as my future bride's unwelcome homecoming, is an understatement.

Adding to my frustration is the fact that for the first hour since we resigned ourselves to my office, all I heard as I tried to fucking conduct business was Maria's screaming, yelling, beating of the damn door right above my damn head. She'll be punished for that, we both know it. And the fact that she carried on anyways only makes me more anxious to get back to her and deliver the penance she earned.

"A few wise guys from O'Hare decided to pay a visit to Uptown, rolled in like they owned the place last Saturday," Ricardo informs me from his seat across the room. He's an old associate I haven't seen since I first left the city. "You remember how Andrea takes to newbies. He'd never met the duo before, wasn't informed they made rank. Needless to say, *you* sent two dozen gladiolas to the boy's funerals just yesterday," I nod in understanding, but before I can say anything, Ricardo goes on. "Now these boys' friends and family want retribution. Word is they're going to take it upon themselves to seek their revenge, even though these two wise-guy idiots started the fight in the first place."

"Mouthing off as a new soldier will always get you six feet under," Federico says next to him, "They deserve to be made an example of for what they did."

Federico is another associate I haven't seen since I left Chi-Town. Once upon a time, these two were my right-hand men. It's nice to see nothing has changed and they've kept the town and my place in shape while I was away. As best they could anyways.

At Frederico's words, my mind trails back to the example I set with Maria. Telling her the truth could very well be my biggest lie when I said that there are things I can't and won't ever tell her.

But she's not inconsequential, never fucking has been. And I would absolutely take the time if I could, to tell her why, how, and when, before I ever made another move in this life if I knew it would settle her. It's just in my line of work sometimes there just isn't enough fucking time. A fact she knows, if she wasn't being so emotional. She has reason to be though, another truth I can't seem to shake long enough even eight hours later to try and conduct business so I can wrap up this meeting and get back to Maria upstairs.

I shake my head and try and focus. "Put a couple of guys up there, but tell Andrea to cool off. I'm not going to spare them long. If he does this kind of shit again, pulling the trigger without more merit, I won't back his ass the next time he needs it."

"Yes, Boss," Ricardo says as he rises and makes his way out of the room.

"What about the loop," Frederico asks.

"What about it?" I snap.

He looks at Collin, and I do the same, but the bastard only shrugs his shoulders telling Frederico to go on.

"Antonio Romano's daughter was raped on State Street last week," I swallow hard and attempt to cool the fire running in my veins. It's not the first time and it won't be the last, but with a child on the way of my own, all of a sudden news like this hits a little too close to home.

"Who's been heading up operations since I've been gone?"

"Tony Nicoletti."

"Fuck, that explains it," I grit out under my breath.

I leave and the whole town goes to shit. I'm surprised Luigi didn't send me back sooner to clean up the mess Tony's made of things. Then again, I guess he had me on more important tasks. My future wife included.

Tony and I never played for the same team back when we

both ran the Chicago side of the business. Never fought for the same side. Mostly because Tony knew I'd always fucking win.

He's been on his own since I can remember, determined to take over the mob eventually and put us all out of business. It's a surprise he hasn't been taken out yet, then again, he hasn't entirely fucked himself over in order to earn a bullet to the center of his thick skull. There's still time though.

He never had the guts to toe the line hard enough with me back in the day, too scared he'd end up six feet under before the fun ever really got started. Guess I shouldn't be surprised he'd step into my shoes the second I hopped a plane back to the mainland. And I guess we're about to see how gutsy Tony's gotten in my absence now that I'm back and plan on staying, for the foreseeable future at least.

"Only way we figure the pedophile got away with it," Federico continues, "is because he's a fucking *poliziotto*."

I keep my eyes locked on Collin's for confirmation that what Frederico is saying is true. It's a big deal to go around blaming the law in any organization, organized crime, or legit operations. I'm not about to give them the go-ahead they need unless I know we're absolutely sure we're right. Collin gives me a nod, looking to the floor with a heated disgust that I equally feel as it begins growing and rising in my gut. Last I saw Antonio's daughter she was barely one year old. That means his girl is nine, ten years old at most.

"Fuck, they've always been dirty mother fuckers," I grit out on a heavy sigh. "What's Antonio asking?"

"What they all ask for, Boss. Vengeance."

I nod my head and look out across the room, focusing on a

small crack in the plaster and thinking, my mind fucking wandering again to Maria. Maria will want vengeance. If not for what I had to do before, then for what I am doing to her right now. And I won't stand in her way when she seeks it.

"Boss?"

"Take Collin," I snap looking up at both men as I lean back in my chair. "Tonight. No fucking witnesses."

They both nod as Frederico rises and they begin to make their way out of the room.

"And Collin," he stops in the doorway, turning and waiting for me to continue, but I take a moment, sitting with the sickness for what's been done, and wanting to choose my words wisely. "When you find the prick who did it, cut off his dick while he's still alive. Slowly. With a dull pocket knife. Send it as a message to the chief of police. If he hasn't heard by now that I'm back in town, he'll get the fucking message loud and clear."

"Any message you want us to send to his wife?"

"His fucking wedding ring," he turns to leave and I add, "cut off his finger, hell his whole damn left hand and ship it back to her."

A sinister smile graces Collin's face. "Right, boss," he turns to exit, but not before calling over his shoulder, "but the chief knows you're back in town, Leo. He's been to see Maria."

He starts to walk away, slowly attempting to escape out of the doorframe when I yell, "And!"

I've never liked the chief of police in this town. Most others, I have the bastard on payroll. But here, the prick likes to act like he's God and it's his sole mission in life to bring down everything and everyone that he feels won't enter the Kingdom of Heaven with him. The fact that he's taking it upon himself to play judge is the fucking irony, but the bastard is too dumb to understand and too careless in his own self-righteous world to even notice.

He gets his hands dirty from time to time, usually with Tony. But arrests the next guy for running the same damn operation. Like I said, judge and jury and it makes me fucking sick knowing that those two had full reign of town while I was gone.

"And," he laughs as he makes his exit, mocking me as my blood pressure spikes, "Ask your wife."

I grip the arm of the office chair tight in my fist as my jaw clenches, and still, the smug bastard goes on. "It'd be best coming from her. Unless, of course, you have a good reason not to talk to her?"

I reach for my gun and pull the trigger just as his sorry ass escapes out the door. Bullets fly, cracking into the doorframe as Collin successfully makes his retreat and slams the door. His muffled menacing laugh is all I hear as I hang my head in my hands and let out an angry sigh.

If I didn't owe my life to that son-of-a-bitch, for watching over Maria, he'd be dead for talking to me that way. It's also the reason why he's not the first suspect on my list of those under surveillance. He's proven his trust in the past, but I'm not an idiot and know people can change, Maria's harsh welcoming proof of that. Until I'm absolutely sure, his ass is still considered a minor threat.

"Life was a lot easier when we just fucked pussy and didn't think of it after, am I right, Chief?"

Any normal man would agree, but being honest with myself means admitting there was a time that I didn't think of Maria after I fucked another woman. That I didn't look at someone else as I claimed her and envisioned Maria underneath me instead. She's always been there. Always haunted me.

In fact, I was cursed more when she wasn't in my life. Haunted by all the ways I hated myself after taking another woman. I've never been able to escape her. Not even now when she wants nothing to do with me and is acting like she would rather I never came back to her at all.

"Bourbon?"

Is he kidding?

"Bring the fucking bottle," I growl as I lift my head and see Declan grab two glasses off the bar across the room.

"Are you ever going to tell her about Vincent and Sofia?"

He pours us two large portions and makes his way across the room, bottle in hand. Setting it down on my desk, I debate his answer for less than a second before knowing there is no deliberation needed. There will only ever be one answer until the time is absolutely right. What's more, I decide on when that is. So, for now, the answer is...

"No," I grit out as I take the glass he's poured me in anger. He plops himself down in the chair in front of me and studies me for a moment before taking a sip off his glass.

"Even if you lose her?"

I release a heavy sigh and push my chair to the side, spinning 180 degrees to face the floor-to-ceiling windows behind my desk. Snow has begun to fall, and I raise my glass to my lips strongly debating the best answer to his question. In the end, the only choice I have is the one that keeps her safe.

"Yes."

"I'd do anything to keep Magnolia," he instantly retorts. "Shit I have done anything. I came groveling on my fucking knees to you. Went behind the bureau. Signed my life away to people she'll never meet, never know about, to ensure I could give her everything she'd ever want."

"If I lose Maria," I grumble, "It's what she wants."

"Even if you have the power, the answers, to stop her from leaving."

"She won't leave, I won't let her."

"You can lose someone even when they're sitting right next to you, Chief," he sighs, bringing a truth to light that just might be my biggest fear.

I bring my glass to my lips and take a large sip, letting the bourbon burn slowly as it makes its way down the back of my throat. The snowflakes have grown bigger, their descent is faster as they fall to the earth and start to stick. An inevitable beginning to their end. Kinda like the way Maria and my relationship has always been.

"If I have to lose her to keep her safe, so be it."

"And if you lose yourself?" Declan's voice has grown angry as I hear him stand, but I keep my eyes on the world outside and the inevitable freeze that's begun. "I've been there, Leo. Hell is no match for what that does to a man. You've never been unlucky. Yet. Welcoming that kind of suicide will surely kill you. That is, if she doesn't first."

His footsteps retreat and I hear the door slam a moment later. Taking another long drink of bourbon, I sit with his words in silence as a blizzard starts and the sky grows darker above. Would I really risk losing myself before risking telling her the truth? Even if I can make sure I'd succeed in keeping her safe? The answer is simple. I'll keep any damn secret I need to in order to protect her and my child. Even one that might one day inevitably be the key to my own self-demise.

CHAPTER 10

TWELVE YEARS AGO

"This better be good, Dec," I fume. "This time, no fucking around."

Hastily, I take long strides towards the back door of the warehouse. It's midnight. Witching hour. And fuck, I feel the devil inside rising as I check to make sure my gun's fully loaded. Stashing it back in its holster, I take my bowie knife from Declan's hand as he catches up to my side. His heavy steps match my own as we reach the back door to the building and pause. Turning our backs against the cool concrete walls, I search out the night around us to make sure we weren't followed. My men do the same from a distance, standing watch by the car, ensuring a clean getaway if we need it.

"Now why would I ever want to fuck with you, Chief?" Dec grits out through bared teeth as he checks his ammunition. "Besides, giving you this tip, my ass is on the line here."

"With who? Don't tell me the feds are relying on you to take him in?"

"Fuck authority, you get first dibs on this one as far as I'm concerned. Especially considering what it concerns."

A tip that I never expected to land in either of our laps. A hint that maybe I'm not alone in this life after all.

"That's why this is a beautiful partnership, Ace. Can't climb the ranks if you aren't willing to do a little dealing on the side. Rub shoulders. Shake a couple of hands. Make sure your people are in the right place at the right time," I pull my black gloves from my back pocket and slip them on fast. "It's that kind of support that'll make an empire only stronger."

"Whose empire?" Declan taunts with a raised brow. "Yours, or Luigi's?"

"Like you said, Dec. Fuck authority. One day, this will all be mine."

I push off the wall and take a step back. Declan does the same, raising his hand as he takes a step towards the door and starting to count down on his fingers, starting at three. Cracking my neck from side to side, I take a deep breath and hold it in. I make my lungs burn as anticipation starts to slither up my spine. I'm more than ready for his ass to get down to one and open the damn door. When he finally does, a surge of adrenaline I've never felt before rushes through me. The key to one of the most important things that I once thought I lost, thought was gone forever, is supposed to be waiting on the other side.

With stealth, we move through the doorframe. We don't make a noise. We don't make a fucking sound as we walk with our guns raised into the room. My eyes scan the inside of the building, but through hanging plastic and rows of chopped cars and their haphazardly discarded parts, I can't make out the man I need to. The man that's about to take a bullet through the back of his cursed head if he doesn't give me the tip Declan was assured he had.

After a moment, a rustling sound catches our attention in the back. I give Declan a stern look and start to make my way towards it. He follows quickly.

"You set me up," I hear a familiar voice say. "I thought we had a deal. A fucking arrangement."

"Don't talk to me like I'm your bitch," another voice says, one I recognize all too well. "The charges will be dropped. Your records cleared. Tell your boss he has nothing to worry about. The price on this bastard's head was higher than what you offered me."

"Since when does the Chicago police take offers they're not instructed to? I thought you worked for me?"

My movements are slow as I look towards Declan and we both stand down, stashing our guns away the further we walk towards the scene at the far end of the room. He knows the voices as well. *These fucking idiots.* If they got in the way of why I came here tonight, they both just signed their death sentence.

"Since the Nicoletti family proved they don't have the power they once let on."

"Keep running that mouth, Rinaldi. When it comes time for election you won't have the backing you were promised. You want to make Chief? You stop the bullshit, or we won't 'get out the vote' as promised. You'll be on your fucking own."

"Children!" I tisk, rounding the corner and pulling a pack

of cigarettes from my slacks. The two men instantly are on guard, raising their guns and taking aim. "What have I told you about fucking fighting on my side of town."

I place the smoke between my lips as I come to a stop in the middle of the room. Lighting the end, I glance behind the two dumb fucks and see the man that held the information I needed, gutted, what's left of him dangling out of the chair he sits in. My jaw clenches. My anger roars as I blow out smoke and gesture towards the carcass of unrecognizable flesh behind Nicoletti and Rinaldi.

"Your handy work?"

"What the fuck's it to ya?"

My hand reaches for the gun at my hip, but Declan releases a heavy sigh at my left. "Fuck, if this goes down tonight, I can't cover this one up, Chief," he whispers under his breath. "Too many eyes on me. One, yeah. Three? Fat fucking chance."

I won't fuck Dec over. I can't. To get to where I'm going in life, you got to have people on your side. The right men in place. The right *kind* of men. Which excludes these two fucks standing before me.

With a crack of my neck, I take a step towards the babbling fools center stage and take another long drag of my cigarette. Their guns are still raised, but Nicoletti's hand starts to shake. I grin at the bastard, enjoying my smoke and trying to rehash a plan that doesn't put my ass, or Declan's, in hot fucking water.

"You test my restraint, Nicoletti," I blow out the smoke and watch it circle his head. "I can't deal with you as I please tonight. But mark my fucking words. You're a dead man. One day. In this life. I'll make sure of it."

"He's just a Russian soldier that owed us more than he was worth, on more than one occasion, Leo."

I glance back at the man in question as Nicoletti finally lowers his gun. Rinaldi is a little slower to follow his lead but eventually puts his away as well.

"We take out pieces of shit like him regularly for half of what was due."

Taking a step forward, I toss my cig to the floor and reach out and grab Nicoletti by the back of his neck. Pulling him close, so my mouth rests near his ear, I place my knife against his stomach and twist the blade. He squirms and I grip him tighter. Rinaldi reacts, but he's too slow as Declan takes a step in his direction, kicking his gun out of his hand before he can ever get a good aim. Dec raises his pistol, cocks it, then cocks his head to the side with a grin.

"He had information I needed," I hiss into Nicoletti's ear. "Information, that can't be provided by anyone else. How are you going to repay that debt, huh? He's on my side of town, Nicoletti. The proper thing to do is to fucking ask before you take liberties in someone else's territory. Maybe then you'd know not to be fucking around with something, someone, that had something I needed. Something your life isn't worth half of."

"I didn't think…"

"You never fucking think," I seethe. "That's your problem. No common sense. You think you'll rise to power by force. By taking what's not yours to take when no one's watching."

My grip tightens, and I see Rinaldi take a step to the right, attempting to get to his weapon.

"Fuck no," Declan laughs at the stupid bastard. "Stay right where you are you fucking cock-sucker. Cops. All the fucking same. Think they can do what they please whenever the hell they want. Think you hold the power when you'll always only be at the bottom of the ranks."

"Yeah," Rinaldi mouths off. "And how would you know."

Declan smiles. If only Rinaldi really fucking knew who he was dealing with. What he doesn't know, might kill him later. But we'll leave that just between Dec and me for now.

My attention turns back to the man who's still struggling to get out of my grip. "The world would be better, if I snapped your neck in two," I hiss. Twisting my blade, I push it against his skin until I see blood pool on his white dress shirt. "Gut you like your friend."

Nicoletti lets out a slight scream as I turn him to look at the fate he's bound to meet if he ever crosses me again. "The information you took from me tonight should cost you your life. It almost cost me mine. It's irreplaceable."

"I didn't know," he stammers. "I didn't..."

"Think?" My blade cuts deeper and he yells. Rinaldi makes a move for it, but Declan fires off a shot, wounding him in his arm.

"Fucking hell!"

"Another move and the next one goes through your fucking head."

I grin. Declan might act like he's working for the good side the law. But in his head, he's just as fucking sick as I am.

"I'll make it up to you," Nicoletti screams. "I promise. I don't know how. But I will. Just..."

I push him out of my hold and he loses his balance, falling to the floor at the feet of the dead body in the middle of the room. He struggles to get up, falling into the pool of blood on the floor. Slipping into the inevitable death bed he made for himself.

"Get the fuck out of here," I yell.

He scrambles up, finally catching his balance, and gestures for Rinaldi to follow as they hurry and make their way to the back door. Rinaldi gripping his shoulder in pain.

"My gun," Rinaldi shouts.

"Fuck no," Dec laughs. "You're a certifiable nut if you think we'd let you leave with that."

I wipe Nicoletti's blood off on my pant leg and reluctantly watch him leave. This isn't the first time he stood between me and the information I needed most. But I swear to God, as sure as I'm standing here breathing now, it will be the last.

"You think you can find me another lead?" I fume as I pull another smoke from my pack and light up.

"One day," Dec sighs. "If I'm lucky. Hell, it was only by chance I came across this one."

"How often do you deal with the Russians?"

"Not as often as you'd think."

"That's something that needs to change."

"Hm," Dec pauses as we start to make our way towards the door, considering what I've just said. "And you think you can change that?"

"If it gets me the information I need, I could."

"Pull your strings, and I'll start pulling mine. One of these days, something will come up."

Declan glances back behind us at the body still tied to the chair. Pushing through the back door, we're quiet for a moment as we start to make our way back to the car.

"What should we do about that?" Declan asks, gesturing over his shoulder.

"Burn it," I hiss, nodding to one of my men as we reach the car. He nods back, gesturing for one or two others to follow him inside and do as I say.

"And, how am I supposed to explain the fire?"

I take a long drag off my smoke, holding it in, letting it burn away the hope, the anticipation I felt before we barged through that door.

"What can I say, Dec," I whisper as the smoke slowly leaves my lips. "Sometimes, the best way to deal in *this* life is to fan the fucking flames. Hope you survive the fire of hell."

"Only the devil himself has that kind of power."

"The devil is no fucking match for the wrath that'll rain down if someone stands in the way of me getting the information I seek again."

"Do you think she's alive?"

"I don't know," I whisper. "But that won't stop me from trying to find her."

CHAPTER 11
MARIA

My chin rests just underneath the bubbles filling the bath. After an hour of screaming, and crying, I have to admit - carrying on like a two-year-old - I checked all the windows in the room and master bath, but it was no use. I'm too high up, there is no easy way down like a ledge or balcony to help lower myself, and I wouldn't take the risk to my child either.

Stuck. That's one word to describe how I feel. Dejected. Used. Abused in more ways than one. Those are only a few more of the million words and reasons I now harbor strong hate towards the man I am supposed to love.

I lift my toe out of the bath and plug the water spout with it. Stuck. Just like me. Releasing a heavy sigh, I sink lower in the bath and think back to another time I lay in a warm bubble-filled tub thinking about Leonardo. It seems like years and mere days ago when we first crossed paths again. Although this time, I have no desire to pleasure myself with the thoughts of him as I wait for his return, that's for damn sure.

I'd poke his eyes out right now, followed by his seemingly cold heart, if given the chance. I struggle a little as I release my toe from the spout. My head turns and my eyes catch the glimmer of my engagement ring in the late afternoon light coming in from a nearby window. With my thumb, I rotate it back and forth on my finger and watch as the diamonds catch the light. I notice the bathwater has started to grow colder, much like it seems the heart of the man who once promised to love, cherish, honor - until death do us part, has too.

When he gave me this ring, I was foolish enough to think nothing could ever stand in the way of how much I loved him. I was naive to think nothing could ever take away how much I *knew* I never wanted to live without him. I focus on the four-carat marquise cut rock, embellished on each side with a single carat that meets several smaller ones as it wraps around my finger, and try and think back to when our love was simpler.

Letting out a dry, callous laugh, I shake my head because our love has never been anything close to resembling simple - ever. But there once was a time I thought our love was bright, so damn bright, and nothing could dull its sparkle. Much like the ring wrapped around my finger that's supposed to be a symbol of our love. I guess I was wrong.

"I prefer you this way, Maria," his low voice pulls me from my thoughts, startling me suddenly and making my heart rate quicken. "Bare. Vulnerable. Waiting. Focused on what I give you."

I take my time before looking up, attempting to harness some courage, some strength to face the way he's making me feel. When I finally do meet his stare, I see him studying me, his head cocked to the side as his eyes lower towards my body under the bubbles. He's leaning against the doorframe, one foot crossed over his other ankle, his suit jacket unbuttoned with his hands shoved in his pockets. God, I can't deny that my heart speeds up even more when I'm trying so hard to deny him. This time, my heart's fueled by desire as my breathing quickens and I quickly place my hand with my ring on it under the water, as if I was caught doing something wrong.

"You can try and hide it all you want," he taunts, biting his lower lip, pushing off the wall, and making his way into the steam-filled bathroom. "We both know I'll take pleasure in forcing you to see the truth later."

"Stop," I demand, sitting up a little straighter in the bathtub, my breasts now exposed slightly as the cold air caresses my nipples.

To my surprise he does. For just a moment, though. But it's long enough for me to gather my thoughts before he takes another step forward, his eyes downcast on my exposed breasts as he licks his lips with lust. "You can't force me to do anything, Leonardo. Not anymore."

"I've never forced you to take part in what your body wasn't already willing to give me," he whispers, as he lowers to the floor next to the tub and gently wipes bubbles off my collarbone with his fingers. He traces them down the center of my chest, his eyes following the path, and my breath catches in my throat. "What you didn't already want."

His eyes lift, lock with my own, just before his hand descends into the water and I shake my head from side to side, at a loss for words, but desperately needing him to understand that *this* is not what I want from him right now.

Not yet anyway. Not until he understands.

What?

I have to admit I'm having a hard time focusing on the reasons I feel guarded myself as his fingers trace slowly lower still. I close my eyes, expecting him to take what he wants anyway. But again, he surprises me when he stops just above my sex, tenderly cupping my swollen stomach and making my heart melt.

I notice as both our breathing increases as the realization hits us that he's holding the life we created.

The life that came from a love so powerful, we'd never be able to deny it even if we continue to keep trying. Doing so would tear us apart when we need to be strong. We'll never be able to walk away from us. Especially not now with the life that's growing in my belly.

"Why do you torture me, mi Amore," he rasps out with emotion causing my eyes to open as I stare back into his conflicted gaze. "Why do you pretend to hate me when you know it kills me inside, Maria? Makes me irrational. Distracted. Makes me feel like I'm losing control."

His grip tightens on my stomach and I flench slightly. His touch is dominating. Demanding. Much like the look in his eyes.

"I don't hate you..."

A grin flashes across his face, the bastard got what he wanted, as he quickly pushes up his sleeve and drops his hand lower in the water to the opening between my thighs. I keep my legs closed, denying him access, causing his stare to mischievously change as that smirk across his handsome face deepens.

"Then why deny me?"

"Because I don't..."

"Love me?"

I swear I see a nervous fear flash through his eyes, a first for us, but he masks it well and doesn't push the matter underwater further. He holds his hand against my center, my clenched thighs still denying him access, and waits.

"I'm not saying..." I let my words trail off, because, honestly, I'm not sure what to say right now. He's always taken the lead. He's always been in control. He's always been stronger than me. Seeing him slightly vulnerable has thrown me.

Letting out a huff, I shake my head a little, looking off to the side briefly and gathering my thoughts before staring him back in the eye. When I do, the same nervous, pleading look is there, hiding behind the surface in his stare, and it shakes me a little more.

"You're the only one, ever, Maria, who has the power to bring me to my knees."

Not surprisingly, his words soften me a little as *my* knees weaken slightly in the water. We're a pair, both of us, as he kneels on his knees and mine widen slightly underwater, giving into what I will always need most in life.

Him.

"Is that all you want, Maria," his voice deepens, grovels even, as his hand begins lowering again in the water. "To take," his finger brushes against my slit. "To punish," he pushes inside me and I gasp. *Oh, God!* "To make me weak?"

He curls his finger, pulling it up, across, and forward inside my wet flesh. My head falls back, my eyes close, as he slowly places another finger inside my folds and then does the same. His name falls from my lips as his thumb circles my clit and I grab onto the sides of the tub, forcing my body to be still so I can feel each and every caress he's giving me.

I was insistent on standing my ground. He calls me his weakness, but I will always be weaker. I will always surrender to his touch. To the way only he can make me feel.

"Maria," his low voice growls, pulling me from my trance as I look his way with hooded eyes. "I've always worshiped you. Why do you think I'd ever stop?"

His fingers increase their pace, his thumb presses down hard, circling round and round with determination, with desperation and I suck in my bottom lip, closing my eyes, trying to not cry out from his breathtaking touch like I need to.

"Look at me," he demands, and my eyes quickly raise to catch his own. "I wish I could tell you everything, but I can't. Not yet. I need you to understand, keeping you in the dark is keeping you safe. That's more important to me than anything else. Even if doing so turns you into a fucking brat."

I sit up straighter in the tub, pull back, and go to argue, but the cocky, breathtaking smile that spreads across his face and the way his fingers are caressing my entrance the only way he knows how stops me as my mouth falls open. He sticks another finger slowly inside my tight walls and leans in closer.

I go to ask him again about my parents. About why he had them murdered. But he levels me with a stare letting me know not to push the matter right now for reasons I know I couldn't possibly understand. Not yet. Not until he is ready to tell me. And a small piece of my resistance begins to trust him.

"You're my only weakness in my darkness, Maria. My only light in hell. I will protect you, defend you, guard you with my fucking life. Don't push me away, mi Amore. I need to hold you closer now, more than ever before."

The last bit of argument flees my mind as I find myself lost in his stare. He continues to fuck me slowly with his fingers. They're thick inside me as he leans forward and circles my clit harder.

"I'll never not be devoted to you. Only you. You come first, mi Amore. Before business," I reach out and grab ahold of his arms, my mouth falling open, his words and his touch pushing me closer to the edge as his fingers quicken inside me.

"In life," he growls, and my lower stomach tightens, my world teeters on the edge.

"In marriage," I crash over and scream out, his fingers working faster, milking me for all I can give him as his forehead lowers, resting against mine briefly before he captures my screams with his lips.

I'm too far gone, too hungry for him after all the time we've spent apart, as our teeth clash, our mouths crash and our tongues fuck each other with so much greed, I feel another orgasm quickly building on the heels of my first. He feels it too because he pulls his fingers from inside me, releases my kiss, and smiles as I try and catch my breath.

"Mi Amore, you're the only one I've ever let myself love.

I've cherished you, honored you my whole fucking life, Maria," his voice is deep with emotion as I look up into his eyes, still rocking on the very last step before falling over the edge. "That doesn't fucking change. Not even when I have to do things you might not understand. I told you before, you're going to have to trust me."

"I always have," I manage in a whisper, my core still tight, swollen, tender, and needing more of his touch.

He smiles, a genuine, heart-stopping smile, and the weight I felt pushing me down minutes ago lifts, but it doesn't fully go away. Not yet. I know eventually, I'll still need answers. But now...

I pull on the lapels of his jacket, bringing him closer to my lips and he grants me the kiss I desperately crave. This time, our mouths meet tenderly. Passionately. His lips caressing against mine in a way I've missed so much since he's been gone.

Gone.

As the thought enters my mind, a whimper works its way up from my heart. The second he hears it, his hands cradle my face as he deepens our kiss, knowing in an instant the way I feel, the heartache we're both mourning from the time we've been forced to spend apart.

Neither of us has to say a word. We've always been able to feel one another. Miles and years apart have never changed that.

I could kiss him like this forever. As his lips caress mine, his tongue dancing with my own, I send up a silent prayer that when it's my time, I'd be blessed to be able to die with his lips desperately pressed against mine.

His thumb comes up and brushes away tears I suddenly feel streaming down my face, but he never takes his mouth away from mine. I cry out a little harder, my sadness over our past mixes with the happiness that he's here, in my arms. All the emotions I've been trying to suppress finally emerge, breaking free quickly having been held prisoner for far too long.

Pulling back, he stands up quickly, stepping into the tub and shedding his jacket as he lowers himself into the luke-warm water. He flings it over the edge with a loud thud and gathers me in his arms.

"Make love to me," I plead, my head resting against his shoulder. I lean back and stare up into the eyes of the man I can't live without and he steals my breath away as he gazes down at me with so much love I swear my heart bursts.

His eyes lower as he looks down at my mouth. My bottom lip trembles, waiting for his response, waiting for him to do as I asked because I can tell he's just as desperate as I am for us to feel connected to each other once again.

"Love," he finally whispers. "That's all you'll ever feel from me, Maria. Our own, desperate, dark, tainted love."

He brushes his thumb across my bottom lip and I tremble.

His eyes raise and capture mine once again. Darkness clouds them as a thrilling desire shoots through my body knowing the look and the electrifying change in the man that's holding me strongly captive in his arms. Before I can think, his hands lower, quickly grabbing around my waist. He lifts me, spins me, and forces me on my knees, gentle not to hurt my stomach.

I grab onto the tub and instantly feel his fingers dancing across my slit. The sound of his zipper lowering has my knees wobbling. I suck in a breath when I feel his crown at my entrance. His hand caresses its way up my back, and I arch into him on instinct as he wraps his fist in my hair.

Nothing compares to this. Nothing compares to him about to fuck me with a carnal need.

I'd trust him even if it kills me knowing that our love is so strong I'd be with him in the afterlife.

That is, so long as he never stops claiming me in this life like he's about to. Right. Now.

CHAPTER 12

IT's BEEN TOO long since I have felt her tight, sweet, heat wrapped around me, I feel like a teenager, so close to release as my cock rests at the entrance of her pussy.

"I don't want to hurt you," I whisper, knowing the need I feel coursing through my veins will make me take her harder than she expects. Harder than I anticipated.

But we both know that's a lie. Her greatest pleasure comes through feeling pain at the same time as pleasure. My hand reaches around her stomach, resting above her cunt, on the real reason I feel the need to be gentle with her.

"Don't you dare," she releases a hiss that turns into a delicious purr as my crown slips inside her tight walls.

I rotate my hips, both of us hissing out as her head falls back from the sensation of my large tip starting to work its way in, caressing her sensitive, swollen flesh.

"I haven't been properly fucked in months, Leonardo. Take me. The only way you know how."

Restraint snapped, I quickly thrust inside her. Her scream echoes off the bathroom walls as she looks forward and tries to get away, her hips forcing forward, but with a tight grip I hold her still and force my length deeper, farther, until I am buried so deep inside her I see her knuckles turn white as she deathly grips the edge of the tub.

"Fuck," I groan, "Properly fucked? Is that what you need, Maria?" She doesn't answer, only moans out incoherent plea-sure as I pull out and thrust back inside her again. She screams but thrusts her hips back against my pelvis needing me to give her more, burying my cock even deeper than before inside her.

"I know what you need," I grit out, gripping her hips fiercely as I pound into her slick heat.

Her ass slaps against my hips. Her screams fill my ears. My own carnal sounds fill the room as I unleash a desperate hunger that's been building since the last time I let myself go inside her. She looks back over her shoulder as I loosen my grip on her hair. A lustful trance clouds her eyes and it fuels me as I grip her hips harder, fuck her faster, lean back, and smack her ass once, twice, three damn times as she screams my name with each burn of my palm across her white skin.

"Properly fucked, mi Amore, is not what your body desires."

Pausing briefly, I hold her down against the front of the tub, watching as my length pulls in and out of her slick folds. The bathwater has run cold and I notice goosebumps on her thighs, her back, her arms, as my eyes raise and catch hers still watching me over her shoulder.

My cock slides in and out, slowly, gently, lazily. Her velvet lips suck the crown back in, just the tip, before I pull it out and watch as her body sucks it back inside beautifully. Her pussy and my cock fucking made for each other, knowing just how to please, to caress, to suck and wrap around and fuck like no other.

"Properly," I hiss, as I reluctantly pull from inside her. She pouts from the loss of connection as I stand and offer her my hand, raising her to her feet. "Means appropriate."

Her eyes flash with understanding as I step out of the tub and motion for her to do the same.

"There's nothing proper about the things I want to do to your body, Maria."

"Then..."

I place my finger against her lips, stopping the rebuttal that I know her smart mouth was insistent on telling me. Her body shakes slightly from the chill in the air as she stands with me in the middle of the master bathroom. I glance down at her perky nipples and my tongue instantly wets my lips with need.

"On your knees, Maria."

Without hesitation, she lowers quickly to the floor in front of me. Placing her hands on her thighs, I watch her shiver again as her gaze falls to my crotch. Ripping through my buttons, I toss my wet shirt on the floor beside her and then kick out of my socks and shoes with haste because seeing her kneeling in front of me is suddenly too much for my aching cock to take. She wets her lips in anticipation and watches, her pupils dilated, her thirst evident.

I take my time unzipping my slacks, she reaches out to help, but I stop her and she obeys instantly, fully aware of what would happen if she doesn't let me have my way. The wet slacks fall to my feet, and I step out of them, kicking them to the side with my dress shirt. My briefs are next. Her mouth falls open and I watch as her tongue rotates around her plump lips as my cock springs free and I step out of the black boxers, kicking them to the side as well.

"Is it appropriate to make you watch," my breath hitches as I grab my length and slide my hand up and down my shaft. She shakes her head no.

"Is it appropriate to force my cock down your throat?" I groan as precum spills over my tip and she inches forward on the floor, eager, wanting a taste, needing to feel my dick in her hot tight mouth.

"No, Sir," she whispers.

"Open wide, Maria. Stick out your tongue."

She does as she's told instantly. I step forward, placing my throbbing cock on her tongue and swirling around the tip until she's cleaned off all the cum.

"Good girl. Now close your lips," she does so with a moan. I force my cock to the back of her throat, tears spill down her cheeks from the intrusion as I hold her in place by the back of her head. "Fucking swallow."

She does and my world goes black momentarily, my knees slightly buckle before I focus back on the saint between my thighs. Pulling back out, I slam my cock back down her throat forcing her still again with a firm grip on the back of her hair.

"Damn, no one sucks cock like you, mi Amore," she lets

out a cry, half pleasure, half pain, as I fuck her mouth on another quick thrust. "But I don't want to cum down your throat."

Her eyes flash up as I watch my dick pull in and out of her pink lips. My eyes graze down the front of her body, watch as her hands travel towards the center of her thighs, and feel my cock twitch in her mouth.

"Don't fucking touch yourself," I demand before hearing her cry and then glancing back into her tear-stained eyes.

Gripping the back of her head, I slowly force my cock to the back of her throat and hold it there.

"Do you like this, Maria?" She shakes her head yes, her fingers shaking on her thighs with the need to feel more pleasure.

"Is it proper, mi Amore, to want to fuck your mouth with my cock?"

She hesitates, knowing the wrong answer could result in punishment. As I pull my cock from her lips she shakes her head.

"No," she whispers as her eyes find the floor. Placing a finger under her chin, I raise her gaze to mine and smile.

"Is it appropriate, to want to cum on your tits," I smile, flicking one of her hardened nipples before pinching down lightly and seeing her eyes roll back in pleasure. Her hands inch forward, eager to stroke herself, and I quickly kneel and grab them both, stopping her.

"How about if I cum on your ass?"

"No, Sir."

With her right hand gripped in mine, I place our fingers against her slit and pull through her wetness. She lets out a gasp I quickly capture with my lips as my tongue fucks her mouth and my fingers fuck her pussy. Her free hand wraps around my length and makes quick work of bringing me closer to release. She circles the crown, pushes down, and pulls up. Quicker, faster. Maria makes me go insane as the sounds of our slick bodies and our moans of pleasure fill the space around us.

Slowly pulling out of her heat, I circle her clit with both our hands and break our kiss. "How about, if I cum in your ass."

She stills. Stops. Backs away and looks into my eyes. I release her hand and with just my own continue to pleasure her. She's tense at first. Reluctant. Until I gather her wetness, roll my fingers backward, and press against her tight hole. Her hips raise and she allows me to do as I please.

"Would you like that, Maria," I slip a finger inside her ass and she groans, her eyes closing with satisfaction.

"Better yet," I whisper, laying her flat on the floor and trailing a line of kisses down her chest. "I have a better idea."

My mouth closes over her clit and her hips buck up granting me better access to push my finger deeper inside her.

"Leo," she pants, as I stick my tongue inside her pussy and fuck her ass with my finger. "Oh my God, Leo, I..."

With my free hand, I stick two, then three fingers in her pussy, my mouth on her clit, and my dick hardens as her wetness travels back coating her ass and making my finger slide in and out her easier than before.

"Nothing I do to your body is appropriate, Maria," I

repeat, as I release her bud and raise up her body, watching as her form rises with ecstasy.

"Do you want more?" I demand. "Say the words, and I'll give you more."

My fingers move faster, claiming her in ways she's too insecure to tell me she wants. I give her time, making sure to give her fast when her body tells me more, and slow when I can tell she's on the brink of losing control.

"More," she finally whispers. I smile as I lower to her ear, my fingers sliding free from inside both her openings.

"Good girl."

Maria

"On your knees, hands on the headboard."

I quickly do as I'm told, scrambling to the center of the massive bed as the shadows of twilight start turning tonight. I can barely make out Leo behind me, but I hear as he climbs onto the sheets. I feel his warmth as he presses himself against me.

A velvet rope is tied around my right wrist and I smile. He places a kiss on my shoulder before his fingertips trail down my spine and I feel another piece of the rope tie around my left wrist.

No longer cold from the bath, Leo toweled me off before taking me in his arms and carrying me to the room. His tenderness melding together perfectly with his darkness and making me remember all the reasons why I fell in love with him to begin with. I feel his fingertip fall down my spine once again before his tongue replaces the trail. When his lips meet my ass, he bites me and I jolt forward, surprisingly wanting him to do it again.

My legs are next. I hear him rise off the bed, my breathing quickening the entire time he's gone before I feel the dip of the mattress as he returns. But instead of ropes, he spreads my legs further apart and places them in a metal bar.

"No ropes?"

"No chance at you breaking them."

"You think I can't take it?"

"Maria," he breathes, leaning over my back and taking my ear in his mouth. "I know you've never felt this kind of pleasure."

His fingers dance around to my clit and he rubs it in a circle, making a moan escape my lips.

"You'll take it," he whispers. "Like a good girl, you'll take whatever my body wants to give you. Take from you."

He spanks my pussy and I let out a light scream, my thighs already slick with arousal. Before I can have a chance to maybe fear what he's just said, I feel both of his hands spread my ass cheeks apart.

"Stay still. Tilt your hips up."

I do as I'm told, his tongue parting my velvet lips a moment later. I resist the urge to move, to grind back and forth, to bring friction to where I need it most, but in the end, my body wins and I move on instinct. I'm rewarded with a smack against the ass as he takes his mouth away from my sex.

"Do as you're told, mi Amore," he harshly demands and my pussy instantly grows wetter.

His mouth finds my sex seconds later, and this time he licks from my clit all the way back across my ass. My mouth falls open, embarrassment filling me inside for where he just tasted. And then I feel him do the same thing again, this time pressing the tip of his tongue against my tight hole.

"Leo," I struggle, attempting to pull my hips away, but he grips them tight, licking a slow circle before backing away. I hear him spit a second later. Wetness pools at the top of my ass crack as it slides down towards my pussy.

"What did I tell you," his strict tone fills the darkness.

I still, waiting for him to do as he pleases. Do as I'm quickly finding out I want him to, as well.

I feel the tip of his cock resting against my pussy before hearing a vibrating noise come to life behind me. My eyes widen, but before I can process what it might be, he slips his length inside me, reaches around my front, and rubs my clit.

"Will you be a good girl if I untie one wrist?"

I'm too lost in the pleasure to answer. I'm drowning too quickly in his touch as my thighs shake and my orgasm quickly approaches. I realize my mistake when he smacks my clit, thrusting faster inside my pussy, urging me to answer with each strong thrust of his hips.

"Ye..yes," I manage, before quickly feeling him reach up and release my right hand. The vibrating rings in the distance, but all I feel is his throbbing cock inside me and his free hand grabbing my own, bringing it down in front of me, and rubbing it against my clit.

"Touch yourself, Maria. Don't fucking stop."

Frantic, unhinged, I do as he tells me, needing to cum more than I ever have before in my life. The darkness. The man behind me. The throbbing between my thighs. It all crashes together in the most intense high after being forced apart for so long.

I feel pressure against my ass, my insides still, my movements slow.

"What did I tell you? Don't fucking stop," he grits out, as he thrusts into me wilder than before, the tip of the vibrator entering my ass a little more a moment later.

I don't dare stop now. I can't. My fingers rub faster. My walls tighten. His hips take with a carnal urgency as he forces the toy deeper and rotates it around. It's ridged, and the swirling of it inside my tight ass, matched with the slow thrusts of his length in and out of my center make me instantly approach climax.

"Good fucking girl."

At his words, I explode. My eyes close and my world goes entirely black. I hear screams. I hear his name. I hear pleas for him to stop, for him to give me more. My eyes flash open as my high peaks. I hear him curse, hear my name fall from his lips. The toys are suddenly removed, and his large hands grip my thighs.

He thrusts hard, fast, as my climax rolls on. I don't want it to stop but don't think I can take any more. He screams my name just before I feel him crash over as he spills himself inside me.

Out of breath, we sit there for a moment in the stillness before he places a small kiss on my backside. Pulling out, he releases me gently from my restraints. My hand, and then my ankles as he throws the items to the floor at the side of the bed. I fall against the sheets, rolling onto my back before feeling him lower himself over my body.

He kisses my lips instantly, tenderly. Expressing words neither of us knows how to say. Telling each other everything we want and need to in the time we've been apart. Just when I think he'll roll off me and gather me in his arms, he starts to kiss a trail down my stomach, eagerly spreading my thighs with his palms.

He licks up my slit and hums with approval. My taste mixing with his own. I can smell our love filling the room and it makes me drunk and just as greedy for more.

"More," I breathe out on a sigh.

It's meant as more of a question, but he takes it as a plea sticking two fingers inside me. I gasp out as I look down between my thighs and catch him already staring up at me.

"I told you," he whispers, placing a tender kiss against my clit as his fingers pull back and forth inside me. "Whatever my body wants to take."

His eyes lift. "You're mine, Maria. All night. Every night. For the rest of my life."

I let out another gasp as he raises up my body, the tip of his already hardened cock pressing against my inner thigh. Taking a nipple in his mouth he sucks down before lightly biting the bud. My hips rise in need as a moan escapes my lips.

"I'll take what I want, when I want," pressing inside me, I wrap my legs around his hips and keep him buried to the hilt. "Any objections, Mrs. Moretti?" he taunts, calling me a name that's more of a promise between us still and I watch as he smiles, my pussy tightening around him from the beautiful way my future name spilled from his lips.

"More a request," I purr.

His eyebrow arches. He steals a kiss before looking back into my eyes. His hips start rotating his length around inside me and I know I'll never get enough. The rest of our life won't even be long enough.

"Never leave me," I manage, tears filling my eyes. "Never again."

"Never again," he echoes. "No more secrets. Trust me, mi Amore."

PART II

CHAPTER 13
LEONARDO

I ʀᴏᴛᴀᴛᴇ the small piece of iron in my pocket through my fingers, across my palm, and then let it fall back into my slacks before picking it up again and doing the same. It's the last thing Vincent Nitti gave me before Alfonso Capone's army raided down upon what was supposed to be one of the happiest days of my life.

Iron, he said, *to ward off evil.*

Looking out the window overlooking the small number of guests arriving for the service, I focus on the team assembled for protection. My eyes focus on one associate after another at their posts around the gardens, making sure they're focused. Sharp. Concentrated on each and every move the small party is making.

I had laughed at the Sicilian tradition of gifting the groom with iron and left it on my office desk that day, which seems like a lifetime ago now. This time, I take no chances.

I won't allow myself to break tradition twice, which is why every damn aspect of this day has been talked about, planned out, and configured to perfection since the night I returned a month ago.

It's Sunday. Not Tuesday, not fucking Friday. Both days are associated with bad luck for marriage in true Sicilian tradition.

Sunday. The luckiest day, bringing prosperity, and fertility. And nothing better stop me from claiming my bride this time.

"Maria wasn't too happy about ripping her Sicilian lace veil, especially since I'm told it came with a heavy price," Magnolia says as she enters the room. "Very hard to find real Sicilian lace these days, but she didn't hesitate when I explained where the demand came from."

She heads straight for the bourbon and pours herself an ample amount before sitting next to her husband on the couch. *To welcome good luck,* I remember Maria's mother Sofia telling me that day. From the sounds of it, she never told her daughter about the tradition before it was too late.

"You sure you only want me and Declan as witnesses?"

"Sicilian tradition doesn't warrant large wedding parties," I sigh. Happy enough with the attention my men are giving to details outside, I finally turn from the window and walk back to my desk. "Besides, you're the best suited for the job, seeing as you provided the wedding rings, and are now tied to the family forever."

I pick up my drink and study both of them over the rim. They exchange a look that worries me. I take a moment, and a second gulp of bourbon, to give them time to hopefully explain themselves before I have to question them.

If I have to ask, it proves maybe this tie isn't the best for either of us and now would be a fucking terrible time to find out that truth.

"Actually Chief," Declan starts, sitting up in his seat and leaning forward resting his elbows on his knees. "Those rings were supplied by someone already tied to the family."

I already knew that, but I wait for him to go on.

"We're just the messenger," he explains with mischief hanging in his eyes. "The middle man in this little arrangement if you can call it that."

I rotate my glass from one palm to the other as I look down and smile. I can always count on Dec to do the right thing. Shouldn't have doubted him for a second. Even if he's not legally tied by tradition, he's the most trustworthy man I've ever met, second to Collin. But I've known Declan much, much longer.

"So you've found out my secret?" Raising my glass to my lips, I take a sip and wait for his answer.

"Wouldn't be any good at my job if I didn't."

"Are you surprised?"

"Hardly," he laughs. "But let me ask you once again, are you going to tell Maria?"

I take another drink and turn, looking out the window as the last of the guests arrive. My mind wrestles with itself, debating the question that's been plaguing my mind since the first time we gathered to watch her walk down the aisle. Eventually, I decide on the only answer I can think of.

"When it's the right time."

"And if it never is? Sometimes you don't always get a choice before it's too late."

My jaw sets harshly as my back molars grind together

thinking of the worst, that it could *ever* be too late. That what we have will ever see an end. I refuse to accept the fact that we won't have the life I've planned for us since the first day I met her when we were both just kids. Back then, she was the only future I could ever see. When she walked back into my life by some miracle years later, everything became about building my world with one mission in mind. To protect her and keep her in it. There's no fucking alternative, no other choice. Never has been.

"Then I'll deal with it," I hiss in response. "And who or whatever attempts to take that away from us will meet a fucking fate worse than death, worse than an eternity in hell. I promise you that."

"In those kinds of situations," Declan sighs, rising from the couch as I turn back around, "death is welcome, but hell is typically what finds you first, Chief."

"A delivery, Boss," Federico says, entering the room and stopping my rebuttal. Declan looks relieved for the distraction. I, however, wouldn't mind still giving him a piece of my mind. "Do you want me to take it up to the bridal suite?"

He sets a large box down on the table and I smile, already knowing what's inside. My last gift to my bride before she walks down the aisle and becomes Mrs. Moretti. Her bridal bouquet. More tradition and I have to say one I'm kind of fond of.

Lifting the lid, I see the massive cluster of gardenias, white roses, coral plumerias, and matching hydrangeas all spilling down a foot or two, and perfectly set off by the white silk ribbon that binds them, embellished with diamonds and of course, pearls. When the ceremony is finished, I've already contacted the master jeweler in the city who will fashion the jewels into a one-year anniversary gift for Maria. A matching set of earrings, necklace, and a fucking tiara meant for a queen, not that I think she'd ever wear it. But wear it she will, at least once, with nothing else on while I take her with greed on our anniversary bed.

She's the only queen that will ever rule over my world. She comes first. Always.

"Gorgeous," I hear Magnolia say as she takes a step to my side and peers inside the box. "I can take it up to her if you'd like? I just got word her dress is arriving. I told her I'd be back to help her with it."

I haven't seen my bride in her dress *this* time, but I did have two requirements for it. Blue. Sky blue. Never white.

In Sicily, only the poor wore white in our ancestor's days. I hired the top Italian designer to not only find enough real Sicilian silk to fasten my bride a dress to rival any other, but to make it the way she dreamed it would be all her life, and to make it as blue as the fucking Italian sky. As breathtaking as her blue eyes.

My other request? Once it was done, the dress didn't sleep with the bride. Not according to tradition. Again. No fucking chances.

I even hired my men to find me four virgins from respectable Italian families. Three days ago they turned down the white bed Maria and I will share later tonight. A marriage bed I haven't taken my wife in since that day, and one I'm going mad thinking about all the ways I plan to enjoy her in later. One I'm suddenly feeling the urge to take her in now before we even get a chance to walk down the aisle.

Closing the lid on the flower box, I lift it and hand it off to Magnolia. She takes it without hesitation and hurries out of the room, Federico hot on her heels as he yells over his shoulder.

"They told me to let you know it'll be a half-hour, Boss. The priest is just arriving."

"Half hour," I laugh as Declan joins me in the middle of the room and hands me another glass of bourbon. "We're Sicilian. It'll be at least twice as long as that."

MARIA

"I've been told our couple has written their own vows, and I'd like to invite them to recite them now."

My throat closes as I turn, step forward, and take Leo's hand in my own. Taking a deep breath, I tell myself not to cry as I lift my head and look up into his eyes for the first time since I walked into the gardens. For the last time, before we're pronounced husband and wife. My emotions betray me as his eyes meet mine, a single tear falls down my cheek and the look he gives me steals the breath from my lungs.

"Maria," his voice shakes just as my hands start to tremble. "My soul has loved you before my eyes ever got the chance to behold you. When I first met you, all my days, all my years, my entire future was made with just one look in your eyes. *Da ragazzo, mi sono innamorato di una bellissima principessa.* (*As a boy, I fell in love with a beautiful princess*). Today, I make the princess of my childhood dreams my queen. There is nothing in this world, in heaven or hell, that I don't promise to give you. I've always loved you. You've always come first. You always will. I was forever wed to you from the moment you took your first breath, and I will fight for our love until the second we take our last. Together, mi Amore, we'll rule. Together, we'll always win. Lucky doesn't even begin to describe the way I feel. *Tu mi completi, Maria. (You complete me)*. Making you my wife, I show the world what you've always had power over, my life, and I declare it with so much pride, so much honor, to be able to call you mine. Forever, Maria. *Finché morte non ci separi, mi Amore. (Until death do us part, my love)*."

Shaking, I suck in a breath as Leo's hand reaches under my veil and brushes away the tears flowing down my face. Those gathered in attendance at our house are quiet, so quiet all I hear are the muffled sounds of the guards in the hall announcing their second round, and that the perimeter is secure. Surprisingly, it gives me the break in the spell Leo's just put me under in order to gather myself, to take a deep breath, before attempting to tell him just how much he means to me.

"Leonardo," I silently cry in a whisper.

The guests may not hear me. The priest might not even catch every word. But I have the full attention of the man in front of me. The only man that will ever matter, and he gives me a nod, an encouragement, instructing me to go on.

"In my darkness, you've been my light. In my secrets, you've been my truth. In this life, the only true love I've ever known has come from you. You love me with a passion I don't deserve. You've cared for me with an unconditional love I've struggled to understand. From the moment I met you, I fell in love with a boy who continued to be my strength even in his absence. Whose love has been the only thing most days that has made life worth living. I promise to love you just as passionately and unconditionally as you love me. I promise to be your strength, as you have been mine. I promise to be your light in the darkness, your truth in every secret this world keeps hidden. What's more, I promise to always trust you with my life, our family's life, and never stop loving you, in this life and our next. Because our love knows no boundaries. Our love surpasses time. Our love is the only thing that has ever felt like home in a world that's always tried to break us apart. With this ring, I give you a symbol of what you've always already had. My commitment. To you. My king. My ruler. My dominant. My husband. My forever love."

Leo doesn't wait for the priest, he reaches out to me, flinging my veil over my head and crashing his lips to my own. Behind us, I can hear cheers from the small crowd. Italian blessings shouted at the top of their lungs.

Evviva gli sposi, *hurray newlyweds.*

Per Cent'anni, *a hundred years,* wishing us a century of good luck.

Bacio! Bacio! - *kiss, kiss!*

But their shouts fade as I melt into my husband's arms and his lips press harder against my own. His grip tightens, his mouth opens, tempting me, enticing my desire for more. As his tongue brushes against mine in the most sensual way, his hands roam up the back of my neck and nestle tightly into my hair. He commands our first kiss as husband in wife like he rules over everything else in life. With final authority as my head falls to the side and he takes more of what he wants. Passionately. Discreetly. A heavenly moment just for the two of us I'll never forget as I hear the priest finally announce us husband and wife.

Leo breaks away and gives me that devilish smile I fell in love with when we were just kids. After all these years, it still causes butterflies to dance in my stomach as he takes my hand and spins me around to meet the faces of those in the crowd. Declan appears at his side and offers him a wine glass wrapped in fine linen. Leo doesn't miss a beat, setting it under his foot and stomping on the glass as more cheers and shouts of congratulations erupt throughout the crowd.

Each broken piece symbolizes how many happy years are to come in our marriage. With the look in Leo's eye as he turns to me, winks, and then starts to pull me down the aisle, I know my husband made sure the glass broke into a million pieces. Even then, a million wouldn't be enough for all the years I can count on him making me happy.

We're quickly filed into our grand entryway, traditionally handed a glass of champagne, the finest Prosecco for Sicilians, which of course I deny as guests begin to file in line to congratulate us. But even if I wasn't with child, I still wouldn't need the champagne, I'm high on my husband. My husband - I still can't believe the word - as he nestles his mouth next to my ear in between guests and whispers the most seductive things.

"Your dress is beautiful, Maria. But I can't wait to taste the heaven that's underneath it."

I try and hide my blush as I'm hugged by family and wished many years of happiness. When I pull back, Leo shakes their hand quickly, before placing his hand on the small of my back and leaning into my neck.

"Would my wife prefer to be *properly* fucked now, or should we wait until later? My cock is dying to be buried inside of you, *mi Amore*."

I gasp out slightly as I greet another close friend of the family. I'm at a loss for words, which thankfully he's not as he ushers them his way, thanks them for coming, and then quickly turns his attention back to me.

"You're trembling with need, Maria. Let me release you."

I whisper his name in warning as I try and focus, shaking the man in front of me's hand. But he leans in against my ear again.

"All I can think about is your pussy against my tongue. My cock in your hot little cunt. I need to fuck *mia moglie, (my wife)*, Maria. And I'm not going to wait until all the guests leave to be buried deep inside you."

I close my eyes and bite my lip, desire pooling at my center. I can't help it, and God, I don't want to either. It's been too long. Okay, it's been a few days. But a few days is a few days too long when you fuck like a God, only the way my *husband* can.

"Fuck it." He growls into my neck, grabbing my hand in his and sinking his teeth into the sensitive flesh by my ear. "You're mine. But it's not official until you're screaming my fucking name."

On his last whispered seduction, his hand finds my wrist as he pulls me out of line and hauls me off towards the staircase. I blush looking back at a couple of guests still lined up to wish us happiness. Two men shake their heads and smile as

Declan and Collin make excuses for our sudden departure. Although I'm sure they know exactly where we're headed.

But it's not their telling looks that bother me. It's not their whispered chuckles of where we're headed that has my stomach twisted in knots. It's the eyes of the woman standing next to them that chill my blood. A woman I've never seen before, and one I notice Magnolia is keeping a stern, evil eye on as well.

But my mind doesn't stay there long as I'm hurried into our master suite, my dress quickly pushed up to my waist as Leo kneels in front of me and pulls my panties to the side.

"This is the first time I taste you as my wife, Maria," my eyes flutter as he traces a finger across my slit. "The first time I claim you as Mrs. Moretti."

He sticks one, then two fingers inside my wet sex and my mouth falls open, but my eyes never leave his.

"I own you now, mi Amore."

"You always owned me, Leo."

"Hm," he considers what I've said as his eyes lock on my center. "Not like the way I do now." He licks up my cunt and my knees buckle. "Now that you belong to me, I can take you how I want to as often as I please."

"Never stopped you before."

His chuckle vibrates across my clit, my legs grow weaker, but he holds me up in his strong arms.

"Making you my wife," his fingers trace out of my sex and across my ass as he sticks his tongue in my sex. I dig my fingers in his hair as he licks my center thoroughly before going on, "my appetite has only increased."

He blows against my sex, his finger tracing back and

sinking into my warm center once again. He looks up and stares me in the eyes as he places another finger inside and stretches my pussy wide, as wide as it will allow. The pleasure boarding on pain and a high I need more of as I look down at him between my legs.

"Any objections?"

I can't speak, can't think as he rotates his fingers around and then drives them up deep inside my core. Shaking my head no, a devilish smile spreads across his sinfully handsome face.

"Good girl."

"I know it's unusual to unite the families on such a big job, Leonardo. If one goes down, we all go down. It's a big risk to take. But one I am willing to consider given Rinaldi's backing."

I glare at the man sitting across from me. Tony Nicoletti. My fucking nemeses if I'm not extra careful. My head turns and my stare lands on his partner. Jack Rinaldi. Chief of Chicago Police. A cock sucking bastard that the world would be better off rid of if I had my chance to pull the damn trigger.

Letting out a heavy sigh, I sit up straight in my office chair as my gaze lands on Collin, Declan, and Nicoletti's men standing in the back of the room. All four lurking in the dark shadows behind the two men sitting confidently in front of me. Collin & Declan trust Nicoletti and Rinaldi less than me, and that's fucking saying something. Taking a long puff or two off my cigar, I let the smoke fill the space between us, hanging there like a threat as I debate what Nicoletti's just said.

"Stock market manipulation is no damn joke, Tony," my condescending tone hisses out between us. His glare deepens. "Sure, we've dabbled before. But what you're talking about could send a lot of good men away for a long time, including yourself. Only a fool would chance taking such a high risk."

He frowns at me, my words not sitting well. Or maybe it's just the last bit. *Fool.* He always was a deluded idiot. I can't say I'm surprised to see that nothing's changed.

"I'm willing to risk it," he finally insists, thinking he has enough backing to get me to do as he says.

"I'm pretty sure I speak for the rest of the major family heads when I say, we're not."

His glare deepens as I set down my cigar and then take my time slowly picking up my glass of scotch. I let him sit with my decision on the matter while I take a nice long drink and watch him over the rim. Rinaldi fidgets in his seat beside him, but when I look his way I don't see the eyes of a scared man who is fearful of the person that sits across from him. Instead, I see the scowl of a cocky son-of-a-bitch that's two seconds away from learning a hard fucking lesson. The only way bastards like him learn anything.

With a pistol held to his head, or a knife held at the base of his throat. Pleading for his life. A life their ego was so sure of only seconds before.

"What makes you think you have the authority to speak for Alfonso?" My eyes snap back to Tony and I stop breathing, my teeth grinding in protest as I sit still, waiting for him to continue. "What makes you think I didn't go to him first? The last time you two met, I heard things didn't go so fucking well. The *Boss*," he taunts loosely, "didn't take well to you taking over a business that's not rightfully yours."

"The only Boss either of you two answer to, is me, capo," I grin, knowing the prick hates to hear the truth, which makes it all the sweeter vengeance. "It's best you remember that or you won't stay alive long enough to try this fucking ludicrous operation."

I raise my glass to my lips again, but before I can take another drink, he says, "is that a fact?"

"Fucking certifiable, Nicoletti," the alcohol burns as it slides down the back of my throat, much like I figure Tony here will burn in hell before I ever say yes to what he's proposing. "You crossed me once, years ago. Don't make me remind you how that ended." Setting my glass down, the memory makes me laugh, my low sinister chuckle rings through the room around us as I look up into his hateful stare. "Hell, I'm still bitter I didn't get to off you when I had the chance. I don't need a reason to pull the trigger this time, *Amico*. You want to test that theory. You go right ahead and push your little operation."

He eyes me for a moment, debating his next words wisely, and it stuns me to see maybe there is a little brain rattling around in his thick skull after all.

"To take over Wall Street, we need all the top families in on this," he pleads his case and I stand corrected on my last crazy thought. "The mainstream security market is harder to break into, but in the microcap market, we've been perfecting our take, our operation, over the last five years. Our company,

Nico Technologies, is the front, secretly paying our 'brokers' large fees. We have a couple inside men we trust. A few news reporters, and journalists on payroll to hype up the public. They inflate the price of the stocks, get people to invest, and we sell them for large profits."

"Who invests and how?"

"City officials, myself included," Rinaldi finally speaks. I roll my neck as my gaze reluctantly falls on his ugly face. My spine cracks a few times in the process, much like I'd love to crack his thick skull instead of ever listening to him speak again. But as fate would have it, he goes on. "Pension funds. Hedge funds from large institutions."

"Where are these pension funds coming from," I inquire. "Don't tell me you've invested yours?"

"Fallen officers," he shrugs. *Fucking prick.* "Officers who get their pensions taken away."

"In return, Rinaldi gets a higher cut than most," Nicoletti explains as I cast my attention back on him.

I'm thankful for the break from Rinaldi because listening to him babble anymore would have me making good on my previous thought. I want nothing more than to reach across the table and put a bullet through the center of his selfish brain.

"But it's a small price to pay for secured gun permits, parking permits, outcomes of certain 'investigations.'"

"I know how the racket works, Tony," I hiss, "There's no need to fucking explain. With the way you walk around town, hiding behind an obvious public deception, it's a wonder you still understand the game yourself."

For as long as I've known the bastard in front of me, he's

put on the front of being mentally ill. No one would suspect a mentally handicapped person to orchestrate a stock market takeover, would they? With a person like the chief of police backing your every move, of course, no one would question it. Or the cop doing the backing.

No one would go up against it. It's a sick twisted union between the two that I've always sworn to blow the cover off of. I've always been able to see through the front, long before I ever found out the truth years ago.

The fucker doesn't miss a beat, though. Picking up his glass set on the edge of my desk, he studies the liquid and quickly continues. "Right now what we really are trying to accomplish is increasing the price of cryptocurrency," Tony continues. "Help our gambling efforts. Your new wife has ties to Las Vegas, no?"

He studies me, a sinister glare on his face and a tight grip on his glass. My scowl deepens as I push back in my seat and think of the best way to handle his comment.

Fuck him and whatever his mentally ill mind is thinking up. Right now I gotta admit I do believe he's fucking crazy for coming to my damn house, on my wedding day, and suggesting anything concerning my new wife.

"Her ties were severed not so long ago," my sigh is heavy as the words fall from my lips, filled with a quickly building annoyance for anything more either of the men in front of me has to say. "Can't say I'm sorry to tell you that. Besides, my wife does as *I* wish. And I wouldn't agree to anything concerning your proposition." Sometimes, getting her to agree involves taking her over my knee, but I leave that little bit of information out.

"She'd never get mixed up in a business transaction that wouldn't - please her husband."

"Hm," he weighs my answer as he also weighs the glass in his hand, switching it from palm to palm and studying it closely. I don't like the suggestiveness of his tone, or his hesitance. Both have my instincts on high alert.

"Wish I could say the same."

He takes a drink, and my eyes lift as the door to the office opens, and in walks a woman who looks vaguely familiar, but I can't for the life of me place how or why. Her icy stare never wavers off my own and I get a sick feeling in the pit of my gut I try quickly to push away. To disguise as she stares back into my eyes.

"You see, my wife...," he nods his head back, gesturing towards the brunette making her way towards us and I can't fucking deny my heart rate ticks up a notch knowing no good is going to come from this little reunion. Yes, reunion. I can't place where, but I know I know this woman. "... She got mixed up in a - business transaction - right before I married her."

Collin and Declan stop the woman mid-room. I can hear their hushed tones as she's frisked and questioned about what she's doing here. Nicoletti's men standstill, my gaze flickering back and forth between them as the man in front of me remains quiet. They both present with a sickening smile across their smug faces. Smiles I'd like nothing more than to slice off their faces.

"Her ties also lead to Vegas," Nicoletti finally continues.

I study the face of the woman, trying to piece together

what I'm being told and what I know inside me to be true. I know her. But how?

"See, back then, I didn't know what I know now. You being the son of Luigi Lombardi and all." He lets me sit with that statement. Her icy stare is still fixed on my eyes as Collin and Declan give me a look telling me she's clean.

Then it fucking hits me. Where I know her from. And one of the last things I said to her so many years ago.

No real man will ever need a woman when she spends her time trying to rise to the top by first starting out on her knees!

All these years later, her fucking name still eludes me. But the venom she spits first, the reason I kicked her out of my bed and erased the thought of her from my life were her words that ring through my ears a second later. I hear them as loud as if it's the first time she's said them.

Never go for the second-tier captain when the underboss is one step closer to the Don!

A bitterness builds in my gut. I give Declan a nod, letting him know it's okay for her to come closer. Call me a glutton for punishment, but I want to see just where the fuck this is going. If my instincts are right, and they always are, some fucker might die tonight after the news she's about to deliver, and I'll be damned if it's going to be me.

Collin and Declan let her pass, and I know most men in my shoes might feel slightly shaken. Maybe even a little nervous, anxious, being confronted with a whore they once paid to blow their load in each and every hole for a few hours. But I'm not like most men.

She was a means to forget about the world and everyone in it for a while. Inconsequential at most. I took what I needed from her, and made sure she was satisfied in return, but the arrangement never meant I would see her again. Never meant I wanted to. Fuck, I still don't. The twisting sickness in the pit of my stomach gets worse, a forewarning of what's coming, not nerves. She makes her way across the room and I notice a figure in white come through the door after her.

Maria.

"At first I was shocked to find out my wife, Sabrina...," there's that fucking name. The whore in Vegas I brought back to Chicago one drunken night, "...was pregnant so soon after our wedding."

My eyes flashback towards Nicoletti's and a fire burns under my skin. Out of the corner of my eye, I see Maria take a few more steps, curiosity getting the better of her. Normally, she never interrupts my meetings, knowing very well the type of punishment that'll bring her. But the taunting realization that I know exactly where this is going clouds my better judgment and makes it impossible for me to turn her away.

I'll be damned if I let him say what he's about to on a day like today. With my wife standing ring-side to a fucking fight that's been decades in the making. Standing quickly, I round the desk and rip him out of his seat by his throat.

Guns are drawn. Tensions explode. My anger fucking roars as I grip Nicoletti's neck a little tighter and tempt him with his own daunting death if he continues.

"You set me up, you fucking sick bastard," I hiss, my fists tightening as a sadistic smile spreads across his reddened face. He can't breathe and I find every amount of pleasure in knowing I am cutting him off before he tells me what he really came here to say. Problem is, the whore he calls wife is dead set on making sure I know the truth. A truth that could ruin mine and Maria's future. And she's determined not to hold back.

"No, Leo," Sabrina taunts as my blood turns cold, my grip tightens until I can feel the back of his spine start to crack.

I look up, frantic, into the eyes of a tramp I fucked only one night to erase the pain of never being able to see the only woman that ever mattered to me again. The woman I now call my life.

"I set you up," Sabrina hisses. "*Occhio per occhio.* (*An eye for an eye.*) Looks like I finally made it in life after all. Mothering the first son of the new Don."

Maria's gasp is the last thing I hear before a shot rings out in the darkness.

CHAPTER 15

MARIA

"I DON'T CARE what it costs, who we have to bribe, I want them to run that damn blood test twice. I want this kept a fucking secret. Pay whoever runs the test whatever they want. This doesn't get out or someone fucking dies, *comprendere*."

"Yeah Chief, you can count on me, you know that," Declan insists. "But what the hell would it matter anyway? She's a nobody from nowhere. So she has your kid? You take what's yours and raise him to know who is really in control in your world."

My back rests against the wall separating me from Leo's office. Swallowing hard and forcing back tears, I look up at the ceiling, completely not believing the twist that was just thrown into our lives. Our wedding day.

A son?

I don't even know the sex of our child yet. Leo wanted to wait. Now, no matter boy or girl, our child together will possibly always come second to a child he fathered without knowing. A child whose mother has raised him only God knows how. A child that will always hold more clout in our life than any we ever have together. Much like Angelo always held a seat over Leo and me before his demise. It's a sick twist in the game we call life, and one I'm not happy to be repeating.

"She's not a nobody from nowhere," Leo's low whisper pulls me from my thoughts and has my stomach instantly feeling ill. I wait, my next breath caught in my throat as my mind races wondering just how much worse all of this can get.

"Who the fuck is she?" Collin's harsh voice demands after a moment of silence.

I look up and see Giovanni approaching down the hallway. His head hung low, he's busy on his phone and consumed with the new news that's buzzing quickly through the house. I'm not sure how Leo intends to try and keep this quiet. But if I know my husband, he'll find a way.

All the wedding guests were thrown out after the shot was fired in Leo's office earlier. No one was hurt, just one of Nicoletti's men hot on the trigger when Leo wouldn't take his hands off their boss. After a few choice words were exchanged, a blood test was demanded, security was ramped up and I was carried off by my husband after I couldn't catch my breath. I suffered a sudden breakdown at the news which only slowly made me suffer more the longer I stayed in Sabrina's presence.

Leo stayed by my side for close to three hours. Assuring me, loving me, promising me that this changes nothing. Exhausted by the day, the tears, and the horror of what that bitch had to say on my wedding day, I fell asleep and woke only a few minutes ago. I quickly found myself restless with a need to know where my husband went, and what more he might be hiding.

I hold my finger up and silence Giovanni as his eyes lift and catch mine. I don't want to be found out yet. Not until I hear what I need to hear. A nightmare I can feel coming next.

"Fuck," my husband grits out in a hushed tone. "It's not important. Not until we know if the child is mine or not."

"Let's just say it's best to be prepared," Collin insists in his thick Irish accent. "Helps us all sleep better at night, right? Best to know what we're dealing with."

"Agreed," Declan sighs. "Maybe I can work to pull some strings. If you know more about her, where she comes from, her family, then maybe we have a better chance at keeping this secret from exploding before it's time."

"If it is true, there will never be a good time. This could ruin many people's lives. Starting with my own."

"So you do know who she is?"

"Oh I know who she is, that's never been the fucking problem. Her name may have eluded me time and time again, but I know where that whore comes from. I know what I'm fucking dealing with, and until I know that child is mine, I'd rather I keep the damn secret than worry Maria over it."

"Maybe you should let me handle it," Collin insists. "Like we did in Dublin, remember, when I was just a small lad and new to the game."

"Too risky."

"For who," Collin snaps. "Her or you?"

"Maria and my unborn child are my only concern."

"Then you'd know this is the only way."

"Perhaps, I just don't know if I can stomach the sight of it."

Leo says something under his breath in response but he says it too low, and I can't make it out.

Giovanni cocks an eyebrow at me and I swallow over a lump in my throat.

"You can't hide in the shadows for long, Mrs. Moretti."

My new last name makes me hold back a sob that threatens to escape and blow my cover. This is not how I envisioned my wedding day going. Hell, this is not how I envisioned my wedding night going. I close my eyes and shake my head, trying to escape the destiny that's quickly shaping our future. A hell we never saw coming.

"Maria!"

My husband's voice pulls me from my self-inflicted torture and I open my eyes to see Giovanni looking at me with such pity it makes me see red. I am not a pity case. We will deal with it, in the end, I know that to be true when all else seems hopeless. Even if I am having a hard time wrapping my head around the news right now.

Pushing off the wall, I give our consigliere a deep glare and force the office door more ajar. Stepping into the doorway, I lift my chin and catch Leonardo's eye as he starts to make his way toward me.

"Amore, I thought you were sleeping?"

Exhaustion and sadness are quickly replaced with fury as I realize this is the second time since my husband has been home that he's continued to hide something from me. He takes my hand gently in his, and I look away, into the eyes of Collin and Declan. Declan gives me the same pitiful look that graced Giovanni's face moments before and I avert my stare, glancing quickly into Collin's. He gives me a suggestive stare, one filled with mischief and anger. Nothing like I was expecting, and it's something that makes me fill with even more unease than usual as he looks me up and down, sizing up the situation in front of him.

"Where's Daniella?" I stutter, Collin's gaze making me feel shaky the longer it stays on me.

"Dublin," Collin answers quickly, and I watch as Leo glances over his shoulder, giving him a look I'm not quite sure how to read.

The answer startles me. "When did she leave? I'm sure I saw her at the wedding."

"Ah, she wouldn't be missing your wedding for the world, Lass," he taunts, and my eyes fall back on Leo's as he pulls me further into the room and his arms. "She left soon after. I thought it best with what might be coming."

"Coming?" I glance up at Leo, a storm of emotions raging between us. One neither of us can fully decipher yet, but we all know we're sitting ducks, just waiting for the worst to pass.

"Ah feck, love, don't act like a feckin eejit, com'on now," Collin continues, making Leo give him a stern look that finally shuts him up.

"Watch it, Fitzgerald," he warns. "I may owe your family a fucking favor, but I wouldn't hesitate to put a damn bullet through your skull for talking to my wife that way."

Collin holds up his hands and laughs sinisterly. "The

gents spoken, has he now. Alright, then. I see my feckin' place here."

"You keep running that mouth, and you won't see much more," Declan says. "Your mother must have been the real idiot to raise such a mumbling fool."

Collin glares at Declan and I swear conjures up more restraint than he normally has to not pull his weapon and end Declan's life for insulting his mother. I may not have known the Irish man in front of me long, but that is one thing I know you should never do unless you're keen on signing your own death sentence. That, and maybe spit in his Guinness.

With nothing else to say, I watch as Collin shoulders past Declan and forces me and Leo to step aside as he quickly makes his way out of the room.

"That's my cue as well," Declan mumbles, my gaze falling to the floor between Leo and me, as I watch him out of the corner of my eye start to make his way towards the door. "I'm sure it's about time I went and found out what kind of mischief Magnolia is getting herself into."

My heart pounds as he steps out of the room, leaving Leo and me alone with our thoughts, unspoken words, and a secret that's building between us. One I fear is quickly tearing us apart when we're just finally getting started. Leo reaches around me and closes the door, locking it as he does and I startle slightly when I hear the somewhat deafening click of privacy.

Taking my hands, he leads me to the fireplace across the room, and I take a seat on one of the couches there, only looking up with worry when I see my husband starting to pace the floor. Forcing myself to take a page out of Magnolia's playbook, I straighten my spine, take a deep breath and lift my chin.

"Out with it, Leo." My demand is harsh, quickly doing the job I wished it would as he stops pacing and stares at me with startled eyes. "No more secrets between us. You promised me."

LEONARDO

I've built my life on fucking secrets. One after the other. They've been my foundation and my fortress for as long as I can remember. They keep me safe. Secure in the knowledge that only I truly know what is going on.

It's my protection. *Her protection.* What she doesn't know saves her, fucking saves us, from what I dread most. Her death.

It's what fueled me as a child. What I drowned in as I grew up. What keeps me awake at night now as I lie in bed going over and over every carefully planned piece of our puzzle making sure I have nothing to worry about.

She's safe. Our child is safe. And I will take whatever secrets I need to the grave in order to keep them that way.

Secrets.

As I stop pacing and look into her eyes, I curse myself for agreeing to a promise I knew I'd eventually have to break. I did promise her no more secrets, and I meant it, but I can't honor it. Not entirely. At least not now. And this is one time I'm not backing down.

"And so the standoff part of this marriage business begins," she sighs after a moment, her eyes rolling as she glances off to the side.

"That depends," I counter, crossing my arms over my chest and studying my new bride carefully as the fire behind her beautifully lights her features. "To begin we'd have to start somewhere. You and I, Maria, have no business to discuss tonight."

Her eyes flash back to mine full of a heated rage. She's fucking beautiful like this. On the edge for me. Somewhere between wanting me to fuck her into submission or grab the nearest gun and blow my brains out. I can't deny it gets me off and watching the defiance in her eyes grow as I wait her out only adds to the building pleasure.

"Excuse me?"

I don't answer. Not immediately. Taking a deep breath, I weigh my response heavily before replying.

"More than any secrets that may make their way between us through the years, we've always had each other's trust." She eyes me with disdain because she knows I've got her right where she doesn't want to be. "Perhaps if we're debating opening up a conversation about business, we should start there."

"Are you saying you don't trust me enough to tell me your secrets, Leonardo?"

"Sometimes, secrets are kept simply because the person hiding them doesn't even trust themself."

Her eyes flare with indignation, never wavering from my own as seconds drag on like minutes and I can tell she's considering ending this conversation with what I just said. Or, perhaps provoking it further.

"Who's that woman, Leonardo?"

My jaw clenches tighter as I stare angrily into my wife's eyes. But my anger isn't for her. It's for myself and all the secrets I'm shielding her from.

"I trust you'd never allow anyone into our lives, let alone our house, that was a threat." She has no fucking idea. "So, who is she? If the child is yours...," her hands instinctively raise and cradle the child in her womb. It takes everything inside me to not rush and kneel at her feet, take both of them in my arms and tell them everything will be okay.

Because truth be told, I am not sure it will. Not yet. Not until I've put more pieces of my puzzle in place. And that's why I'm standing firm on withholding my secret. One day, when it's all clear, she'll understand. She just has to fucking trust me. A constant annoyance that we tend to dance around too often. That one simple yet complicated word. Trust.

"You're the only mother of whatever children I may father that will ever matter, Maria. I will love my children equally, but you? You're my life. My beginning and my fucking end." My voice is stern. Authoritative. "You are my wife, Amore. Who she is. What she is. Doesn't fucking matter."

"It matters to me," she screams and I can't hide the flinch that jolts its way through my body. "It matters to our unborn child. How do I know, boy or girl, they won't be cast aside to make room for the 'firstborn?'"

Her outrage makes something inside me snap. In two

strides I'm bearing down on her with more madness than I have ever felt before when she's pushed me to my limit. She shrinks into the couch as I tower above her. With fire in my eyes that match the inferno rushing through my veins, I study her.

I would never cast my flesh and blood aside. As far as firstborn? Maria is my queen. Any child I have with her takes my throne, but only after I'm gone.

If the bastard child from a one-night stand wants to be the one who pulls the trigger ending my life because of it, so be it. But I will love him just the same as any of my other children. I will make sure he will never be treated the same way as Maria or myself were in the past. That's a fucking promise, and I know she feels it as she shrinks into the leather and nervously looks up at me.

"We don't even know if the child is mine, Maria." She tries to act tough, tries to sit back up tall, but the way her body shakes betrays her as she falls back against the cushions. "Whatever issues you have about either of our pasts need to be fucking dealt with. I won't have you bringing up old wounds just to justify newly spilled blood, if and when your problem with the chain of command in this family gets in the way. Complicates things. If the child's mine, we'll deal with it. Together."

"I don't believe you," she seethes, sitting up straighter as her jaw sets in stone-cold defiance. "I don't trust you..."

"Watch your fucking mouth, Maria."

"Let me finish. I don't trust you won't be forced to make a decision we both might live to regret."

"Regret?" I whisper, her words piercing a small piece of my heart and forcing me to back away slightly. She takes the newfound space quickly, rising from the couch and hastily making her way towards the exit. "The only thing I regret, that disappoints, saddens me, is the way you're running away from me now."

Stopping once she reaches the door, she glances over her shoulder. "Then tell me your truths, Leo. All of them."

"The only fact that holds more weight than any other, more than blood, business, marriage, is that I love you, Maria. That's a promise that I can make you and keep when the life we live may make me have to break your heart."

With a soft cry, she rushes out of the room. Another curse falls from my lips as I watch her go.

I lied. I could never break her heart. Truth is, keeping secrets from her is what's breaking mine.

CHAPTER 16
MARIA

RUSHING OUT OF THE OFFICE, I feel like I'm drowning. I feel like our marriage is failing, sinking fast and it has only just begun. Choking on my tears, I look up and quickly righten myself, swallowing back any last bit of the meltdown I'm holding inside when I catch the disapproving arched eye of Magnolia. She's standing in the corner, discussing business no doubt with Declan and Giovanni. Business I am forced to stay out of.

Holding my head high, I manage to force my feelings to the back of my mind. Turn them off completely. I force myself to look away from her critical stare as I put one foot in front of the other and cross the entryway of the house. When I look back, she gives me a proud smile and I can't help but wonder what fires she's walked through in life to make her so bulletproof. So cold.

I've never wanted to be seen as cold. But I'm learning that this life doesn't always give me the chance to choose. The power lies in the ability to flip a switch, conceal, bury the way I feel if it means a better chance at survival. I'm learning that. Although it would seem I'm learning it the hard way.

As I push through two french doors, I glance back her way and see her studying me curiously. She whispers something to Declan over her shoulder, his eyes lift and study me as well, but I hurry outside because I don't care to be the center of any more of their judgment. I don't want to be dissected, told I'm not doing things right, told I'm too fragile or not educated enough on this life to understand. To be taken seriously.

Their accusations have been nothing if not constant contraindications since we got to Chicago. Take care of yourself and the baby. Stand up for yourself and be stronger to take over the empire. I'm so sick of it all it's suffocating me. As I reach the outside patio, I hurry quickly across the center courtyard and look back to see Leo studying me out of his office window.

Just the idea of still being watched, as if I'm not smart enough to take care of myself has me quickly picking up my pace. I took care of myself for decades before I was free of the man I used to call my father. I've survived worse. I've been treated better.

I shake my head as I come to a bench at the far end of the garden and sit down exhausted. It's all been so tiresome. And I feel like I'm at the lowest I've been since we arrived. I wonder if it'll always be this way. If I've been stupid to get involved in a life that I only tried to escape growing up.

The only difference is - I love him. There's no denying ever that I'm hopelessly in love with Leonardo, and our unborn child. I love them more than I could ever love myself.

"Fecking savages, ey? The lot of 'em."

I look up to see Collin leaning against a tree, one foot propped up behind him as he flicks the butt of his cigarette. The ash lights up the night before it falls to the ground and he takes another drag. Collin never talks to me much. Especially not concerning business. Not since we've been here, and definitely not even before, when he was paid as my protection by my father, Vincent. God rest his soul.

He addresses me, sure, when we're forced to be in a room together. He gives me an anxious, nervous feeling, I am still trying to navigate around. He's made me mad sticking his nose in business that should be none of his concern. But actually talk to me? About business? Never.

I give him a curious eye because I'm not quite sure why he's addressing me now. My gut does the same butterfly roll it always does when he's around, and I try and shake it off, tell it to go away. He takes another drag, exhaling the smoke slowly as he gestures back towards the main house.

"Nicoletti and Jack Rinaldi," he says, explaining himself when it's obvious I am not completely following. The last word is said with a hateful sneer. "The fecking cunt. Never did like the bastard."

I've known Collin for close to five years. He's older than me, but not by much. I'd be lying if I said there wasn't a mysterious pull to him. Something just under the surface you couldn't help but be curious about.

"You don't trust him?"

He arches a brow, taking another drag of his smoke as he continues to stare back at the house. My eyes study him, briefly appreciating the way he looks. I'm married, not dead.

Although I would never be tempted to touch. Especially not now. My heart will always belong to Leo.

Collin's shorter than most men. Five-foot ten, eleven at best. But he's stocky. Built like a brick. A boulder all rounded out and edged in the perfect places. If I had to describe him, I'd say a little Tom Hardy mixed with the finest parts of Cillian Murphy. His arms are covered in sleeves of some of the most beautiful tattoos I have ever seen. I've always wondered what they mean. I've always been curious if there were more than were visual to the eye, but again, I've never let my eyes study him long enough in order to find out.

His dirty brown hair has a hint of blondish red to it. The sides are shaven with the top longer than most, falling just past his ears, and typically slicked back like he's wearing it now. He glances at me out of the corner of his eye, his crystal blue irises making it hard for me to concentrate on anything else.

Cigarette resting between his teeth. He pushes up the sleeve of his white dress shirt, revealing some of the strongest forearms I have ever seen.

"Shite, that tool ain't pretending he's an eejit, he fecking really is one, love."

He pushes off the tree with a smile that makes me glance over my shoulder at the office. Leo is nowhere in sight.

Is Collin actually talking and being nice to me? Has hell frozen over? Obviously, I decide, as he takes a few steps in my direction and sits down at my side.

The only interaction we've ever had before was forced. Dutiful. Always purposeful because Collin, it seems, has always been sent to watch me.

In Vegas.

Here in Chicago.

But he never lets himself get close. Never opens up. Even with Daniella. I've watched them over the years, and there is no doubt in my mind that he loves her. But he's guarded. He doesn't trust easily. He doesn't open up easily which makes me wonder even more why he is talking to me now.

I sit next to him, a shiver rising up my spine and wonder if that's just the way men are in this lifestyle? Because now understanding it more than I used to, I see Leo's that way with me as well sometimes.

"'It 'twas a nice wedding, ey?" He eventually says, nudging my shoulder. "Got everything you need now in life, isn't that right, Stunner?"

Stunner. I shake my head and blush a little as I look down into my lap. He's been using that nickname on me since we met, although he hasn't said it in a while. Not really since he started dating Daniella. And never when she's around.

"Maybe," I whisper as he takes another puff off his cigarette before tossing it to the ground.

"Maybe sounds like a fecking lie to me, ya brat," I look up at him quickly only to see him smirking. Shaking my head I return the grin. "Maybe," he says, leaning in a little too close. I can smell the bourbon on his breath, inhale the smoke as it hangs on his skin, "maybe, ya got a wee secret of your own, Mrs. Moretti."

I swallow hard and try not to act phased. "I came out here to escape secrets."

My tone comes out harsher than I expected, although I can't say I'm upset about it. I'm hopeful it puts him in his place as I rise and start to make my way towards the back of the garden.

"Not entertain ideas of more."

Collin is quick on his feet and at my side in an instant. I glance at him, curious as to his intentions of following.

"You know," I sigh, "you don't need to watch me anymore, Collin. I know Daniella is gone. But I'm sure Leo has more than enough eyes on me at this moment."

I stop in my tracks and face him. A revelation suddenly registering in my mind. "That is unless you're the eyes Leo hired to keep on me?"

The idea has my blood firing through my veins like I haven't felt in a few minutes. Thank God for the small intermission. Collin hangs his head, his palm coming up and resting on his strong chin as he scratches the stubble there and raises his eyebrow, giving me a mischievous grin.

"No, Stunner, I wasn't hired to watch 'ya. You came out into the garden and found me, remember? Not the other way around."

True.

"Then why the 'stick like glue' spectacle you're putting on?"

"Is that how this looks?" He grins wider, taking a step back, arms held out to his side, and making an emphasis of putting space between us. "Bollocks, don't be daft, Lass. I've got no ill intentions but wishing you good luck on your marriage is all. Nothing more, now. I swear it."

I study him closely, a smile tugging at the edge of my lips. He sees and lowers his arms, then his head, and takes a step back towards me. "Ay, but ya see, it's the lack of intentions of the dishonorable you got to look out for most, Stunner. If ya know what's good for ya."

He gives me a wink, as he licks his full lips and takes a step closer.

"You're crossing a line, Collin," I stutter, watching as his right hand comes up and brushes a piece of hair back out of my face. I try to disguise my shaking, my knees wobbling as I clutch my lower stomach and look over his shoulder back at the house.

"Lines were meant to be crossed." His voice is demanding. Controlling. It forces me to look back in his eyes when that's the last thing I want to do.

"He'll kill you," I whisper.

"I'm a dead man anyway, Maria." The way he says my name has my body involuntarily shivering. I take a step back just as he takes a step forward. "The only one that'll pull the trigger is you if you whisper a word of what's about to happen out here to anyone."

"Of course I would..."

Collin backs me up against a nearby bush, my back is pierced by the thick leaves and branches and makes me arch into him. He takes the opportunity to wrap his thick left arm around my waist and pull me in tight against his frame. I go to scream, but his right-hand cuts off my air supply as it quickly wraps it around my throat.

"No," he chuckles, leaning in and resting his face against my neck.

His right hand loosens, testing me, giving me just enough breath in my lungs to yell if I really wanted to. But I'm too paralyzed by what's happening right now to think straight.

"No, you wouldn't." His breath is hot on my neck, sending chills down my spine. "Not when we've both wanted each other longer than you've ever known Leo. In this game, you've got to ask yourself, whose side are you on? I know where I stand, and I'm tired of hiding it."

I struggle against his hold, but he just wrestles me back. His laugh grows louder as I realize how powerless I am to his strong body.

"It'll hurt less if you take it, like a good fecking girl," he hisses out, raising my skirt slowly, causing sickness to rise in my throat.

I welcome it. I want to throw up. Quickly. Right in his face if it means I'd get his hands off me.

Have I appreciated the look of him from time to time before Leo, back in Vegas? Yes. Have I given him any inclination besides that that I'm interested? Definitely not. If anything we've both done nothing but fight since then. Hatred fueling an unspoken truth between us that I thought screamed we both couldn't stand one another.

"It's the fight that gets me hard, lass," he growls in my ear. "It's what fuels me. Made me realize you fecking want it. Don't you Maria?"

Pushing against his frame with all my strength, his grip on my neck loosens slightly. My instincts take over quickly this time as I scream at the top of my lungs. A moment later, his fist wraps around my throat tighter than before as he holds me still and forces me to look into his eyes.

"Now, that wasn't very nice, was it," he glares at me. "The punishment I'll give you won't be as sweet as his, lass. Won't be as tender. I fuck harder, take faster, and won't hold back for your benefit. Your body? I'll make it mine to use. How I want. When I want." He glances down between us and my heart stops. "No matter who's child your fecking carrying."

A shot rings out, followed quickly by another, and instinctively I close my eyes. Just as I do, I'm thrown to the ground, deadweight sits on top of me holding me still. Scared. Panicked. I stay still, quiet. Waiting to hear the sounds of more gunfire, of men screaming and fighting, but it never comes.

"Maria!"

My world is still black, the dead weight sitting on top of me won't move. I'm too paralyzed by what just happened and the body on top of me. I can't answer.

Body?

"Maria!"

I try and shift my weight, finally alert enough to feel the tugging on my arm as the body is rolled off myself and I'm quickly being pulled to my feet.

"Fuck, Maria, look at me," Leo demands, but I can't.

All I can stare at is Collin's body on the floor beside me. His head cocked to the side, blood oozing out the back and quickly pooling under his head. Leo stashes his gun in the waist of his slacks before grabbing my arms.

"Maria!" He demands a final time, making me shift my shaky gaze and look him in the eyes.

"You shot him?" I mean for it to sound more like a statement, but it comes out questioning, like I can't believe it. "He's dead?"

"He deserved more than that for..."

"He was your friend."

"His hands were all over you," Leo snaps. "All over our child."

"You never hesitated…"

"I'd never fucking hesitate when it comes to protecting what's mine. What's most important." He looks down at the ground between us, his jaw ticks in anger. "More than his life will pay for what he was just threatening."

I catch motion behind my husband and look up to see Declan and Magnolia quickly rushing out into the garden. Declan takes one look at the scene and stops in his tracks. Shaking his head, he says a word or two under his breath to Magnolia just as she reaches his side.

"No one else has to pay," I stammer, glancing back at Leo and watching as his eyes cloud over, a look of vengeance over-shadowing the love and concern that was there a moment ago when he first found me. "He…" I begin and then stop when the look grows darker. "I don't know what got into him. Honestly, but he paid more than he had to, Leo. His family is not to blame for his mistake."

"Mistake?" He bellows. "It's a fucking crime, Maria. Make no *mistake* about that. He was trying to…"

"But he didn't."

"Why are you defending him?"

Why? I honestly don't know. Maybe because Collin was always there to protect me before. He never failed. Not once. He stood in between me and the man who raised me on countless occasions. We never got along well, but he always had my best interest. Always made sure I was safe. Until he didn't.

What got into him tonight is a mystery. But we've all been stirred up trying to make sense of the cluster fuck that has become our lives since Alfonso crashed our wedding the first time. Collin didn't have to pay for the insanity with his life.

"Daniella..."

"Is better rid of him," Leo snaps, grabbing my arm in his as I almost trip over Collin's body. He stalks quickly back towards the house and I try to keep up with him as he ushers me towards the door.

"Take care of it," I hear him whisper to Declan as we pass.

He gives Leo a quick nod and I decide it's best not to speak of what just happened anymore tonight. Even if my hands are still shaking, my mind still tumbling trying to grasp why and how Collin would turn on us all in an instant.

Maybe he wasn't the man my father thought he was. Leo has never dismissed him since they met, but he never confided in him either like I see him do with Declan. My husband always knows more than he lets on, and I'm guessing this was one of those topics he kept under wraps instead of discussing.

Secrets. Always more secrets.

"Did you know Collin could be a threat?" I ask as he continues to usher me up the stairs to the master bedroom.

"Did you?" He raises his brow at me as he pushes open the door to the master suite and gestures for me to walk through. "You spent more time with him than me, Maria. If anything was going on that I needed to know about, I would hope my wife would tell me before I had to kill an innocent man that may have been acting on intuition."

"Are you calling me a whore?" I demand, turning quickly to see him close and lock the door.

He keeps his back turned. His head held low. To any other person, it would look like I just hit him with a low blow. That he's hurt. But not Leo. I take a step back, both thrilled and anxious for what I know comes next.

"Whore?" his voice hisses out in a low menacing tone. He turns slowly, blood staining his clothes, his eyes hooded as he meets my stare. I look down and see I'm just as soiled. Blood streaking my dress. Pools of red in some places and splashes of it in others. "My wife is nobody's whore, except mine."

A thrill shoots through me at his words. They're dirty and awful, but God, they make me want to be dirty and awful just for him.

"You said..."

"Intuition is a funny thing, Maria." He takes a few steps forward and I shake with anticipation. When he gets to my side, he circles me like a hawk circling its prey and it just adds to the excitement running through my veins. "For instance, I understand, without reason, that you get off sometimes on being treated like a dirty slut."

He's behind me now, and I spin quickly, intent on meeting his eye and telling him off. But he grabs me around my waist and holds me in a tight grip.

"I bet your panties are soaking wet," I gasp out and he grips my dress, raising it slowly up my thigh. "Your pussy, fucking throbbing, needing my fingers, my cock."

He traces the lace fabric and groans, I'm wetter than he

expected. I know that by the hiss that escapes his lips a moment later.

"Tell me this is only for me, mi Amore, and not because of the way he was touching you."

The thought crosses my mind, is it? Though I'd never admit it if it were true. But it only makes me wetter with need as I gasp out the second his fingers find my clit and start to rub in delicious circles. Maybe I have denied telling him about my feelings for Collin in the past, but he's keeping secrets from me too. More than I believe he's letting on. He stops abruptly, his thumbs finding the sides of my panties as he lowers them to the floor.

"Step out," he demands, his fingers quickly tracing back up my inner thighs after I do as he says. He quickly enters them back inside me, one, two, three, and I purr a moment later as he finger fucks me harshly and rubs my clit with his other hand, holding my back tight against his frame.

"Hm," he growls hot in my ear as he stands behind me. "You like the idea of two men, Maria." I shake my head from side to side, desperate for him to be wrong and to make myself believe it. "Too bad for you, I don't fucking share."

He forces me forward in one quick thrust. "Grab your fucking ankles," he hisses out, and I do what he says quickly.

A moment later, he smacks my ass so hard I yell out and almost lose my balance as I stumble to catch myself on the floor in front of me. Just as I regain my composure, he thrusts inside so deep I scream.

"Leo!"

Smack!

"My cock is the only fucking cock you'll ever need

Maria," he demands as he pulls out and thrusts back in harder than before. My scream echoes off the wall as he holds my hips still, making sure I take every single inch of him. He pulls me tight against his pelvis, his cock hitting the back of my pussy, tears pricking my eyes from the pain. The pleasure.

"Yes, Sir," I manage to whisper just before his hands rub the pain away from where he punished me. A spanking I know I deserved.

"All you have to do is tell me what you want, Maria, and I will give it to you." He rotates his hips and I groan out in pleasure.

"I need," I pant as he picks up the pace, "I need..."

He pulls out of me quickly and raises me to look him in the eyes just as he comes around to stand in front of me.

"Only you," I whisper.

Consumed by everything. The lies. The secrets. The past, present, fear of the future, I know that to be true. All I've ever needed is him. That will never change. No one could ever make me want them like I want Leo. I wasn't wet until he touched me. I could never desire anyone the way I desire him.

"And all I'll ever need is you, mi Amore," he whispers, brushing a stray strand of hair out of my eyes. He lifts me in his arms and carries me a few steps towards the bed. Laying me down gently, he climbs on top of me, slightly to the side to be gentle with my small swollen stomach.

When he kisses me, I see heaven. When his tongue meets mine, I taste all the beauty that I could ever need or want in this world. He takes his time, enjoying himself, his hands roaming my body, his lips touching every inch of my skin.

When he enters me again, I feel immortal.

When he whispers his sexy wants, demands, desires in my ears, I swear I see stars.

Later, when we climax together, I know no matter what, secrets and all, I could never love or trust anyone as much as I love Leonardo.

"IT's FUCKING FOOLPROOF," Nicoletti says a month later. "I'm telling you, it's like this crypto bullshit was made specifically with the mob in mind."

I lean back in my chair and roll his comment around in my head a while, letting it simmer while I weigh all the risks and benefits. Taking another puff off my cigar, I glance down at the ice in my tumbler and give the glass a little shake. Buying a few more seconds never hurt anyone. Besides, I'm still not sure I want to back Nicoletti's crazy-ass idea.

"We can't fail, I fucking promise," he continues when I still haven't given him any inclination that I care about his ludicrous operation. In reality, I really fucking don't. I'm only here because the cocksucker black-mailed my family soon after the last time I sat in the same room as him.

He's holding my son against me. The son I learned days after our last meeting was my own. We expected as much, Maria and I, and doing so made the shock easier to bare.

He's threatening to never let me see him, a fact that's he's made good on until now, and is the only reason why I finally agreed to a discussion. The only reason I didn't blow his fucking brains out the second he kept what was mine away from me is because I'm not equipped yet for a full-out war between families. Secrets still laying low and simmering until the right time. Soon, though. Very soon.

He's brought me to a breaking point with the little secret he's been withholding until now, my son, and it's making me agree to a negotiation we both know I'm not keen to make. My secret, however, has the ability to change everything, though he'd never guess the cards I'm holding. A fact that makes this little sit-down between gangsters so much fucking sweeter.

"Nothing is foolproof, Nicoletti," I finally assert, blowing out a thick cloud of smoke from the cigar I'm holding and watching as it fills the space above my head. "A plan like this, is only as good, as foolproof, as the man who undertakes it."

"There is power in size, Leonardo. Uniting the families..."

"It would be a fucking mistake, one even you're not fool enough to make."

His jaw locks, his back molars grinding together as he looks at me with so much hatred. Silence settles across the room. All that can be heard is the ice in Declan's glass as he raises it, finishes taking his last sip of scotch, and then deposits the tumbler on the table.

"So that's your decision then?" Nicoletti seethes. "You won't even attempt to try, not even once in order to have a presence in your son's life?"

With a heavy sigh, I sit forward and set my glass down on the table as well. My cigar is discarded in the ashtray immediately after. Looking up, I rest my elbows on my knees and roll my head from side to side.

"Start at the beginning," I hiss. "I'll need to know everything. Don't leave a single thing out. Not if you want to live to see the outcome of your asinine operation."

I lie. I plan on killing this fucker anyways. He's a dead man. Sure as the look on his cocky face as he smiles at me thinking he's won. He's so sure he got his way it's fucking comical.

"Our brokers create fake orders on Wall Street...," he begins.

I rest back in my seat and give Declan a look. One he knows well. One that means I'm done before we're even getting started. He shakes his head and laughs under his breath. I pride myself on control. On restraint in certain situations in order to glean a bigger reward.

Nicoletti has always tested that restraint. Always made me want to snap his neck in two the second I see him. A fact Declan knows well having spent time with me previously when I first reigned over Chi-Town.

"...We influence the price. Create optimism. They're instructed to place large buy/sale options with no intention of filling them. It tricks the other brokers to influence their customers to sell where we want them to and then buy stock where we're directing. Our brokers then cancel the large orders and glean the profit off the rest."

"It's the way we've found we can influence the market to move in the direction we want it to," Jack Rinaldi adds. My eyes glance to the right and catch his. The look I give him causes a startled expression to pass across his features and he shuts up quickly.

Good.

"With cryptocurrency, we can launder the funds electronically across borders with no barriers," Nicoletti continues.

"Crypto, like Bitcoin," I suggest.

"Not necessarily," he sighs. "Bitcoin is the only cryptocurrency that currently keeps a public ledger. It's too risky. I'm sure once we cleaned it, we might get away with no trail. But with all the other options available, why chance it?"

Well, at least the prick has some fucking brains.

"How do you clean it?" I ask.

"We use what they call mixers," he shrugs. "Tumblers. It's considered chain hopping. 'Cross-currency.' It sends it through a set of various addresses. We move the funds from one crypto to another making it impossible to track. In doing so, it breaks the links between transactions."

"How do you know they can't trace it back to you?"

"We login anonymously. Each time, our men are given a new address to make a deposit. By doing it this way, the companies are basically handing us the eraser to wipe our slate clean. It can't be linked to an individual."

"Sounds too good to be true," I suggest, raising my eyebrow and waiting for Nicoletti to say what I'm expecting him to say. That it is. That there is more to it. But instead, he sits silent and waits me out.

"How can they not link it back to the stocks?"

"Some of it that we can claim legitimately we don't have to worry about the trail back to the market and we just move it," he says, picking up his glass from the table and motioning for a nearby soldier to fill it up.

When the young boy does, he gestures around to the rest of us, Declan, Jack, myself, and the kid runs his errand as fast as he can. Filling our glasses almost to the brim, but I'm not fucking complaining. It's sixty-year-old scotch. The kid can keep pouring as far as I'm concerned. Stand by, and then fill it up again.

"The stuff we're concerned about, we invest in online gaming first."

"How?" Declan asks quickly.

A little too quickly. Good thing for him, Nicoletti has no fucking clue he's in the presence of an undercover agent. Although the look he gives my friend may just say he's coming on to him. Something Declan's quick to cover up as he picks up his glass and looks uninterested a moment later. After all, working one too many years undercover, you learn to put on a mask more than you ever really take it off.

"Buying credit," Rinaldi answers for Nicoletti. "Virtual chips. We play a game or two. Maybe transfer some online to an opponent. Another man we've purposely put there. Minor losses for huge gains. They cash them out. There is no more trail to Wall Street."

"So why do you need me?"

The two men in front of me look at each other and smile. I knew we were getting to that question, and I knew before I even set foot in this room that I'd hate to ask it.

"After the funds are clean, we need to legitimize it. Make it part of something real. Integrate it."

"Naturally," I shrug.

"I've burnt many bridges..."

"More times than you should've been allowed," I cut Nicoletti off to which he just sneers at me across the table.

"The operation has grown larger than expected," his smirk deepens. "I've used some of the bridges I haven't burnt across the globe to move what I can so far, but with more brokers turning to the mob, eager to make a buck due to the recession, their services are now not enough."

"What are you asking?"

"Most of my money is legitimized through bars, clubs..."

"Not just any kind of clubs?" I ask, knowing where this is headed, having been informed of his previous operations before this meeting, and wanting to make sure I am ahead of his questions.

"That's right," he smiles. "Not just any. One kind of club in particular," he says, taking another sip of scotch. "And only one kind of club in the city that can handle this kind of operation."

I know the club he's talking about without him even having to say it. And the answer is no fucking way. There isn't a chance in hell the Rossi family will do business with Nicoletti's blood.

"It's impossible."

"Not with your backing."

I glare at him for a moment before sitting up a little straighter. "You're saying you're going to hold my son against me if I don't go to the Rossi family and ask them for you to use Fottere, their sex club, as a means for you to legitimize your underground, money laundering, Wall Street take over, ludicrous operation."

He shrugs. Completely unfazed. Nicoletti had their son killed ten years ago. One of his men had fallen in love with their daughter. The son was protecting her, stopping his men from kidnapping her.

He was shot, point-blank, through the center of the back of his head, and this girl was never seen again.

My men, Federico and Ricardo, the bouncers at the Rossi's club, found their son and saw Nicoletti's men fleeing the scene. Lots of blood was shed that night. Unfortunately for the Rossi family, it wasn't the blood they'd like since Nicoletti sits across from me now still breathing.

"They'll listen to you."

"Not when it comes to you they won't."

His eyes snap up to meet mine. A deadly fire brewing in them. "Then tell them it's for you. They'd do anything for the big Boss." So now I'm the Boss, huh? When he needs something. "And I'm sure you'd do anything for your son, your firstborn, so he doesn't live a life like you did growing up."

My jaw ticks as I force myself to stay still. To not show emotion. In time I'll seek my vengeance for all he's saying. Right now, I need a clear fucking head if I'm going to accomplish the retribution I seek.

"You'll be paid heavily for your alliance."

"I don't want your money."

"If you'd rather..."

"Where's my son?" I demand.

"With his mother."

"You bring me my son," I force out through clenched teeth, about to agree to something that will put a lot of good men, a good Italian family, at risk. "We have a fucking deal, Nicoletti."

He frowns, rising from his seat and gesturing for a man in the back corner of the room to come forward.

"You bring my son to me. At my house. Where he belongs." His eyes widen. "Or no deal."

Nicoletti turns quickly, looking at me a little surprised. "Sabrina..."

"Was always a whore. Can't say I'd think any higher of her as a mother."

"She won't like it."

Rising, I button my coat jacket and regard his statement, knowing it makes no bit of fucking difference to me. Picking up my glass, I drain the last of the scotch, and motion for Declan to follow me to the door.

"Do I look like a man who gives a fuck, Nicoletti?"

He says nothing as I take a few slow strides towards the exit. When he still hasn't answered once I reach the door, I turn and see him still looking at where I was sitting, debating if what I'm asking, the price I am asking him to pay, is worth his payout. In the end, money will always win over family with him, and that is a fact that will eventually be his final downfall.

"My son, Nicoletti," I insist. "I'll give you one hour. After that, we have no fucking deal."

CHAPTER 18
MARIA

I PACE THE FRONT ENTRYWAY, more like waddle in my state, my stomach more than doubling in size this last month, and wring my hands in front of me.

What was he thinking?

I would kill any man who ever tried to take my child away from me. The saying "over my dead body" was definitely invented by a mother protecting her young. Since the beginning of time, the animal kingdom has shown us that the male species will gladly sacrifice whatever they need to be king. The female, however, can manage to rule as a queen without a man and with any number of children in tow, fighting till the end to protect what's hers.

I look up and see Leo casually leaning against the banister, watching me, studying me, nonchalantly looking me up and down as if he didn't just demand a child be taken from his mother.

"Calm yourself, Maria," he whispers, exhaling smoke from a cigarette loosely set between his fingers. It's a habit he's picked up recently, and one I have to admit makes him so much sexier at times, even if I do worry it might kill him later in life. "I'm welcoming home my son after way too long. I don't need to meet my other child before the time's right."

"I'm thirty weeks pregnant, Leonardo," I snap. "Trust me, the time is fucking right."

His eyes widen with my curse before a sexy grin spreads across his lips.

"Let's not tempt fate then, mi Amore. I've never been a father before. Even though the thought of a large family," he suggests, eyeing me up and down like he's ready to fuck me where I'm standing, "thrills me, I'd like to take it one step at a time. One child at a time, if I can."

"Sometimes, you don't get so lucky."

"Sometimes, I enjoy taking my wife over my knee to remind her who's fucking boss."

I stop in my tracks and glare at him just as he flicks the butt of his cigarette to the floor and crushes it slowly with his shoe. He talks a big game, but we both know he cares more than any man ever cared about a woman, a boy, and an unborn child. A fact he likes to keep hidden, just between the two of us.

Leo looks up and sees Declan passing in the hallway. Magnolia walks slowly behind him. They've overheard our little debate and she glances up at us, obviously taking a liking to what she sees, or rather, what she thinks she's seeing, and stops, folding her arms over her chest to watch.

I've grown a lot since she first stepped foot in this house. I've matured even more since Leo came home. But what I haven't conquered is my tongue. The need to talk back when he pushes my buttons, like he's doing now, no matter who's watching.

"You took a woman's child today, Leonardo."

"My child."

"A child who's only ever known one family, one he is being ripped away from right now as he makes his way here. If he's making his way here. I can't believe a mother would hand over her child so easily."

"You don't know the kind of woman Sabrina is, Maria. The kind of woman that's been raising my son for the last five years. Besides, I thought you'd be happy to bring him up as our own. Considering..."

"Kidnapping is where this all started Leonardo!"

"Wrong! Lies. Secrets. Rape. That's where this all started, Maria."

"Well, you sure as hell won't tell me your secrets," I seethe, hitting him where I know it counts. "Are you telling me you raped the woman that bore your son?"

He's at my side in an instant. His harsh grasp stinging as he takes both my arms in his and shakes me once to make me look him in the eye.

"I am not my father, Maria," he hisses and a shiver runs down my spine as his breath feathers across my face. "That boy will be raised by me, he will know he is my flesh and blood. You will be his mother. Soon, you'll be the only mother he'll ever remember. Ever know."

"Don't be too sure of that."

He cocks his head to the side just as the doorbell rings and considers what I've just said.

"Instinct tells me that boy hasn't been raised by a good

woman," his hands drop, he leans in and kisses me on the cheek before brushing a strand of hair behind my ears.

"Trust me," he whispers, as Giovanni enters the entryway and heads for the door. "Boys who grow into real men know the fucking difference."

When the door opens, my eyes lower and take in the stare of a scared little boy and my heart stops. A scared little boy who has the same eyes as the man I love. He clutches his mother's hand tightly and it kills me that we are about to do what we are about to do.

My gaze lifts and locks with Sabrina's. I don't know what I expect. Tears. Red rings around her eyes from crying on the way over, bawling her eyes out ever since she was told her son would no longer be hers. But that's not what looks back at me.

Her eyes are hollow. Empty. Void of any love and affection and cold as ice, obviously caring less about the exchange that is about to take place. I have to admit, Leo might be right in his assumptions, and his actions. The woman before me is heartless. I can see it. But more than that, I can feel it.

"Come in," Giovanni ushers our guest forward, my eyes drifting to the left and finally landing on Nicoletti's.

His smile is sinister, his gaze staying a little too long on my stomach causing me to hold my hand on top of my own child as if that could protect us both. Leo senses my unease as his hand quickly finds my lower back. He steps into my side possessively and my heart beats easier knowing he's beside me, even in the presence of the people before us.

A wicked man, his whorish wife, and a little boy whose world is about to change in ways he doesn't even know yet.

My gaze falls once again on Sabrina. Just like that first night I saw her in my house, on our wedding day, there's something familiar about her that I just can't put my finger on. Or, maybe I don't want to remember.

"Luca," Nicoletti says, but the boy doesn't respond. "Luca, fucking listen to me!"

"Hey!" My husband shouts, stepping forward and getting in Nicoletti's face. "Watch the way you talk to my son."

They stand off against each other, toe to toe, for several seconds that seem more like hours until Sabrina's chuckle starts to fill the room.

"Always had to act like you had the bigger balls, didn't you, Leonardo?"

His icy gaze falls on her instantly but he doesn't respond. Instead, he takes a step back and falls to his knee. Eye-level with Luca, he attempts to get the boy to look at him, but it's no use. His big eyes wander around the entryway. Up, down. Side to side. Anywhere but into Leo's gaze.

"Luca," Leo tries, but it just causes the boy to shake slightly as he backs away and casts his gaze to the floor.

"What did you tell him about me?" Leo snaps.

"Only that he'll be staying here now. That his home isn't with us anymore," Sabrina sighs.

At that, Leo blanches slightly, his jaw set tight as he stares back at the boy in front of him. He reaches for him, but Luca flinches and so he stops.

"What's wrong with him then?" Leo demands. "Did you tell him lies? Lies to make him hate his only father?"

"Not exactly," Nicoletti chuckles as one of his soldiers walks inside the front door and drops a few suitcases in the entryway. Nicoletti regards him for a moment, giving him a slight nod, informing him to wait outside for him, and then turns back to us with a heavy sigh. "He's been diagnosed as having delayed motor development."

Leo slowly rises to full height, his gaze still downcast on the boy for a moment. A boy who is now, once again, glancing around the new space that surrounds him.

"Why?" Leo grits out, and I catch an air of tension building as it quickly grows stronger between us all.

I look up to see Magnolia, a moment ago forgotten, as she makes her way out of the shadows and into the entryway, obviously wanting to hear what Nicoletti has to say. But he doesn't continue. Just glances at his wife, Sabrina, and a look is exchanged that I'm glad Leo doesn't witness as he continues to stare down at his son. Our son.

Sabrina drops the child's hand and he doesn't move. Doesn't reach back for his mother. Doesn't even act like a child normally would that is about to be left all alone and taken away from the only world he's ever known.

"I said, why?" Leo demands a little more harshly, catching the ear of Declan who I now notice is suddenly standing close by just in case he's needed.

Giovanni goes to close the front door, but Nicoletti holds up a hand stopping him. He takes his wife's arm and starts to lead her toward the exit.

"Answer me, Nicoletti," my husband demands, and my heart rate spikes as I watch in fear of what might come if he doesn't. "What is wrong with my son?"

With a roll of her eyes, Sabrina finally responds.

"Shortly after he was born, he was diagnosed with two

things." Her voice is cold. Dismissive. Careless as she talks about the child she carried. The child she brought into this world and she's now discarding away like he is nothing. "Cardiac anomalies, and slowed physical growth both resulting in delayed motor development."

"I don't like to repeat myself," Leo says through clenched teeth. "But for the third time damn it, someone tell me why."

Nicoletti and Sabrina exchange a look, one that breaks my heart. This time, Leo sees and takes a step forward, quickly guiding Luca behind him to protect him in a way only a loving father could. Luca takes no notice, just stands there and glances off into the distance. Completely unaware of what is going on between everyone.

"I'll find out sooner or later," Leo hisses. "So you might as well tell me, Sabrina, because this sounds like a crock of shit. A cardiac abnormality, ok. That can be hereditary. But mixed with the rest, I'm not fucking buying it."

For the first time since she walked in the door, I see the woman before me get nervous. She glances at me, then behind us at Declan and Magnolia. Finally, her gaze falls to the floor as she fidgets with the sleeve of her blouse, tugging it up slightly to scratch her forearm.

And that's when I see it.

My eyes widen as I take a few steps forward.

"Maria," Leo demands, trying to stop me before he knows what is going on. Trying to protect me always, like I suddenly feel the urge to protect our new son.

I reach out and grab her arm. Nicoletti tries to stop me but Leo is at my side in an instant making him take his hands off me. I look behind me and notice Luca has been ushered to the shadows. Magnolia kneels in front of him, talking to him, although he's not paying attention. Declan stands by her side, his hand on his waist, no doubt on a trigger.

Looking back at Sabrina, she tries to pull her arm from my grasp, but I just hold on tighter.

"You want to tell him," I hiss, "Or should I?"

I cock my head to the side, hatred for a woman I barely know coming off of me in spades. And fuck, I can't shake the fact that she looks so familiar, it haunts me. Her eyes darken. Her nostrils flare. She takes one step into me and I swear if I thought I'd get away with it in my state, I'd wring her fucking neck. Her eyes flash with something that brings my past to my present, but I shake it off and try to focus only on the rage that's building inside my gut.

"You go right ahead, sweetheart. After all, a queen knows everything. Doesn't hide anything from her king. Am I right?"

Her mocking tone hurts momentarily, but it doesn't linger. I push up her sleeve and nod towards her arm. Leo looks over my shoulder and curses under his breath.

"Is that what I think it is?" he whispers, his voice deathly and taking on a tone I've never heard before. "Were you using while you were pregnant with my son, Sabrina?"

Her eyes flash to his. Anger. Bitterness. Hurt filling them as she considers not answering.

"You weren't there," she shrugs. "Couldn't have stopped me even if you were."

He reaches around me so quickly, that I almost stumble to the floor trying to get out of the way. His hand grips her throat as he forces her back out the front door.

"Take your hands off my wife!" Nicoletti demands.

His gun is pulled, I glance behind me and see Declan's is raised as well. He never takes his eyes off the back of Nicoletti's head and I pray he pulls the trigger. Rids us all of everything that's come here to haunt us. But I know he won't. Secrets still untold, I'm not an idiot to understand doing so would start a larger war. One I trust my husband to end before it ever really has the chance to get started.

Leo gives Sabrina a shove out the door and her hands quickly go to her throat. She hunches over, attempting to catch her breath, and then stares back up at Leo with dark eyes. Nicoletti is at her side in an instant. Giovanni is quick on their heels to close the door behind them.

"You're lucky," Leo hisses, trying to catch his breath as he addresses Sabrina. "I won't kill you in front of my son."

She glares at him as I step up to his side. But just before the door closes, just before she's blocked out of Luca's life forever, I smile and add.

"But I will," the look on her face is worth everything as I continue. "I didn't carry him for nine months, but I will be his mother for the rest of his life. You cross him, me, or any of our children again, I'll fucking kill you. I'll send you back to hell where pieces of shit like you belong. And I won't think twice before I pull the damn trigger."

The door closes and I turn around, ready to embrace the boy I'm eager to get to know. A boy I can't wait to hear one day call me mom. As I walk toward him, my eyes lift and catch Magnolias. A proud look stares back at me. One that matches the smile in the eyes of the man at my side as we embrace our son. I smile a little wider knowing I put it there.

CHAPTER 19

"Where the fuck have you been? I've been waiting a fucking hour," I hiss out in a whisper as I raise my glass to my lips and shoot back the shittiest whiskey I've ever tasted.

I grit my teeth as it stings down the back of my throat. It's my third, and still just as bad as the first sip. My phone vibrates in my pocket, but I ignore the incoming text now that he's finally here.

My eyes raise and watch the show in front of me as he slides into the seat to my right. The woman on stage is nothing compared to the masterpiece that's at home warming my bed, and as I watch her start to strip, start to touch herself, I'm suddenly very ready to make this meeting as quick as possible so I can get back home to fuck Maria while I still can.

That is, before the baby comes and I'm laid high and dry for weeks having to jerk off, fuck her mouth, her ass, instead of making love to her like I'm suddenly obsessed with now that she's my wife.

"Fecking shite, ya' know how hard it is to get through customs mate, I shouldn't have to tell 'ya."

I glance his way just as Collin gestures for the bartender to bring him over the same as what is in my glass. I think about warning him, telling him he's better off staying sober, but he goes on before I can stop him.

"Would've thought ya needed more time, Boss," he sighs, glancing up at the woman on stage just as my phone vibrates again in my pocket. "Must admit, I was surprised to get word so quickly. Surprised to get raised from the dead so quickly."

The bartender sets his glass down in front of him and I watch as he takes his first sip, almost spitting it out on the counter in front of us the second it hits his lips.

"Feck, that shite is awful. You honestly going to tell me you've been sitting here drinking this piss for the past hour?"

Shaking my head, I look back in front of me. The woman is now completely devoid of clothes and doing things with a pole I have never seen before. And hell, I've seen a fucking lot.

"I see why you come here now," Collin almost groans. "Must admit, the view is fecking spectacular, mate."

"And how is Daniella?"

"Feck off," he tosses over his shoulder at me and I stifle a laugh. Leaning back in his chair, he adjusts the crotch of his pants and takes another sip of his shitty drink. "She's in Dublin. I'm here. And this view is fecking stunning, ya? A love lost is a life regained. Besides, love can feck right off as far as I'm concerned."

"Right." My voice is laced with heavy sarcasm as we both get lost in the view in front of us. Out of the corner of my eye,

I see his brow raise as he looks in my direction, debating whether or not to tell me more. In the end, the heart wins. It always does.

"Walked in on the whore banging an ol' buddy of mine," he divulges with bitterness. Leaning towards me, his eyes darken as he says, "Tits and ass, all over the place. Lettin' that wanker feck 'er in places I never could. Places she's never let me." He returns his full attention to the woman in front of him and gives her a wink when she starts to crawl toward him. "Figure, a good ol' feck with no fecking strings is just what I need, right."

I nod my head and turn in his direction.

"Well, before she's on her knees sucking your cock," I gesture towards the woman on stage and he gives me a sly smile as the girl starts dancing only for him. She's caught on that I'm definitely not interested, and Collin is rock hard and ready. Although she has no idea what she's getting into with him. I'm absolutely positive. No woman ever does. "Business first, you bastard."

"Aye, yes," he sits up straight and gives me half of his attention. "Don't tell me she fecking suspects anything?"

"As far as anyone knows, besides Dec that is, you're dead," my phone vibrates again making my damn annoyance grow. "Let's keep it that way. Whores have big fucking mouths. Sucking you off isn't the worst thing they can do."

"Again, feck off," he laughs. When I don't respond, just level him with a serious stare he shrugs his shoulders and pays better attention. "I get it. No feckin' problem."

"I gather besides Daniella, business in Dublin worked out well?"

He nods, continuing to keep a secret I hope doesn't get out. That is, not before I can pull off a damn miracle. Collin is the only man closest to me that could pull off this kind of stunt. Maria would have expected something was off if it had been Declan. Besides, Dec is slightly more straight-laced than fucked in the head like the rest of us. Who am I joking? We're all fucking mad, it's the only way to survive this kind of life. In the end, Collin had the connections and previous experience with faking his own death. My only regret, letting him put his hands on my wife in order to get the job done.

"You going to tell me why I'm back from the dead so soon? Or do I have time for a lap dance?"

Rolling my eyes, I can't say I don't blame his urgency. I remember the need to lose myself in someone in order to numb the sting of a woman you won't ever be able to forget. It's kind of what got me into the mess I'm now facing. So, before I lose Collin's attention completely, I figure it'd be better to hit him with just what he needs to know, get the answers I want, and get back to my beautiful wife.

"The Fitzgerald family has done more dealings in sex clubs than the Lombardi's, Nitti's, and Moretti's," I begin. He eyes me curiously, nods, takes another sip of the awful whiskey, and turns his attention back to the stage. "I made a promise to Nicoletti to help him with his operation in exchange for my son."

"Aye, so the wean was yours after all, ey?" he smiles, and a sense of pride fills my once hollow chest. "Fecking hell, you're a dad, mate. Never thought I'd see the damn day. Same for you doing business with Nicoletti, right. That's a day neither of us ever thought we'd see, even long after the good Lord decides to send me to fecking hell where I belong."

"It's not a promise I intend to keep," I whisper.

He looks my way, studies me for a moment before saying, "Aye, I see now."

"I need to use the Fottere club uptown as a front. The Rossi family trusts me, but we both know they have more dealings with your father. His club in Dublin backs theirs."

"Well, then you'd be wanting to take that up with me ol' man, but you already know that," Collin sarcastically laughs. "And you'd also be knowing, we don't so much as get along, now do we?"

"It's not your dad's name that matters, it's your family's. I need you to talk to the Rossi's, explain the situation, front as my man on the inside. Nicoletti has never seen you. He stays mostly out of sight to put up his act, his stupid mental show."

He gives me a look telling me I'm a damn idiot, men in our line of work have ways of getting any information they want. Nicoletti may act the part of a moron, but he didn't rise to where he is by being a fool. I'm surprised at myself for not thinking of that first. I don't know where my fucking head is, maybe on the phone that's ringing once again in my pocket.

"Wear a disguise," I grit out, fumbling with my slacks trying to pull the phone free. "Fuck, if you can fake your own damn death, I know you can do that."

He nods, and just as I'm finally about to get my phone out of my pocket, it stops ringing. Rolling my eyes, I see Collin's attention is once again turning back to the stage as he waves for the bartender to pour him some more shitty whiskey and the smell of wet pussy starts to invade my senses. Obviously our little cock-tease likes the look of Collin as well. Her pheromones are overpowering, and not calling to me in any way whatsoever. Collin on the other hand is already adjusting his crotch and very eager to get off.

"They're calling a meeting in order to make sure everyone knows what they're doing and how to make this operation, laundering the cash through the club, happen as clean and easy as possible," I say a little too loud, trying to get his attention back on business.

Normally I'd worry someone overheard, but I own the damn strip club. I've known the men who run it for decades, and we're the only two besides the bartender here. A plus for Collin and the stripper he's set on fucking the second I leave.

"I need you in place by then. Running things."

He nods. "When is that?"

"Soon. I'll get you word as soon as possible," I rise from my seat and drop a few bills on the counter. His nod is all the answer I need that things will be set up how I need them to be, when I need them to be. "For the fuck," I goad with a demeaning laugh. "And your trouble."

"Don't pay for the feck, mate," he smiles as the woman in front of him drops to her knees and grinds towards his face. "Never have."

He runs a finger over her pussy, an action that's completely not allowed, but no one's going to stop him in my presence. He finally glances up my way.

"My troubles thank you though, Boss."

I turn and start to make my way to the door, my phone vibrating in my pocket with an incoming text once again.

"Feck, it's good to be back in the states," I hear Collin say just as I glance behind me and see the stripper straddling him as he buries his face in her tits.

I nod to two of my soldiers as I stride towards the door. They've been in the shadows keeping a watchful eye. I'm not afraid of Nicoletti, but I don't trust him either. That's for damn sure. Pushing out into the evening, I look up as my driver exits the car and comes around to open my door the closer I get to the limo.

Finally pulling my phone from my pocket, I glance down to see three missed texts from Magnolia and a handful of missed calls. What the fuck? I expected this type of hounding from an eager wife. And I got to admit, I am just as eager to get back to her after leaving the strip-tease I just did. But just as I am about to open the texts to see what the hell is going on, I receive an incoming call from Declan.

"Where the fuck have you been?"

"Funny, I was just asking someone else that same question," I laugh as I climb into the car. I wait for Declan's response, which oddly doesn't come, just as the driver situates himself before pulling away from the curb. "I'm on my way home. What the fuck couldn't wait until..."

"Fuck going home, get your ass to Chicago Memorial."

My blood turns cold. "Maria?" I demand.

"Is in labor. Better tell your driver to step on it. From the way she's screaming, it won't be long."

Ten fingers. Ten toes. A full head of strawberry blonde hair, and blue eyes looking up at me that I swear are identical to her mother's.

She starts to cry, just a little bit, and I pull her up to my face quickly, quietly shushing her in her tiny little ears as I sway back and forth in front of the hospital window. It does the trick, and I smile to myself, feeling more equipped suddenly than I ever thought I would at being a father.

I breathe my daughter in. So pure. So innocent. A fresh start. A new life and it does something to my heart that I have never felt before.

Glancing up as a nurse enters the room, I continue my light dance with my daughter as she goes about checking on Maria. My wife lays peaceful napping and I can't deny that right now feels like the closest to heaven I will ever get the chance to be.

Another noise sounds from the small bundle in my arms, and I look down to see her beautiful cherub face practically smiling as I hold her close. I know it's not a real smile, but the idea that I could be the one to make her happy does something to me that I haven't felt since the first day I fell in love with her mother all those years ago.

"Your wife is due for more pain meds," the nurse whispers as she comes up to my side and gestures for me to give her my daughter. I pull back from her, not entirely sure why she's insisting I hand her over. "I need to check the baby's vitals. She may also need to be changed..."

"I'll do it," I hiss a little too harshly and feel sorry for the older woman when I see her take a step back in fear.

Swallowing some of the possessive fatherly feelings I am

suddenly consumed with, I follow the nurse over to her bassinet and lay my daughter down in her bed. As I go about checking her to see if she needs changing, the nurse sets about checking what she needs to and I'm relieved that she sees enough of the dominance, the need for control in me, that she doesn't press taking my daughter from me again.

"Did you decide on a name?" she asks, as she sets about her tasks, looking up at me briefly to study me over her glasses.

"Francesca," I smile down at my daughter. "It means 'free one.'"

The nurse just nods, oblivious to the depth of the meaning of the name. Free. That's all Maria and I will ever want for our children. To live a free life and not be weighed down by the secrets, the lies, the business we run.

"And your son?" I look up at her just as she finishes and takes over swaddling Francesca tightly before handing her back over into my arms again. "I saw him earlier in the hall-way. What's his name?"

"Luca," I sigh, my heart heavy with the knowledge that his life will not be as free as Francesca's. Not with the burdens he'll carry. Not with the obstacles he'll be forced to overcome because of his low-life mother.

"*Light*," the older woman smiles down at my daughter, her hand adjusting the cap on her head.

The gesture makes me take a step back for some reason. I may be new to this father thing, but I know what my daughter needs. And I'll give it to her always, without her ever having to ask.

"That's right," I whisper, agreeing with the nurse about

the meaning of Luca's name. "He's been dealt a dark hand, but if I can do anything about it, I'll change it for him. I wanted him to have a name that reminded him he'll do just fine, be alright in life, if only he follows the light."

I was bred, raised, and trained to do anything for my family before I ever had one to call my own. Now, that greed, that dominating desire to ensure nothing ever harms them has grown a million times more intense than I ever thought it would.

"Leonardo," my wife's groggy voice pulls me from the woman in front of me. My eyes lift and I instinctively start making my way toward her.

"Mi Amore, rest," I say, sitting down next to her on her bed. "*Dormire*, your body needs it."

"Francesca," she breathes, sitting up straight in her bed and reaching out her arms. I put our daughter in them gently as the nurse makes her exit, giving us privacy.

"Lei è bellissima, Maria," my voice comes out strained, my emotions getting the better of me as I stare at my daughter in my wife's arms.

Maria lowers her top and guides our daughter to her breast, her motherly instincts taking over and making my heart swell at the sight. She's going to be a better mother than I ever imagined, I can feel it. As the weight of that feeling gets the better of me, I lean forward and place a kiss against my wife's forehead.

"What was that for?" she smiles, as I lean back and return the grin.

"For loving me," I whisper, taking her hand in mine. "For giving me life," she stares into my eyes so lovingly it knocks the air out of my lungs. When I can finally continue, I add, "For giving me a future. For forever being my light."

A knock sounds at the door, but I'm not ready to break the moment and get lost in my wife's eyes a little while longer. A lifetime of unspoken words exchanged perfectly between us as she stares back at me with a smile. When the knock sounds again, she covers herself and tends to Francesca as I rise from her hospital bed.

"Come in."

Magnolia enters first, making a b-line straight for the baby. Declan follows, ushering Luca in before him. I look down at my son and smile. This is the first time we have all been in the room together, and having my whole family under one roof makes me want to kick Magnolia and Declan out. Makes me want to wrap us four up in a bubble so nothing can ever threaten the happiness I'm not accustomed to feeling. So no harm will ever come to them.

I could care less about me, and by the look in Declan's eyes, it would seem that's right where this conversation is headed as he gestures for me to step aside.

"We got a problem."

"I don't deal in problems. Take care of it."

"Not a problem I can handle without you."

I glance back over my shoulder. Luca is standing at the end of the bed. Emotionless, staring straight ahead at Maria and his sister. Maria hands Francesca off to Magnolia and gestures for our son to come closer, but he doesn't budge. A wave of burning anger builds in the pit of my gut as I turn back to Declan.

"I'm a little fucking busy right now."

"Can't wait," he shrugs as he shoves his hands in his pockets. "Daniella..."

"Is a whore who got caught red-handed from what I'm told."

"Then you weren't told everything."

My blood turns cold. "What the fuck does that mean?"

"Means I told you so."

I glare at him. Entirely not in the mood for games and his dumb-ass antics. "What did you tell me, Dec? Get to the fucking point."

"Betrayal, Chief. It never comes from an enemy."

I study him, my brain struggling to keep up after the events of today. "Our newly resurrected friend told me he caught her cheating. Nothing more."

"I don't think he knew," Declan sighs, turning to watch Magnolia swaying back and forth with Francesca, a hurt look disguised under a longing only I can understand graces his face before he goes on. "Word is, Daniella's been the rat far longer than just since we got to Chicago."

"Vegas?"

"Vegas," he confirms. "And before."

He nods to his wife and smiles when she holds the baby up a little higher so he can see her better before kissing both her cheeks.

"How big is the threat?"

"She can blow the cover off the secret you've been hiding."

I stop breathing. My blood rages through my veins. He feels the hostility and turns to meet my eye.

"The man she was caught fucking works for Nicoletti,"

he sees the look in my eyes, knowing I'm wondering how Collin overlooked this important fact. "That's the thing about love, right? It's blind. I'm not sure our friend would have noticed anyway, but given he caught his girl with another man's dick inside her, I'm thinking his judgment was blurred."

"How do we know he worked for Nicoletti?"

"The man's dead. Contrary to popular belief, sometimes it is easier to get a dead man to talk than a live one," Declan laughs. "Oh, Collin spared Daniella. But the bastard took his time killing the adulterer. That is, after blowing off his head. It was hard to get an I.D. Happened a week ago, and word just got back to Nicoletti."

"Which proves we have two problems."

Declan mumbles his agreement as he nods his head a few times. "Ghosts won't remain ghosts for long. Not if Daniella wants to squeal."

I shake my head, taking a moment as I turn and look at my family. Consider all that's at stake. Maria has finally succeeded in getting Luca to come to her side of the bed. Francesca is now back in her arms as she talks to him and shows him his sister.

Daniella must know the cards we're hiding. She lived in my house for months. Kept Collin's bed warm. I don't think he'd tell her such an important secret as pillow talk. But I can't be too sure either.

Even worse, she's been in on faking Collin's death since we made the decision. Question is, how much does she fear the Moretti's and Fitzgeralds, and how much faith does she honestly have in her boss, Nicoletti, to protect her as she tries to stab us in the back. From the looks of it, not much or she'd have already blown the lid off everything.

"What do you suggest?"

"Silence her."

"How?" I grit. "I don't take too well with pulling the trigger on women, Dec. I've done it once or twice, when I've absolutely had to, and the shit still doesn't sit well with me."

"Fucking hell," he seethes. "That's not what I was suggesting. Before it ever comes to that, I say we send in the only woman we know that's cold enough to deal with a traitor and not get herself killed in the process."

"I've always admired the way you're so keen to offer up your wife."

"For business, yes. Pleasure? I'll kill any man who lays a fucking hand on her." I laugh knowingly. "Honestly, she's the only woman I've ever known that has bigger balls than any man I've ever met, and that includes the two of us. That's fucking saying something."

I nod my head once in agreement. Still watching Maria as she wins my heart over again in life with how flawless she is at being a mother. "Regardless, the job needs to be moved up to ensure no fucking mistakes happen," I add.

He nods again.

"How soon can we get the paperwork signed and every-thing in place?"

"One month. Maybe two."

"That's a long fucking time to wait."

"Which is why we need to move fast. Magnolia and I can be on a plane tonight. Have the problem contained by tomor-row, noon at the latest."

I turn back his way and study him, cocking my head to the side. "I understand the debt you owe me, Dec. But I can't help feeling like there is more in it for you than just paying off a gentleman's agreement."

"We bag Nicoletti, I get a promotion at the bureau," he finally divulges. "And," he continues before I can respond, "Watching my wife work has always been my kryptonite."

I turn back to my family, watch my wife with my children, and can't help but fucking grin like a lovestruck bastard. I feel the fucking same, there's no denying it.

PART III

CHAPTER 20

SIX WEEKS LATER

"REMEMBER," Magnolia says to Maria as Declan and I watch them from our spot across the room, "Eyes, nose, throat," she points to each as she moves down her frame. "Solar plexus, groin, knees."

"What about the foot?" my wife asks.

I look at Declan and we both exchange a grin. We've been standing in our home gym for about an hour now for what my wife calls her daily "life skill training." Ever since about a week after the baby was born, she's been determined to learn how to feel more confident in our way of life. I told her she should take time to heal, I would protect her like I always have. Until she was ready. But she wouldn't have it.

Seven days after our daughter was born, she started meeting Magnolia here every day at noon. I have to admit, it's an appointment I look forward to as well while I stand back and watch her grow more and more into her own skin. Her

222 / EVELYN MONTGOMERY

confidence rises like my dick in my slacks as she wrestles around with Magnolia on the mat.

"Yeah, sure, feet," Mags shrugs. "But, in all honesty, your attacker will probably come at you from behind and be wearing some sort of heavy boot, not fucking sandals. Better to aim where it's going to count most."

She takes an aggressive stand in the middle of the mat, and Maria tries her best to imitate the pose. She's fucking adorable. Pushing herself so soon after Francesca's birth. Determined to learn all she can and become stronger.

Declan and Magnolia returned a month ago, after the threat with Daniella was handled in typical covert FBI fashion. The *threat* is now state-side and awaiting sentencing. A punishment I am all too happy to dish out myself. That is after all the bullshit is all over and every secret is finally out in the damn open.

"If you can break loose and get around them, come at them from the back, you want to go for their Achilles tendon," Magnolia explains. "But you'd have to break free first to give yourself that advantage. Now, come at me. And this time, don't swing like a frail little bitch."

Maria jolts forward, slightly pissed off from the name she's just been called. Her arm flies out in front of her as she attempts an upward jab at Magnolia's face, but Mags is faster and grabs her wrist, turning her around and pinning her quickly against a nearby wall.

"Hard not to get off on watching two women fight and pin each other down," Declan sighs next to me. I hate to agree, but the evident bulge in my slacks would say otherwise. There's just something about watching, sweat glistening on my wife's dewy skin, her hair a mess, clothes that look like they were painted on, that makes me fill with the need to take her in a very primal way.

"Now," Magnolia hisses out of breath. "What do you do?"

Maria steps forward with one foot to get her balance as best she can while facing the wall, and then uses her free elbow to strike back at her attacker. She pauses, elbow raised in action, waiting for Magnolia to let her go.

"That's right, right?" she questions when Magnolia won't release her hold.

"Keep fucking striking until I let you go, darling," Magnolia grits out, igniting a fire in my wife's eyes that makes me grin with pride.

I clear my throat and cross my arms over my chest. Declan coughs into his fist, before adjusting his cock, and then proceeds to watch our women duke it out. Hell, we'd both be lying if we said it wasn't one of the biggest fucking turn-ons.

Maria grunts as she forces her elbow backward.

"Again!" Magnolia shouts.

My wife repeats the action. Once, twice, three more times before she picks up her right foot and steps back hard, right on top of Magnolia's toes.

"Fucking hell!" Mags shouts as she finally releases Maria and I then watch my wife wiggle free.

"I thought you said feet don't count," Maria taunts as Dec and I stifle a laugh.

Magnolia gathers herself momentarily and then reaches out, and grabs Maria by the throat. A surge of adrenaline rushes through my body, wanting to make sure Magnolia is not hurting Maria. Wanting to protect my wife and make sure she's alright.

But I push it down, back where it came from. If she's going to walk with me in this life, she'll need to learn on her own how to survive when I'm not always there to watch over her. Besides, she's learning from the best. Something I wish could've taken place before Alfonso Capone's raid on our wedding day almost a year ago now.

"Fucking fight," Magnolia shouts, and I watch as Maria remembers what to do, stepping back to gain her balance right before she traps Magnolia's fingers with her bicep close to her ear.

She pivots away, bringing her elbow down to break the chokehold. Quickly, I see my wife raise her elbow and slam it straight forward into Magnolia's face. Mags catches my wife's arm before it can make contact, stepping back a moment later and stopping the fight.

"Good, at least you finally got one thing right," Mags teases, causing Maria to retaliate with an evil scowl as she pushes out of Magnolia's hold.

"Rossi said the paperwork for the club should be good to go sometime next week, two weeks tops," Declan says as we watch our wives continue to fight on the mat in the center of the room.

"Good," I sigh. "Any word on Nicoletti?"

"He wants to sign documents and proceed with the first transaction as soon as Rossi is good to go."

We both cock our heads to the side and watch as Maria is tackled to the floor, Magnolia on top of her, holding her hands above her head. My wife kicks up between Magnolia's thighs and Declan and I wince as Magnolia frees Maria and they both scramble quickly to standing.

"Do you think loose ends will be tied up by then?" I question.

"It's cutting it close, but I was able to pull a couple of strings."

"None of which are going to hurt your promotion, I hope?"

"What's the fun of playing both sides if I don't use the resources to get what I want?"

Magnolia lunges at Maria, who instantly jumps back in fear. Magnolia rolls her eyes once before saying, "Don't fucking hesitate. If you fight, fucking commit. You're all in or you're fucking dead. Become the aggressor. Remember that."

Maria glares at her before charging forward and wrapping her arms around Magnolia's middle and then pushing her up against a wall. Magnolia anticipates it and wraps her arms around Maria's neck, cutting off her air supply.

"And have we used the right resources to get what we need to ensure this job's done right?" I ask, pulling my eyes away from the women and turning to face Declan at my side.

"Wouldn't play both sides of the law if I wasn't any fucking good at it," he shrugs. "The history we have together proves that."

"Our track record is reckless sometimes. I need to make sure nothing reckless comes out of this deal. For my family's sake."

"This whole deal since day one has been nothing but reckless," Declan laughs.

"Right, but what my wife doesn't know can't hurt her. When she finds out the truth, that's another story."

"You think she's not on to you yet?"

"If she was," I sigh as I turn around and take in my wife still struggling to get out of Magnolia's hold, "Trust me, I'd know. Maria's pure. Sometimes I think too pure for this way of life."

Maria has spun around and is facing us now, Magnolia is at her back. Her chin comes down like a vice against Magnolia's forearm. She uses her hands to grab at Magnolia's elbow and wrist. Taking a step to Magnolia's side, Maria hunches forward and then releases her elbow up into her attacker's stomach, making contact as Magnolia huffs out a breath completely unprepared. She releases Maria, who spins and shoves the palm of her hand up cracking Magnolia's nose as her head jolts backward.

Up until this moment, they've been playing fair. Pretend. Now, my wife's had enough as she unleashes a fire that I'm all too used to seeing when I'm on the receiving end.

"Don't hesitate," she screams as she punches forward once again. Magnolia blocks it this time, taking a step back and trying to regain her balance. "Commit!"

Maria gives Magnolia a one-two punch, which Declan's wife blocks perfectly. Without hesitation, Maria drops to her knees and sweeps her right foot out and under Magnolia's who then goes flying and lands on the mat upside down.

"All in," Maria shouts as she puts a foot to Magnolia's chest. Out of breath, she sneers, "Remember that."

Declan's wife smiles up at Maria and wipes the blood off

her nose. "That's right, darling. Looks like you're not a whiny little bitch after all."

Lesson done for the day, I take a few steps towards the two women in the center of the room as Declan follows.

"Too pure," Declan laughs under his breath. "Give your wife a knife in the next fight and she'll be unstoppable."

"Knife?" Maria questions as I take my final step toward her. "When do I get to learn that?"

"One step at a time," Magnolia huffs as my wife helps her up off the mat. "Besides, I want to make sure you're ready, not planning to stab me in the back when I'm not looking."

She gives Maria a teasing smile before she follows Declan off towards the door. I watch as they go, admiring the power they hold as a couple. A power Maria and I will one day hold as well when she's ready.

"What were you two talking about?" my wife inquires, dragging my attention back to her and the sweat that's pooling seductively across her collarbone.

I pull her into me and kiss her lips. "Nothing you need to worry about." I trace my finger through the sweat on her skin, dragging it lower, down to her cleavage that's larger and more mouthwatering than ever since Francesca's been born.

"When you make comments like that, typically I do need to worry."

"The only thing I'm worried about," I whisper as I back her up against the nearest wall, "Is how much longer I can hold out before I need to feel my cock inside you."

Her eyes close as desire takes hold, and her head falls back against the wall. We've never gone this long without sex. Only when we were forced to in the time we've spent apart.

But being next to her, day and night, watching her grow as a mother, a wife, a partner in this life – it's been unbearable. The need to possess her is aching inside me, more than it ever has before. I take advantage of her exposed skin and suck along her neck, licking, savoring, and tasting the sweet sweat on her skin.

"I need a shower," she whispers, embarrassed, but I think she tastes sexy as fuck.

"You need to be *properly* fucked."

She lets out a laugh. "I thought there was nothing proper you wanted to do to my body, Leonardo?"

"There isn't," I whisper, my hands gripping the sides of her yoga pants, pulling down ever so slightly, slowly, waiting to see if she'll permit me to push this any further. "That in mind," I tease, looking up into her eyes, my face aligned with her pussy, I trace a finger over her slit and ask, "Are you going to tell me to stop?"

Breathless, she urges me to keep going with a nod of her head. Once I've stripped her bare, I rise to standing, placing a gentle kiss against her velvet lips as I go. My eyes lift and catch hers as she raises her right leg and wraps it around my thigh, pulling me into her core and placing both hands on either side of my face. "Would you listen if I told you to stop now?"

She grinds down against me, the crown of my dick in my slacks gliding up across her slit. "No," I groan. "Not when you're acting like this I won't."

Placing my hand under her other thigh, I pull her other leg up in the air. She straddles me as her hands instantly fall to my zipper and she pulls me free with desperation.

"God, Maria," I hiss, as she circles my tip and pulls me towards her entrance. "It's been so long, I'm not going to fucking last."

Slamming up inside her, she screams out as her walls tighten around me.

"Leo," she pants as I take her viciously up against the wall. Her back arching as each thrust of my hips pushes her up before she falls back down. Pulling back, I circle her nub and feel her instantly grow wetter.

"Watching you fight, Maria," I whisper, rubbing her clit faster and seeing her eyes cloud over as her head falls forward and she stares me in the eyes. "Watching you see for yourself, what I've always seen in you," her mouth falls open as she looks down between us. I do the same, my balls tightening as I watch her wetness grow thicker, pooling around my cock. "That you're stronger than you once believed. It's fucking beautiful," I hiss, my fingers gathering her cum and running it back up to her clit. She sucks in a breath, and I look up, catching her eye as her orgasm starts to rip through her body.

"Breathtaking," I grit out. My climax on the verge of breaking free. "Makes me so damn proud to call you mine."

My head falls to her chest as I thrust up faster, violently chasing my orgasm. Seconds later, it comes in a rush. Stealing my breath. Stopping my heart. Crashing into me stronger than I have ever felt before. My screams match her own as we find our release. The only release we'll both ever need. Each other.

CHAPTER 21

LEONARDO

TWO WEEKS LATER

"No means no, you got that? It's probably the most important rule tonight."

"I'm not worried about myself Dec," I hiss out, as I throw back the last sip of bourbon and button my suit jacket. "I'm more worried about some cock-sucker putting his fucking hands on my wife."

I look up at him and he just gives me a smug smile. Shoving his hands in his pockets, he shrugs as if sharing his wife is an option when we both know we'd kill any bastard who tried. The adrenaline rush of claiming our women is what we fucking live for. In public, and definitely in private. Unfortunately for me, tonight's events have us in a much more public setting.

"The rule works both ways, Chief. Every patron of a sex club knows that. You don't abide by the rules, you get your ass thrown out. Fast."

"What rules might that be?" Magnolia sasses, knowing well what rules he's talking about as she enters the room. She's followed by Maria, and I curse under my breath as my eyes lock on hers, still not believing I let Magnolia talk me into her going with us.

If I had it my way, she'd be locked in her room with our children until this was all over. Posted guards would be at the master bedroom door and every damn window.

"I'm curious too," my wife says, giving me a come fuck me stare that instantly has my dick rock hard and ready for her.

The thought of where we're going, what we'll be seeing, *experiencing,* all night, proves an aphrodisiac I know I won't be able to watch other people fucking around and not want to be inside her. Not want to claim her. Make her scream louder than any bastard in the place ever thought a woman could. Even though the thought of her in a fucking sex club infuriates me and has my blood quickly coming to a raging boil.

Magnolia thought it would look suspicious if she didn't come. A meeting of families, where I've also planned Nicoletti's impending demise, would look questionable if the new wife of the Don was not in attendance. And fuck, I hate to say I agree with her.

Since Dec's promotion is riding on bringing down the man I am about to meet, and since he's been acting as my right-hand man undercover, it's only natural he comes along. Magnolia, of course, wouldn't let him walk into a sex club without being by his side. And I have to admit, I'm glad she'll be there. For Maria's sake if shit gets too crazy.

Still, I don't fucking like it, not one fucking bit.

"Our man inside wanted all patrons briefed before entering the club," Declan continues. The man in question is Collin. Although the ladies aren't aware of that yet. "There are rules, and if you know them, obey them, you'll be fine."

"I still don't like..."

Declan holds up his hand stopping me and I have to swallow down the rage that threatens to break free, threatens to unleash on his face. Magnolia and Maria study me for a moment with disapproving stares. I sternly look into my wife's eyes and deliver a silent warning. Don't push me. If she does, I'll be taking her over my knee before we ever even reach the club.

"No means no," Declan repeats. "With that in mind, never underestimate the power of touch. If you don't want to get touched back, keep your hands to yourself. Or better yet, your spouse."

He eyes Magnolia who gives him a wicked smile and then looks at Maria.

"I'm not planning on touching anyone," she exclaims in slight horror. "Not even myself if I can help it. Who knows what kind of fluids have been passed around in a place like that. I'm scared to touch anything."

My laugh cuts her off and she turns towards me quickly, a fire burning in her eyes.

"Trust me, mi Amore, you'll want to be touched," I take a step into her and whisper in her ear. "You'll want to be fucked. Your hands, your fingers, will betray you. They'll be eager to be inside you, just like I will. I'll remember you said that when you're begging for me to fuck you hard in a dark corner."

"I'll never..."

"No cameras, no recordings," Declan cuts her off as I lean back from her and smile. "Everything will be locked up in lockers."

"Lockers?" Maria questions. "What will be locked up in lockers."

I groan as I crack my neck from side to side and look up at Declan. He just smiles at me, knowing the hell I'm walking into, and the little bit of information that's been withheld from her very well might push me over the edge.

"Well, Mrs. Moretti, evening gowns are alright for entrance. Tuxedos are a must for men," he gestures between us two and she nods her head in understanding. "I trust Magnolia fitted you with appropriate undergarments?"

My eyes lock with Magnolia and she gives me a sinister smile.

"Um, yes," my wife stutters. "But..."

"Once granted entrance to the club, clothing is considered optional for men. Not permissible for women. You'll be granted entrance only with the undergarments you have on."

"Fuck this, I'm not letting anyone..."

This time it's Maria who holds up her hand stopping me. Her eyes are still trained on Declan, but she holds me submissive in an awkward change of events while she gathers her thoughts.

"What else?" she finally asks, and I let out an angry sigh as I start to walk towards the door.

"No one is required to play the first night..."

"No one will be playing," I insist, as I take my jacket from Giovanni and shove black leather gloves on my hands.

"Hygiene is a must, for all club members," Magnolia finally chimes in.

Declan and Magnolia frequent sex clubs often. They don't share each other. But they like to watch and be watched. I've dabbled in the past, but this is the first time since I found the love of my life, that I will be walking back through the door of one, and my mind is fucked trying to think of how I'm going to pull off this job and keep an eye on Maria at the same time.

"No exceptions," she continues as I take Maria's coat and gesture for her to turn around.

She does slowly, and as I wrap her shoulders in mink, I pull her close to me and breathe her in, sending up a silent prayer that tonight goes according to plan.

"Of course, we don't have to worry about that, we live by high standards. But club-goers must have fresh breath, a clean body, clean hair, and come prepared with condoms and lube. Oh they have some there for you to buy if you'd prefer," she shrugs as Declan helps her into her coat, "but it's way more expensive and not always our preferred stuff."

Magnolia eyes Declan over her shoulder and I swear the man fucks her with his stare right in front of us. No doubt these two will be staying to partake in the action after we've accomplished what we came there to do. As for Maria and myself? I can't wait to get the job over with so I can fuck her in my bed, secure in the fact that all threats have been taken care of, put out, and finally fucking stopped. At least for now.

I'm no idiot. In our way of life, there will always be some sort of threat.

"There is a two-drink max," Magnolia continues as we start to make our way towards the door. Our driver is outside, the limo idling as it waits, and with every step further into the evening, my heart rate ticks up and makes my chest ache in a way I have never felt before. "Safe sex is mandatory. Everything can happen, but nothing has to. Understand?"

Maria nods, and my chest aches a little more. Magnolia gives me a knowing smile and then climbs in the back of the limo as Declan turns to look at us.

"Only watching is frowned upon. Like Magnolia said, you don't have to 'play' your first night. With others that is. But you'll be looked at awkwardly if you don't partake in each other."

"Not fucking happening," I grunt out as Declan climbs into the limo with a laugh.

"And what if I want to," my wife turns to me and says. I cock my head to the side and study her. She can't be serious. "What if I want to 'play?' You said you'd always give me whatever I want." Her hand raises as she adjusts my tie and averts her eyes. "What if that's what I want," she whispers.

"I told you," I grit out. "I don't fucking share."

"I'm not talking about sharing, Leo," she breathes heavily, her dangerous thoughts and desires taking over. "I'm talking about you," she takes a step forward, "and me," she purrs, leaning into my ear and cupping my hardened dick in her palm. I hiss out slightly and close my eyes as she starts to stroke me through my slacks. "Touching each other, watching, being watched. Letting the world see how powerful the new Don is. How good he fucks."

"Maria," I breathe as she continues stroking me and I have to tell myself not to fuck her up against the car. "That is sharing, mi Amore. Letting someone watch, see what's mine. I'm not going to cross that line."

"We'll see," she teases, pulling away and stepping around me to climb into the car. "Claiming is the most carnal thing we all do, Leonardo. A real King always stakes his claim."

Fuck me.

If I survive tonight, claiming my place in life will be the least of my fucking worries. I've already staked a claim. To her, and my position. What she's asking, what she's insinuating, makes it hard to say no when everything inside me screams yes.

MARIA

"Ground rules have been set before your arrival?" the gentleman in front of us asks.

I swear he looks familiar, but with the mask covering his face, it's hard to tell. He's not American. His voice is strained like he's hiding something. But I can't tell what.

Magnolia hands me my mask and I look down to notice my hands are shaking. Leonardo takes it from me, stepping behind me gracefully and tying it around my eyes. When he's done, I take a deep breath as his hands lower, wrap around my waist, and ground me. Lacing my fingers through his, I force myself to breathe once again as everything the man in front of us is saying starts to blur.

"Mi Amore," my husband breathes into my ear. "I'm not leaving your side all night. Don't wander off. Don't leave mine. Understand?" I give him a nod as he places a kiss on the side of my neck. "Promise? Because I know good girls do very naughty things to get spanked."

I smile to myself, my nerves suddenly lifting. "I promise," I whisper.

"Then I promise to give you what you want." My heart stops, waiting for him to continue. "Be rough with you, just like you like, just like you asked, in so many sweet ways."

His hands slip from my waist and I suddenly feel one in my palm. He wraps his strong grip around my frail fingers and I know I'm safe, I know everything will be alright. No one commands power like Leonardo. The fact that someone is threatening him, threatening us and trying, makes me suddenly feel like laughing as I turn and meet his eyes.

"Everything beyond those doors is about communication & trust," the man at the front of the room says, addressing the four of us. But I keep my eyes on my husband. "You'll find three different types of areas to partake in. Semi-Private rooms where you can discreetly watch or sign up to be watched. All themed for our patron's enjoyment. Private areas to fulfill some of your wildest fantasies, that you might not find at home. Either with a new partner, or two, or the person you brought with you tonight. And then there is the Voyeur room, where everything is on display in a group setting. There is a buffet to make sure you are energized for your activities, and to fuel you if you are famished."

As he continues to talk, I realize there is so much more to this kind of life than I ever thought imaginable.

"We make no guarantees of playing with others. We ask that if you're interested, please have the woman approach another couple. It's less intimidating. Don't have high expectations. Don't be shy. You don't have to try a new fetish, take a time out when needed and rethink if necessary. And if you do play with others, don't hang around too long afterward, it makes for uncomfortable situations and makes my job harder."

He levels us with a stern look and I swallow hard.

"Welcome to Fottere, Ladies, and Gentlemen," he smiles. "Ladies, the locker rooms are right through that door," he gestures to the right and my hand starts to shake. Leo feels it and grips my hand a little tighter. "Gentlemen, I invite you to have a drink at the bar while you wait for your women. I understand you have business here at Fottere tonight. Once all the people in your party have arrived, we'll be ushering you into a private room. Until then, we invite you to partake in the activities."

I let go of Leonardo's hand and give him a small smile as I follow Magnolia to the room off to the right. As I watch him walk through the entrance of the club, I can't help but think, mixing business with pleasure just reached a whole new level.

CHAPTER 22

"After the papers are signed, we'll wire the money. If it all goes through smoothly, we'll consider this new arrangement final and I'll have your cut wired to your account by tomorrow morning."

"I told you, Nicoletti, I don't want a cut, all I wanted was my son."

He hears me but he's not entirely listening. His eyes are on the show center stage. One woman and three men. All holes filled and sounds of pleasure screaming through the open room. I turn my back on the scene, knowing Declan has me covered, his eyes still glued to the show on stage.

Arranging a meeting in a place like this was a smart move on Nicoletti's part. Hard to think straight with all the tits and ass on display and being enjoyed for everyone to see. I adjust the bulge in my slacks, the one that's been rock hard since Maria's touch back at the mansion, and then throw back the bourbon in my glass.

Motioning for the bartender to pour me another, he

gives me two fingers, warning me it'll be my last if I take it. I give him a look that could kill, and very well may murder him if he doesn't do as I ask. He quickly walks my way and pours me more than a fair share, of which I am very grateful.

"Giving up your son was easy on my part, Moretti," he says, my attention snaps back to him, amazed he's even answering with the way I hear the orgasm taking place behind me. "I insist on giving you something for your trouble. Sweetening the deal, and making sure we understand each other."

"We've never understood each other, Nicoletti. Why should we start now?"

"Because this arrangement is only the beginning." I turn his way, and an icy glare meets my eye. My jaw clenches, waiting for him to continue. "Your cooperation is appreciated. But don't tell me you thought your connections are all I wanted from you."

"No one tells me what to do," I warn. "Cooperation be damned. I got what I want out of it. My son. Nothing else you have to offer could persuade me to give you anything else in return."

"Are you sure about that?"

I level him with a stare. The sound of sex penetrates the space around us. Drugs the rest of the room. Pulls them under with its voodoo that's inescapable. But I'm no prisoner. I'm not phased. My attention is perfectly focused on the bastard in front of me.

"What if I told you Vincent and Sofia's lives were spared. That Alfonso kept them alive as collateral."

I take a deep breath and shove my right hand in my pocket, easy not to give myself away.

"Vincent & Sofia are dead to me," I manage with a stern voice.

"Hm," he prods, eyeing me with a sick fucking grin that tells me he might know more than I want him to just as Declan pulls his attention back to our conversation. "What would your wife have to say about that?"

His eyes lift, catching a sight he's enjoying by the way his fucking face grins. I turn, noticing what his eyes are admiring, and snap. Declan is quick to respond as he pulls me back by my shoulders and keeps me from murdering Nicoletti right where he stands.

When I look up, Nicoletti's hand is rubbing his chin, his eyes appreciating my wife's mostly naked body. I push off Declan as hard as I can but he keeps me still, keeps me grounded from blowing the job before it's time.

"Not yet, Chief," he rasps in my ear, but only lets me go when he knows I won't cause any trouble.

"Keep your fucking hands and your eyes to yourself, Nicoletti," I warn, sticking a finger in his face before turning to get to Maria's side. His laugh registers at my back as I make my way towards her, and it takes all my restraint to not turn around and blow his head off. If I fuck up the job at hand, so be it.

"Fuck," I groan as I come to her side and take in her nude teddy fixed with black lace barely covering her nipples and pussy. "Turn around," I growl.

When she does, her plump ass greets me. Bare and completely uncovered. I snap the string of her thong, barely able to keep from taking her right where she stands, and then smack her fine ass quickly before she turns around to face me.

When she does, a blush stains her cheeks and I pull her into me quickly, kissing her madly and staking my claim, showing the room that she's with me and no one else.

She kisses me back in a way I've never tasted before. Heightened. Erotic. Stimulated more than I've ever felt her. Her hands roam down my frame, cupping me and I pull away quickly, stopping her before she can go any further.

"This turns you on, mi Amore?"

"You turn me on, Leo. This," she gestures around us, her eyes wide and taking everything in, "Is the most arousing foreplay I've ever experienced."

I take her hand and pull her to the far side of the room. "You haven't seen everything," I whisper.

Looking over my shoulder, I notice her eyes are on Nicoletti who is still eye fucking the shit out of her and guaranteeing the fact that I will take my time killing him later.

"I thought we were here to talk business?"

"We are. But we're still waiting on one more guest."

"Does Nicoletti know that? It looks like he's trying to get the man who greeted us at the door to take him to the back room."

"Declan will take care of it," I pull her around a dark corner and push her up against a wall. "Does my wife want to see more, or first, can I do with her as I please?"

Her eyebrow raises as she gives me the sexiest smile I have ever seen. "What did you have in mind?"

"I want to taste you," I breathe, my fingers finding the lace surrounding her pussy and pushing it to the side. She gasps as my fingers enter her slick cunt and I stare deep into her eyes. "I want to savor you until your body shakes."

Dropping to my knees, I pull my fingers from her pussy and stick them in my mouth. Her hands find my hair just as I push her hips up against the wall and hold her firmly in place.

"What if someone sees?" she breathes.

I glance up and grin. "Isn't that what you want, Maria?" Her eyes widen but she doesn't say no. "This pussy deserves flat tongue, slow licks, and to be properly sucked."

She groans as I do just that, licking up her center slowly before sucking her clit into my mouth.

"Any objection?"

I'm giving her an out, which I know she won't take. And fuck the meeting because I'm fucking my wife's pussy with my tongue first. She looks too good, smells too fucking amazing, and tastes out of this fucking world.

Sticking my finger back in her tight cunt, she whispers, "No."

"Good girl."

I look over my shoulder and catch the eye of a few patrons. From the shadows, they can't see more than my body, her face, and the motion of us both enjoying her release. I wouldn't want it any other way. I'm not ready to share her. I won't ever be.

Their eyes are glued on us and I look up and notice the second she realizes too. She licks her lips. Her hands shake in my hair and she sucks in a big breath.

"Lose yourself in me a little bit more tonight, Maria," I groan as I start to finger fuck her tight hole before my mouth

246 / EVELYN MONTGOMERY

closes over her clit. She's so fucking wet. Wetter than I've ever felt before. Her climax is building fast. Her shy purrs quickly turn to loud moans.

"They're watching," she breathlessly says above me.

"Good," I growl, sticking my tongue deep inside her and flicking her clit with my fingers. When she's almost there I pull back and she pouts, earning her a smack to the pussy.

"Oh God," she screams.

"That's right, I'll make you mine, Maria, with every fucking scream."

My mouth descends on her swollen flesh again. This time I let her have her release, and when she cums, a part of her she never knew existed is born and given to me. She rides my fucking face best she can. Her pussy is greedy as it grinds against my jaw. I hold her hips in my hands and suck down so hard another orgasm explodes on the heels of the first. I hear the sounds of others getting off to us behind me and feel myself harden to a painful height. She screams my name and all I want is to fuck her. To rise up and lose myself inside her.

"Fuck, Leo, I ..." her breaths come out in pants as she comes down from her high. Licking up her seam one more time, I back away from her and run my finger across her swollen core. She bucks her hips, tender from her orgasm.

"Do you want more?" I look up and say.

"Yes please."

With a grin, I rise to my feet, grab her chin and pull her into me. "Business first, mi Amore. Then more pleasure."

Collin, who greeted us earlier this evening, shows us through the sex club as we make our way to the back room where the documents will be signed and the money wired. His accent is disguised. His face is covered with a mask. But to anyone who knows him well, it's not hard to figure out he's not who he says he is. At least not for me.

Maria's given him a curious look once or twice and I know it won't be much longer before others are on to our trick. More reasons for us to make this meeting quick. Finish business between Nicoletti and me once and for all and move the fuck on with our lives.

"We have two sets of rooms on each side of the hallway, five on each side, ten in total," Collin explains, trying to sound as American as he can, but I catch the slight give of his accent now and again. "On the left, you can enter into a viewing room after selecting from a list on our master keypad for what type of entertainment you'd like to see. These rooms are closed off to others, except the viewer who pays a higher price for the show. Those who are selected to play, enter through a door in the back."

"What kind of show," my curious wife asks bashfully and I can't help but grin as we stroll behind Collin hand in hand. My cock is still painfully hard from the pleasure I was giving her a few minutes ago. I've awakened a beast in her, and I can't say I mind where this is taking us.

"Vaginal, oral, anal," Collin suggests. "Masturbation. We close the body count off at three per room. Any more than that and we notice things have a tendency to get out of hand."

"Three viewers?" she asks.

He turns to her and smiles. "Three partners."

I watch as her cheeks flush. "Oh." She eyes him again curiously, and this time he sees the prying in her stare and quickly moves on.

"On our right, these rooms are open for everyone's viewing pleasure and any club-goer can sign up to partici-pate." I look over to the right and notice as everyone else does the same the further we follow Collin down the hallway.

"As you can see, we have rooms set up as stages. The first is an office."

I take in the woman on her knees sucking a man off behind a desk. He looks up just as he fists her hair in his hand and pushes her head down further, no doubt blowing his load down the back of her throat.

"We have a library," Collin continues.

As we pass I look at Maria, whose eyes widen and she turns away quickly, flushing an adorable shade of red. When I glance back to see what she's just seen, a woman dressed as a librarian is bent over a desk. One man is under her, licking and finger fucking her pussy while another one thrusts hard into her ass.

"Did you like that one, Maria," I whisper in her ear. "It's been a while," I say, tracing her ass with my finger, dipping lower until I can feel her juices pooling against my fingertips. "But I still remember how well you took my cock in your ass."

She lets out a tiny moan which earns a stern look from Collin.

"Next," he says clearing his throat. "A bathroom, complete with a glass-enclosed shower, two shower heads, and a large glass tub. All see-through for our viewers and quite popular for couples."

He continues. "Next, an orgasm denial room, self-explanatory there. Finally, our BDSM setup, because it's rare to find a club without one."

As we pass the third room, a couple is just starting their show. They're slowly stripping and I hear Maria gasp as the man lowers his pants and she sees the head of his cock is pierced.

"Don't get any fucking ideas," I rasp in her ear. "Not fucking happening."

"I wonder," she breathes, completely dazed as she watches him start to stroke his cock. "What would that feel like?"

"A good Dom can take you without anything extra and you'll never miss it," Magnolia says in front of us.

I pass by her as she slows to catch up with Maria and I start to walk with Declan, but train my ear to keep listening to their conversation. We pass the next two sets of rooms, but they're empty for now. With nothing to see, we keep walking to the room in the back. Nicoletti is in front of us with Collin, and if my assumption is right, my unexpected guest will soon arrive.

"But..." Maria whispers, making me start to take a tally on how many ways I will make her pay later for even thinking I couldn't please her in every fucking way imaginable. And definitely without a fucking piece of metal stuck through my cock.

"No buts," Magnolia insists. "You're a submissive. You know the voice. That's all you need."

Declan looks at me the same moment I look at him and we both grin.

"Every good dominant has it," she continues. "It makes your heart race. Your face flush. It's what we crave. What we get nowhere else. It quiets our minds. Prompts us to pay attention to what matters most. His control is our release. It keeps us in a suspended state where we can forget everything except the pleasure we're feeling. The release we're getting. With a voice like that, you know you'd do anything to hear him say 'good girl.' That's worth more than a cock piercing," she laughs, making me smile as I stop and she passes, following Declan into the room.

"Real satisfaction comes from being fucked so hard, you forget you have a safe word," she tosses over her shoulder.

"Safeword?"

I laugh. "We've never set boundaries like most Doms and Subs," I explain to Maria. "We've never established safe words. I guess I never felt the need," I shrug.

"There are no boundaries with us, Leo," my wife smiles. "There's only ever been trust."

And what a road we spiraled down getting to that, I think.

"No need for safe words when you have that," I whisper, pulling her closer and stealing a brief kiss. "If my life ended tonight. That would be enough."

"When my life ends," she smiles, melting into my arms and making it hard to let go. "It'll be enough just knowing I'm the last one you loved."

"You're the only one I've ever loved, Maria. The only one I've ever worshiped. A queen I'll never be worthy of. In this life, and our next."

"How does it feel, Moretti," I hear the man across from me sneer as I stand next to my husband. "Signing your life away. Giving up control. Reign. When you've fought for so many years to keep dominance over something you had no power to control to begin with."

Anger rises inside me as I watch Leonardo sign his name on the contracts. The papers I also signed right before him. I look up and bite my tongue, wanting to give Nicoletti an ear full but knowing better than to speak for my husband. Leo's a man that handles himself perfectly in every single situation, and one I am still learning from as we continue on our way through this kind of life.

"Signing my name gives me control, Nicoletti," Leonardo sighs as he flips a page and scribbles his name on the last dotted line.

The lawyer present, gestures towards another line, and I watch as my husband regards it questionably for a moment, and then signs again. He tosses the pen on the table in front of him and stands up straight. A strong tower, a force to never be reckoned with, as he squares off across the table with Nicoletti.

"The Rossi's have signed over control of their club in trust to me for this business arrangement," Leonardo gestures towards Mr. Rossi who signed first and is now standing by nervously awaiting his cue to exit. "If at any time the terms of this contract are not honored, I have the right to stop your little business arrangement in its tracks. All I need is the smallest reason, one I'll be looking for regularly. It seems to me that you just signed your life's work over to me. Let's not forget who's really in charge here."

Nicoletti takes the pen and starts the process of signing the same papers. His smile and his cocky demeanor worry me as he flips each page, diligent to initial and sign where he's supposed to. The tension in the room builds, the silence making every second worse as we all wait for the deal to be done and wait for the money to be transferred so we can get on with our night. On with life.

"Funny," Nicoletti finally says after a few minutes. "The need for control. The need to be in charge. We're all guilty of it. Like gluttons, we devour every chance we get to feel the rush that dominion over another can give us."

He flips the last page, signs, initials, and then without a thought moves to the last space, the one that I saw my husband questioning earlier, and signs again. Happy with himself, happier than I think he should be, he places the pen on the table, braces his hands on each side of the contract, and looks up at us with an evil smirk.

"There's nothing like it. Ruling over the weak. Knowing

you have made yourself more powerful. Unstoppable. The final course of judgment between life and death."

"The weak choose death by their own self-demise, Nicoletti," my husband attempts to explain with slight irritation. "Power comes from proper justice. Rules come by common fucking sense. Followed by the intuition that if you fuck with them, you'll be dealt with. It's the same in everyone's life. Not just ours."

My husband leans in across the table and levels Nicoletti with a glare. The room buzzes with unease, with hostility as the two men stare at each other.

"But you've never had either, have you? Common sense. Intuition. It's what's made you weak your entire life. Only the weak seek ways to climb to the top by stepping on the less fortunate. A man who knows his real power, his strength to truly reign, does so by building a trustworthy army underneath him. You've stepped on everyone to get where you are in life. But I'm not fucking weak, Nicoletti. I'm not stepping down from my rule. You try to fuck with me, fuck with my family, you will be stopped. You will be brought to justice. Death. By your own, foolish, self-demise if that's the way you choose."

Nicoletti's jaw ticks. He studies Leonardo for a moment. His eyes raising slowly a second later to catch Declan's. I glance behind me and notice he's poised and ready. His hand on his waist, prepared, ready to take aim and pull the trigger if necessary.

I quickly glance at Magnolia. She raises her eyebrow with a mischievous smirk. One that hints at the fact that I don't know half of what the three of them know. A few months ago it would have bothered me. A year ago I would have wanted to storm out of the room and cause a scene that could do far more damage than good.

But I've learned to trust the madness that surrounds my husband. I've learned to have confidence in him because what he's done, what he'll continue to have to do, has always been done with one thing in mind.

Family first.

La famiglia e tutto.

The family is everything.

Nicoletti finally stands up straight, buttoning his suit jacket and regarding what my husband has just said.

"Fool," he spits out, angry and on guard. "A true fool doesn't realize when he's finally been taken down." I glance at Leonardo, his hands still braced on the table, and see his jaw tick with rage, but he never takes his eyes off Nicoletti. "He preaches about power when he's just been stripped of every capable way he has left to enforce it."

"Stop proving my point by mumbling like a cock sucking fool," Leo snaps. "What the fuck are you talking about?"

Declan nods toward Mr. Rossi, giving him the signal to leave. He quickly makes his way to the door and is ushered out of the room by Collin who follows close behind.

I realized it was him by the unfortunate slip of his tongue. When I entered the room earlier, he quietly called me "Stunner" as I passed by. Either that or this was the plan all along. I'm just now being fed bread crumbs as it starts to unravel.

The lawyer gathers his papers and quickly exits as well. Jack Rinaldi, who has been quiet this entire time, is on his heels, most likely going to see to it that the wire goes through successfully. The only people left in the room are me, Leo, Declan, Magnolia, Nicoletti, and his two bodyguards.

"You've accepted my percentage," the man across from us finally says.

"As insisted."

"Hm," Nicoletti regards my husband before he slowly places his hands in his pockets. He studies Leo as if waiting for him to understand what is being said without him having to say it.

Nicoletti underestimates Leo. He's the truer fool at the table tonight. I've known my husband almost my entire life, and in that time, the most important thing I have learned is that he's always one step ahead. Always prepared. Always thinking about every possible outcome.

It's why he's so feared. So esteemed. So trusted by those around him, even when he seems like he's playing along. Taking their bait. Much like he's doing now.

Instead, he's studying. Calculating. Becoming more powerful right before their eyes. Only they are too foolish to notice.

"Then you'll be enlightened to know that by signing your consent for me to wire your cut," Nicoletti finally says, "you've signed control of your bank accounts over to me."

My heart plummets as I look quickly to my side and stare at my husband. But his face never changes. His focus never wavers as he continues to stare down the man across the room. A man that could ruin everything we've built with that kind of control.

There's a knock at the door and one of Nicoletti's body-guards opens the door. A tall figure fills the door frame. My whole body begins to shake as I take a step back on instinct, but Leonardo's hand jolts out and steadies me at his side with a firm grasp.

He never looks my way. He never takes his eyes off the change of events happening in front of us. Just holds me still at his side. A warning to stand my ground next to him. With shaky knees, I do as he silently says as I look up and into the eyes of a man that tried like hell once to end my life. End Leo's. And steal the reign that is rightly my husband's.

Alfonso Capone.

"True power doesn't lie in wealth and riches, Nicoletti," Leonardo hisses. "It's in the people you trust most in life. The people you surround yourself with, and the ones that will always prove loyal. Always take your side."

"THE WOMEN CAN LEAVE," Nicoletti snaps. "Our business is not their business."

"My wife's my top priority," I hiss. "Always has been. Everything else is beneath mi famiglia, Nicoletti. She goes where I go. She hears what I hear. Either now, or later when I'm claiming her as my own in my bed. So tell your henchman when he comes back in the room, fucking Rinaldi, to stop looking at her like he's about to rape her the second I turn my back. Then maybe, just maybe, I'll kill him quickly later tonight, instead of drawing out his suffering for the thoughts he's thinking in his mind."

"Women are weak," Nicoletti snaps back. "They shouldn't be granted the privilege to discuss the business of men."

"My business," I grit out, taking a step back from the table and starting to make my way towards him, "will always be her business."

I eye Alfonso, who gives me a deep glare as I make my

way toward him. Fucking bastard deserves the worst for what he's done, and he smiles at me knowingly as I approach.

"Then, again, like an idiot, you prove my point," Nicoletti laughs. "A fool. You'll forever be crippled by your weakness."

I look up just as Collin quietly opens the door to the room and slips inside. He gives me a nod. An exchange. The trap is set. But one of Nicoletti's bodyguards sees, becomes frantic as he turns back around to warn Nicoletti and quickly pulls his gun from his side.

His death happens so fast I almost miss it, as Collin reaches out quickly and expertly slices his throat in stealth silence. He's quick to silence the other bastard as well the same way. It all happens so quickly, the knife quietly placed at the soft spot on the side of his throat, just below his jaw. Collin pulls it across to the right, slicing and silencing him once and for all. Except he doesn't die as quickly, and doesn't make as little sound like the first. Blood gushes from his throat as Collin pulls him back into the shadows and covers his mouth with his gloved hand.

The noise of the club outside helps to muffle any shuffling coming from them as Collin pulls the dead weight into the dark shadows. Maria reaches out and clutches my hand. The scene she's just witnessed is too much for her to take. I give her hand a squeeze of reassurance as Nicoletti just stares straight ahead, oblivious to what's gone on behind him with Alfonso standing by his side.

He's so confident it's sickening. A confidence that will inevitably get him killed tonight.

I glance at Maria, worried she'll react without thinking, possibly give what's happening away. When she doesn't, just grips my hand tighter, I play into her strength. Play into Nicoletti's words as I drop her hand, confident she'll be alright, and then take another step in my opponent's direction.

"A real man understands that a woman, the right woman, is only a strength, never a weakness. It's taken me years to realize that. But once I did, it's a hard truth to ever let go."

I look back at Maria and notice my wife's eyes leave the scene happening in the shadows and meet mine. A smile spreads across her face. A light that I haven't seen in such a long time shines in her eyes as she takes in all that is happening, all that I'm saying, and continues to stand tall as my queen.

"Your wife makes you soft, Moretti," Tony hisses as I turn back his way. "She's always brought you to the point of death. First when you were kids. Later as you faced off against your own father. Lastly, when Alfonso captured you the first time. The odds have never been in your favor. Tonight, once again, you've proven how weak you are. How easy it is to overtake you. All because of your one idiotic flaw. Your love for a woman."

I turn my attention on Alfonso, capturing his stare with intent as he nods his head in an apparent agreement with the man at his side. He hasn't spoken yet, and it irritates the fuck out of me watching him stand mute next to Nicoletti.

"You take his side," I gesture towards the man in question as I address Alfonso. "You stand against the family." It's not a question, more of a statement on his previous actions and the way he's acting now. "Stand against the rightful heirs, the bloodline that is the only deserving ones to the name, the title, the rule."

"I take the side for every man that's entered this life in hopes to one day make something of himself," he sneers. "Fuck the names. The titles. The blood. Every day, more blood is shed that's not Moretti blood. That's not Nitti, Lombardi, De Luca blood. I stand with the rest of *mi famiglia*. The ones that don't have a voice of their own. The ones struggling to be heard while the rest go on ruling as if they don't exist."

The silence stretches out around us. The strain between families grows as we wait each other out. All of us are intent on making the weaker man stands down first. Finally, I nod my head a few times and take a deep breath.

"*Capisco*," I sigh. "*Meglio solo che male accompagnato.*" (Better alone than in bad company).

Alfonso smiles knowingly and gives me a look that makes me believe he's a little too sure of himself. He's counting a victory when the issue at hand hasn't been laid to rest.

Yet.

"Power lies in the people you surround yourself with, right Moretti?" Nicoletti taunts. "I made sure before I ever came to see you about this arrangement to first surround myself with the most powerful as well. The sides of our Italian families that could prove even more powerful than your own. A man who is guaranteed to take you down once and for all. Alfonso Capone."

I glance at Capone and he just smiles back at me. Victory shinning in his eyes.

"It was an arrangement that's proved more powerful than

I originally thought," Nicoletti continues as my blood runs cold. "As we've worked together over the past couple of years to bring you to your own self-demise, once and for all. You see, if you haven't realized, he didn't take too well to you accepting your position without considering him. And I personally found it fucking thrilling working with him to plan that raid on your wedding day over a year ago now. Unfortunately, you and Maria escaped. A mishap I'd like to rectify now."

The door behind the two men open yet again, Collin steps aside, and in walks Rinaldi, Sabrina, and - Daniella? Collin's rage is evident as she passes by without even so much as a second glance. I watch as anger burns in his eyes and he stares at her as she makes her entrance. Sabrina's eyes match Daniella's. Way too overconfident for my liking. Rinaldi, though, is oblivious to the fact that the guards are lying dead in the shadows. He's too focused on the game at hand. The win he's so confident in, just like his idiotic partner, Nicoletti.

"What," Rinaldi taunts as he notices my questioning stare lingering on Daniella. "You don't think I know things. Have connections."

I glance behind me at Declan, the look on my face more serious than it's ever been before. I thought the matter of Daniella was taken care of. Handled. Detained for me to enjoy ruining later.

His eyes meet mine and the look he gives me makes me worry. Makes me feel like we're fucked. All this time we'd been playing a hand, sure no one knew the cards we had up our sleeve. Now, from the look on his face, I can tell we're both not too sure after all. Something went wrong because the rat that we both thought was contained is now walking through the back door with a fucking grin on her face that could prove lethal if something somehow slipped through the cracks.

"Everything cleared," Rinaldi says, taking his place once again by Nicoletti's side. "No hiccups. No issues. Slid right through like fucking butter. Easier than any transaction we've done so far."

"Perfect," Nicoletti grins. He turns and gestures for Daniella to step forward.

"I thought you said 'no women,'" I grit out under my breath. "What the fuck is she doing here?"

My eyes lift and catch Collins, but his face is unreadable. His expression is void of any life. His eyes are black as he stares at the back of the head of the woman he once loved.

Fuck that.

Still loves.

I can see it clouds his judgment as he stands behind her with his hand on his weapon.

"Business is done, Leonardo," Nicoletti laughs slightly. "I got what I wanted. You handed it over beautifully. With the help of my mistress here, the job would've gotten done, with or without your help, Amico," he gestures towards Daniella and I see Collin flinch, his hand a little too eager to pull the trigger.

I give him a look he thankfully notices as he briefly catches my eye and stands down.

"Mistress?" I pull a pack of cigarettes out of my pocket, taking the time to choose my words wisely.

I slowly pull one from the pack, roll it between my thumb and two index fingers and then put it between my lips. I look up at him, but he doesn't elaborate. Lighting the end, I take a long inhale, and then hold the smoke in.

I think about Collin. Nicoletti. The man this bitch was fucking back in Dublin. She's nothing more than a two-bit whore. I decide Nicoletti has a type as my eyes rise and set on Sabrina's.

Noticing where my stare has landed, Nicoletti looks behind himself at his wife. But she doesn't look phased by the comment at all, just stares back at her husband adoringly, raising one of her brows in a challenge. Slowly blowing out the smoke, I gesture toward my son's mother.

"One woman doesn't satisfy you?" Sabrina's eyes snap up to mine. The same look of rage I put in them years ago when I kicked her out of my bed is now back and on full display. Leaning in toward Nicoletti, I can't force myself to bite back the comment that eventually escapes. "She always was a lousy fuck. Can't say I blame you much."

"You fucking bastard..."

Sabrina takes a step forward in fury but her eyes flash behind me and she suddenly stops.

Glancing over my shoulder, I see Maria. Sight trained. Glock raised. Finger on the trigger and a dead shot aimed straight at Sabrina's head.

A glance at Declan tells me he didn't hesitate to hand her his gun when she asked. There's no way she had it hidden anywhere with what she's wearing. Hell, my hands, my mouth would've found it earlier if that were the case. Magnolia is just as bare, but if I know that woman well, and I do, she's hiding something somewhere. A trick I will have to ask that she share with Maria for the future.

"You take another step, I'll kill you, and I won't think twice," my wife breathes. "I warned you once. Twice is already two times too many for a bitch like you who deserves to burn in hell."

I turn back to face the group in front of me with more pride than I have ever felt before in my life. My heart swells in my chest thinking of the amazing woman that's standing behind me. A woman that has more than come into her own in this life. One I was proud of the first day I ever met her, and even more proud of now as we walk through this life together.

"All this time, I've been thinking you looked familiar." Maria cocks her weapon. My first-born mother's smile falters, and her confidence slowly fades. "Tonight, it's finally clear. *I know*." Sabrina takes a step back. "Do you want to tell him, or should I?"

"There's nothing she can say that I don't already know, Maria."

My fucking heart skips a beat. It's not that I wasn't going to tell my wife. It's that between Luca getting dumped on our doorstep, our new daughter, the fucking job, and keeping secrets I'm still trying to cover up, there just hasn't been damn time. This was not part of the original plan, and it threw me for a loop. Question is, will Maria believe that, or is this something that can haunt our marriage forever?

"I didn't know..." Sabrina starts with a shaky voice.

"Quiet!" My wife shouts. I glance back at her and expect her hand to be shaking. Her confidence slipping facing the revelation she's suddenly confronted with. But she's steady. In control. Dominating the situation, and it's sexy as hell.

"Lies," she whispers with a laugh as the gun in her hand lowers slightly. "All lies. My whole life was built on them. Not anymore," she takes aim and Sabrina flenches. "Regardless of the lies, sister. I believe you. You didn't know what me and Leonardo had when you were cast out of the family before me and him met. Because of your addiction. Your disgrace you brought to the family by sleeping around and spilling secrets."

Sabrina looks at me, worry filling her gaze as Maria pauses. I laugh under my breath, because why the hell is she looking at me to save her? She may be the mother of my child, but like I told her all those years ago when she was too quick, too eager to suck my dick. *No real man will ever need a woman when she spends her time trying to rise to the top by first starting out on her knees.*

I only learned she was Maria's half-sister when the paternity test came back. I had my assumptions all those years ago, knowing she was connected to a large mafia name. Can't say that wasn't part of the draw. Fucking a whore that was part of the bigger picture.

Although I never would've thought it was Nitti's blood that ran in her veins.

Luca is Maria's nephew by blood. Half-sister or not, Sabrina fucked with Maria's family when she used while she was pregnant with my son. Not only that, Sabrina used him as blackmail to get what she wanted, from a man that gave his heart away long before he ever took her into his bed. My heart will always belong to Maria. She black-mailed us both.

266 / EVELYN MONTGOMERY

Her secret proves to be her own demise now that's uncovered.

"You didn't know what Leonardo and I have," Maria continues. "Otherwise you never would've tried. My husband is faithful. And so am I."

"You see, the problem with a mistress is you can't trust her to be loyal," I say. Nicoletti regards me for a second, his smile slowly slipping. "Maybe some give the illusion they'll be faithful if only to continue to collect on the goods you're so graciously providing."

"I have no problem pleasing my mistress, and my wife," Nicoletti snaps back, and I look behind him to see Collin's anger growing with each mention of Daniella belonging to Nicoletti, and not him. "They both know what will happen to them if they step out of line. They want to be unfaithful, they do it while also signing their death certificate. Fear, Moretti. Fear is how you make your women listen. How you make people listen"

Maria and I grew up in fear. We were raised in a horrorish hell and forced to walk through a panic, terror-ridden life. That's not the way I'll ever choose to reign.

"You should know that all too well, Moretti," Rinaldi spits out. "Fear makes the best submissive."

My eyes flash to his and I see them running up and down Maria's body.

"You look at my wife like that again, and I won't hesitate to pull the trigger that ends your life. *Capire, Amico.*"

"We're not *friends*," he laughs. "And I wouldn't take orders from you now, anyways. Not that I ever did before. We own you, *Amico*," he taunts back. "You're ours now. And there is nothing your wife, or your two undercover friends, can do about it."

My heart speeds up but I resist the urge to turn and look Declan and Magnolia's way. I refuse to give any inclination that what he's saying may be right. If we're lucky, they've only received a tip that Dec and Mags are agents. Hopefully, they don't know the truth. Not yet. Although Rinaldi did somehow manage to get Daniella out of custody. My bet is leaning more towards the fact that we're totally fucked.

"What more do you want?" I ask, turning my attention back to Nicoletti.

"We want what everyone wants," Daniella suggests, and I regard her with anger as my jaw ticks with hatred. "Power. The seat at the top. You stand down, Leonardo. Now. Or else face the consequences."

I take a drag off my smoke, simultaneously taking a step back as if debating the idea. I let time slip by. Casually taking another deep inhale, I let them think I'm debating the ultimatum they just threw on the table.

"No, can't do that," I exhale. "Won't do that, as a matter of fact. But I got to admit, I admire the balls it took to ask. All things considered."

Daniella eyes me suspiciously. I glance at Nicoletti, but he's oblivious. When I look back Daniella's way, her gun is raised and aimed straight at the middle of my forehead. I don't even flinch. Taking another drag off my cigarette, I drop it to the ground and snuff it out before raising my hands, suggesting I'm accepting defeat.

"Your wife can't kill Sabrina and me at the same time,

Leonardo," the whore grits out. "In fact, you're outnumbered. There's four of you and five of us."

"Five," Collin exclaims, his Irish accent evident and causing the woman in front of me to jump. "Five, Lass. Don't tell me you'd be forgettin' myself now?"

She turns her head slightly to face him. His hand comes up as he removes his mask and steps forward. I can hear Maria's slight intake of breath behind me and pray she holds steady. I'm not sure if she figured him out yet, but if she has I'm hopeful she's not mad about the way she was played in order to orchestrate this setup. One that hasn't fully been revealed. Yet. With my hand poised, ready for anything, I watch the reunion unfold in front of me as Daniella keeps her aim on me and her sight on Collin.

"I'm not sorry for the things I've done," Daniella says on a shaky exhale. "Your family's done worse. They're an evil bunch. The lot of them." Turning back my way, she cocks her gun and I watch as her hand shakes a little more. "I'm not sorry for what I have to do now, either."

"No real man sends a woman in to do his dirty work, Nicoletti," I hiss, watching as the woman in front of me breaks down further. Her words are stronger than the way she's feeling inside as her grip slips on her gun. "The beef between us is personal. You've always wanted what I had," his eyes go to my wife and my blood boils. "Don't bring an innocent woman into this."

I glance at Alfonso out of the corner of my eye and see that he seems to be enjoying this all too much. A fact that makes me slightly more shaken up than I should be when I'm facing a loaded gun.

"What makes you ever think a woman is something you can control, Moretti," Nicoletti laughs. "That she can be trusted. Hell, I'd bet your own would sell you out if it meant keeping herself safe."

Daniella's hand tries to steady itself, her hand gripping the butt of the gun tighter as her finger rests, shaking slightly on the trigger.

"Aye, I second that," Collin whispers and I watch the pain, the regret flash across Daniella's eyes. "A woman can't be trusted. Especially when she goes and stabs you in your feckin' back."

Daniella's finger on the trigger shakes stronger than before. I watch as she pulls the metal back slightly, time stretching in the most agonizing way. I'm seconds away from finding out if all the secrets, all the lies, all the bullshit we deal with in the name of *mi famiglia* is worth risking it all for.

A shot rings out, and I make a fucking rookie mistake. I blink. When I refocus, Daniella grins, her eyes fucking delighted before they fall cloudy, dark, drained of life, and blood pools at the corner of her mouth.

"Daniella," Nicoletti demands as she starts to fall to the side. He catches her in order to break her fall. "Daniella!"

My eyes raise and catch Collin's. His hand shakes as he drops the gun that just took her life to the floor. He refuses to look at me, only watching the woman he loved in the arms of her lover while all the life she has left drains from her soul.

Nicoletti's eyes rise and catch mine. Sabrina stands by shaking, completely caught off guard like the rest of us at what just happened.

"You fucking bastard," Nicoletti seethes, rising to his feet and pulling his gun from his hip.

I pull mine just as Alfonso Capone pulls his and takes aim. Nicoletti's eyes widen when it finally registers which side Capone is on.

"Nothing personal, Nicoletti," Alfonso smiles. "Just fucking business."

Pulling the trigger, he shoots off a round straight through the center of Nicoletti's forehead. Movement catches my eye to the right, turning quickly I fire off a round wounding Rinaldi. Alfonso is quick to back me up, a deal that was made before we ever planned the raid on my wedding day, and shoots the Chief of Police in the chest. Right in his crooked heart. Sending him to hades where both he and Nicoletti belong.

A woman's yell assaults my ears. Screams blur with the sound of gunfire. When I look up, Sabrina has a knife raised and is charging fast in my direction. Arms raised, nails like daggers aimed at my face, I quickly take a step back before she can reach me when another shot rings out, followed by a second, and then a third.

Blood pools quickly on the bodice of her dress. She looks down stunned, meeting an unforeseen fate that I can't say I'm unhappy to see. I turn just as Maria drops the gun to the floor, Declan is quick to pick it up and reach out to steady her as her knees give out.

"Maria," I shout, rounding the table and clutching her in my arms. "Are you hurt?"

The past haunts me like a nightmare as I search her body, clutching her face in my trembling palms and pleading with unspoken words, needing her to answer me. Her head falls back, her eyes stunned before she shakes slightly in my arms and looks back into my gaze.

"Answer me," I demand.

Her light laugh is music to my ears a moment later. It's small at first, growing wilder as life comes back to her eyes and I clutch her tighter in my arms, bringing her into my chest and swearing I'll never let go. I kiss the top of her head and breathe out a shaky breath. My heart only now beginning to beat again knowing that she's okay.

"I just killed my sister," she exhales deep, her body trembling as her laugh morphs into a slight sob. "I just ended her life."

I smile tenderly at her, knowing all too well the shock she's experiencing, and knowing just as well that it will fade over time. She's pulled the trigger once before, with Luigi, but it takes a whole lot more getting used to than that, if you ever really get used to it at all. The fact that it's her half-sister's life she just took will sit heavier than Luigi's life. Even if she never knew her growing up, and only seemed to remember fragments of her sister from her life when she was young, before she was kidnapped and blocked most of it out.

"Leonardo," Alfonso rasps out a second later, pulling my attention from my wife. I glance up to see him gesturing towards Collin who is still standing in the same spot, still staring down at Daniella's lifeless form.

I pull Maria into me and kiss the top of her head, taking a moment just for us. When I'm sure she's okay, I rise, releasing her towards Declan and Magnolia. Magnolia's already sternly telling her she did what she needed to do and she should stand tall, be proud, as I turn my attention to a different matter at hand.

I step over Nicoletti and Rinaldi's bodies on the floor and make my way over to Collin. He doesn't move a muscle. He doesn't blink. I swear the bastard has stopped breathing as his stare never wavers off what he's just done.

"Don't feed me any Shite, Moretti," he finally grits out through clenched teeth. "We're fecking even now, you and I."

He bends over, picking up the pistol that he just used to end Daniella's life, and shoves it at me.

"She was a rat, Fitzgerald," I whisper, taking him by the shoulder and forcing him to turn away from the scene behind us. "You said so yourself. A love lost is a life regained."

"Aye, and if that love was your life, Moretti, then you're just damned to hell," his eyes are black as they regard me and what I've just said. "A walkin' dead man who's just biding his time until he can be with her once again."

He gives me a crazed look, a warning, before pushing me off his side he starts for the door. He kicks it open with his boot and stalks off into the darkness. Into his own personal hell. Dragging him quickly under and I hate that it's partly my fault.

Declan steps to my side a moment later and lets out a heavy sigh. "Let him go, Chief."

"I had no intention of following," I groan. "The job is done."

"Is it ever really done?"

I give him a deep glare, feeling like his words hold more weight than he's letting on. "Nicoletti and Rinaldi paid the heaviest price," I continue. "Fitzgerald is raised from the dead. He can go back to Dublin. Back to his life. Debt-free. For all I fucking care."

"Something tells me the debt he carries now is larger than any debt he owed you, Chief."

I watch the door close behind Collin and can't deny the burden I think I'll always feel for the outcome of events here tonight. I've walked a dark path. I've lost the love of my life and swore I would never again see her face, feel her love, and get a second chance to make her mine. What happened tonight took any chance Collin had away forever for him and Daniella. It changed him in a way I'm not sure will ever be rectified.

"Sorry you won't have a man to turn into the FBI," I say, changing the subject as I turn and meet Declan's eye, and we both glance to the floor at the bodies, the mess, that will need cleaning up.

He shrugs. "Hell, I'm a sure thing for that promotion anyways, Chief. Plus, I got to see my wife in action back in Dublin. It's a win-win. Now that all the bullshit is behind us."

"Staying to play, I take it?"

"Nothing like a good fuck after an adrenaline rush," he laughs as we start to make our way back to our wives. "But no, actually. I have a little side tip that I need to look into. One that you might be interested in as well, depending on the way it turns out."

"Do I even want to ask?"

"Never know what you need to know if you don't take the time to ask questions and listen, am I right, Chief?" Declan smiles. He glances at Magnolia and Maria as we reach their side. "But you two should stick around. Watch the show. Maybe have some fun of your own."

My wife's eyes find mine and I smile.

"No," I grin wider. "I have one last surprise for my lovely bride, and it doesn't involve fucking her for the world to see." Maria blushes and it makes my cock twitch. "Maybe next time."

"There's going to be a next time?" she asks, still slightly shaken up as I pull her into my arms.

"If you want," I promise. "But first, there's one more matter of business we need to address."

"Since when do you discuss business with me?"

"Since now," I firmly state, giving her a firm smack on her ass to warn her against her sass. "In this life, we rule together, Maria. From this moment forward. No more secrets."

Her eyes lift, her breathing quickens, wondering what I'm getting on to. "No more secrets," she breathes. "Only you and me, and our famiglia."

ENTERING THE HOUSE, Leo grasps my hand firmly in his. I've changed back into my evening dress, and he glances back at me as we enter the foyer and smiles.

"I must admit, Mrs. Moretti, I do like you naked, trimmed in black lace and tempting my cock to be buried deep inside you," turning around, he stops me in his tracks and holds me close. "But you're breathtaking just like this, in ways that don't compare."

His eyes travel down my frame as he backs away slightly and devours me with his gaze. My cheeks flush because even after all the time we've spent together, even in the future when years turn to decades and our children are all grown up, he will never stop being able to take my breath away.

"You're so beautiful it fucking hurts," he whispers, his right hand snaking up my torso, around my shoulder, up to my neck, and fisting gently in my hair. "I know what's under this dress. What's hidden behind the silk fabric between your legs."

His hand falls between us and rubs against my clit. I suck in my breath, feeling him harden against my thigh and realizing he never did get his release tonight. More than that, I'm craving the feeling of him buried deep inside me, which is something else I was denied, and something I suddenly so desperately need after the events of tonight.

Making love to Leo makes me feel more alive than anything else in life. I need that now more than ever, and I can tell he does too by the look in his eyes.

"As much as tonight was fun," my husband taunts, taking a step towards me as I take a step back in unison. He rubs my sex harder, making my head fall back and my swollen flesh throb against his fingers. "I have to admit I prefer keeping you all to myself."

"I can live with that," I purr, as his lips find my neck and he kisses my goose-pimpled flesh tenderly.

"You telling me you don't desire more?"

His hands raise, molding my breasts in his palms as he pulls down the bodice of my dress and sucks my nipple into his mouth. I think I hear myself say his name, but I'm too lost in a haze as his fingers find my center again and press against the fabric of my dress. His hot wet mouth continues to pleasure me as his tongue swirls around my nipple.

"Mr. Moretti?" A voice calls from across the room.

I still. I freeze. I feel Leo smile against my breast as he gently raises his hand from between my legs, careful to keep me close so I'm not to be exposed and then raises the top of my gown back into place.

"Yes Giovanni," he smiles as his eyes meet my stare.

"Your guests are in the den. They arrived a few hours ago, Sir. We anticipated you'd be back earlier."

"Couldn't be helped," my husband smiles at me, before stealing a kiss and pulling me to his side. Flustered, I try to keep my gaze adverted so as not to catch the eye of Giovanni. A blush creeping up from my neck and flaming my cheeks. It was one thing to have strangers watching. But I'm realizing it's another to be caught by someone we know.

"I'll inform them you'll be with them shortly."

Leo nods, "Make sure you stick around too, Consigliere. There's something I'd like to ask you before the night is done."

Giovanni nods back, slightly shaken up, before and I hear him walk away quickly. Looking at my husband, slightly embarrassed for what our consigliere just walked in on, I feel my face heat as he seems unfazed by the intrusion. Still, a low simmer brews in the lower stomach. My wetness pools between my thighs.

"I said I wouldn't share, mi Amore," he grins. "I want your body reserved for me, ready to take my sins. But I know the pleasure you feel, the thrill you want at the risk of being seen. Being caught."

My mouth falls open and he shakes his head with a smile. Placing a finger under my chin, he closes my mouth and steps closer, kissing my lips softly.

"Your panties are fucking soaking, aren't they?" he whispers, causing my thighs to clench and me to realize just how drenched I am.

"If it wasn't for the surprise I have for you," he growls, backing me up against a table in the entryway. "I'd force you to your knees right now, Maria, and fuck your shocked little mouth into submission until I came down the back of your pretty little throat." I moan, and he goes on. "I wouldn't care who walked in. Who saw, as I bent you over this damn table and thrust inside your tight wet cunt. Fingered your tight ass until you came so hard, screamed so loud, the staff would come running to make sure you weren't in pain."

"Oh my God, Leo," I breathe, placing my hands against his chest and taking a deep breath, desperately wishing he could make good on all he's saying.

"You know what they'd find, Maria?" I shake my head, my breathing increasing as he sternly looks me in the eyes. "Me on my knees, licking your cum off your pussy, before forcing you to ride my cock while they stood there and watched."

"You said you wouldn't share," my breathing is labored as he smiles wider.

"Who said I'd let them see your pretty pussy, Maria?" His sexy grin grows. "Just me. On my knees. Between your thighs. While you screamed my name over and over again out of your little, tight, beautiful, fucking intoxicating mouth."

My chest rises and falls as he stares me back in the eye. He doesn't back away, just presses his cock between us. I grind into him on instinct, needing him to give me what he just promised and I feel him throb with the same need as he forces himself up against my lower belly.

I start to raise my skirt, to hell with the surprise. I need him. Right here, right now. But his laugh stops me a moment later, right before his hand falls to mine and he grips it, forcing me to drop the fabric of my dress as he pulls me off the table. He takes off quickly towards the den and I struggle to keep up with his quick strides.

"Pull yourself together, Mrs. Moretti," he teases, with a mischievous grin over his shoulder. "Push all thoughts of pleasure aside. You'll want a straight head for your surprise."

"And if I'd rather be fucked on the entryway table by my husband?"

He laughs again but doesn't stop walking.

"That can be arranged, but first, no more secrets, remember? No more lies."

We reach the door of the den and he pauses. Raising my hands to his lips, he kisses them tenderly before giving me a smile that will always melt my heart.

The doors to the den open. By who? I'm not sure. When my head turns, my gaze locks on three people.

"Mom?" I gasp, looking into the eyes of my mother, Sofia Lombardi.

"Dad?" I scream.

My father, Vincent Nitti smiles at me, tears building in the backs of his eyes.

The third person steps forward and the world stops spinning. Looking into her eyes is like staring straight into my husband's. I grab onto his arm as my head feels heavy, and I swear I might faint.

"Maria," Leonardo says. "I'd like you to meet my mother. Gia Moretti."

LEONARDO

I watch diligently as my wife meets my mother for the first time. Her eyes widen in shock like mine had when Alfonso Capone came to me and Vincent over a year ago and told us he believed she was still alive. Capone had learned that the man who raised me, my mother's lover, was murdered when they were taken. But somehow, by the grace of God no less, she had managed to escape. Survive.

Alfonso knew this only because he never stopped looking for Gia Moretti, even after she was presumed dead. He never stopped looking because he never stopped loving a woman he fell for as a young man from the moment he first laid eyes on her. Much like the way I feel for my Maria. He had intended to plead for our help, but it was my mother!

It was a long shot, he had warned, but he felt like he couldn't live with himself if he didn't at least try to do anything in his power to see if she was alive. If what he was saying was the truth, long shot or not, I was more than game to take the chance.

I learned, after her kidnapping, that she never returned to Rome out of fear of Luigi. She was told by the men who took her that I was dead, murdered like the man who raised me. I was told she mourned me all these years, but never gave up hope that maybe the men were wrong. She came looking for me once, Alfonso had explained. But that was back when Luigi had me under his thumb and she quickly fled Italy, believing that he had turned her only son against her.

She's aged now, but she's still just as beautiful as I remember, and I can't help the tear that manages to fall free as she steps forward and embraces me for the first time in decades.

"Figlio mio, Oh come non ho mai smesso di pregare per te negli anni in cui siamo stati costretti a separarci."

(*My son, Oh how I've never stopped praying for you through the years we were forced apart.*)

I grab her close and breathe her in. She still smells like gardenias. Still brings me more comfort than I ever knew, besides Maria. And as she releases me and turns to my wife, I know that life can't be any sweeter than if I had forced its hand myself.

"Maria," she smiles. "You're just as beautiful as I remember from when you were a little girl."

She kisses her right cheek, and then her left, embracing her in the same tight hug she gave me a few moments before.

"I never had a daughter, but I always felt like you were the closest to having one of my own with how much I love your mother." She pulls back and smiles, my wife was evidently taken aback by this sudden revelation as I see her shaking in her arms.

"Scusami," she laughs slightly, "your mother, your father, they are the ones you should be embracing. I'm just so happy you and Leonardo ended up together. We always wished you would. Always thought the two of you would make the greatest star-crossed lovers." With a wink, she adds, "I see we were right."

"That we have, *madre*," I smile, pulling my mother to the side so Vincent and Sofia have a chance to embrace their daughter. "It's always only been, Maria. Of all people, you know that."

"Maria," Sofia cries, as she steps forward towards my wife. "I'm so sorry we kept this secret from you. I'm so sorry…"

"Sabrina?" my wife asks. "My…"

"Sister?" Nitti responds. "I'll explain everything…"

"Not now," Maria cries. "One day. But not now. I'm just so happy you're alive."

My wife takes off running into her mother's arms, her father quickly closing her in from the opposite side and embracing her between them. For the first time in my life, everything seems perfect. For the first time since I can remember, I have everything I could ever ask for and absolutely want for nothing as I watch our families finally come together. Finally unite.

Fucking blessed.

That's how I feel.

How can a man that was once so cursed become saved with the touch of one woman? One beautiful soul I don't deserve but will spend the rest of my life praising.

I let Maria have her moment with her parents, as I embrace my mother in a tight hug.

Finding my mother was not Alfonso's only problem when he came to meet with Vincent and me. Tony Nicoletti and his henchman Jack Rinaldi proved a major threat that needed to be handled. Alfonso told me of his plan to take over the family, with his help. Told me the way he had been conducting business not only in Chicago, but around the world, trying to gain traction in the mob and one day be strong enough to take over the new Don.

The bad blood between Nicoletti and I runs deep. We've

always been competing. Always racing against one another trying to rise to the top. So it wasn't that much of a surprise to me that Nicoletti had gone to Alfonso with a plan for my demise. His downfall? The love Alfonso had for my mother and an alliance he swore to me if only to ever feel like he was avenged for not protecting her in their past.

Alfonso was a man Nicoletti thought could take me out once and for all. But when Alfonso told me about how Nicoletti planned on taking out everyone that mattered most, starting with Vincent and Sofia, and ending with Maria and then myself, the solution was simple. The same way the solution presented itself with Collin in order to trick Maria.

Fake Vincent and Sofia's death. Lie about a feud. Alfonso's attempt at a takeover. With the illusion that Alfonso was not on my side, Nicoletti would turn to him, and Alfonso would in turn help take Nicoletti down in his own foolish demise.

Nicoletti won't be the last, I'm not *foolish* enough to believe that. But with the people surrounding me now, Vincent, Sofia, Maria, Gia my mother, whoever comes next doesn't stand a fucking chance.

"I'm happy for you son," my mother says a moment later as we watch the reunion unfold in front of us. "I couldn't have wanted any more for you than if I would have been there to raise you myself."

She glances at me out of the corner of her eye and smirks. "Well, maybe not everything was done to my liking, but..."

"Madre," I laugh. "Those years, they made me the man I am today. I went through hell but came out a fighter. I have the love of a beautiful woman. I have two children that look to me to guide them. I have you back in my life, raised from the dead. What more can a man ask for?"

"Francesca is *bellissimo*," my mother beams. "I rocked her to sleep waiting for you to return. Luca, he reminds me of you when you were a little boy."

I release a heavy sigh. My heart is just as heavy as it always is every time I think of my son and the troubles he will have to endure in this life. "He's troubled, *madre*."

"So were you, Leonardo." She turns to me and levels me with her smile in a way I've missed so much. "And look how good you turned out."

"That's debatable," I laugh. "You've just met my wife. I'm sure there are stories she can tell you that would completely change your blessing."

"I don't know," she smiles, turning back to face my wife. I do the same and notice her smiling back at me so beautifully it makes my once cursed heart skip a beat. "From the way she looks at you, Leonardo, you could do no wrong in her eyes. She trusts you. And you trust her. That's the secret to making your relationship survive."

Survive.

All Maria and I have ever done is survive since the moment we met all those years ago. Now, it's time for us to finally fucking live.

"*Scusami*," Alfonso's voice lightly calls out behind us a moment later. I turn with a smile, quickly shaking the hand of the man that made all of this possible.

"I'm sorry for the leg," he smirks, gesturing towards the one he stabbed with a knife all those months ago. "And the hand."

I laugh, studying the hand in question after he releases it and looking at the missing nail on my thumb.

"I've survived worse," I harass. "Can't say my mother will let you off the hook as easily for torturing her son, though."

"Ah, but it was a means to a beautiful end. No?"

He eyes my mother, a look I recognize deep in his eyes. It's the same way I look at Maria, and by the way I notice my mother looks back his way, I'd say the feeling is mutual and there's a story there I'm dying to find out one of these days. That is, if Maria doesn't unveil it first.

"I'm sorry what," my mother stutters a moment later. I glance in her direction, then in Alfonso's. When neither of them has spoken a word, I turn my back on them and figure it's best if they work the awkwardness out on their own. I smile to myself as I walk a few steps away. Besides, there are some things a son *doesn't* want to know.

"What are you smiling at," Maria teases as she walks toward me.

"My world. My fucking life. My every dream come true," I whisper, pulling her into my arms and kissing her deeply, "*il mio amante per sempre*, Mrs. Moretti." (My forever lover) She purrs in my ear and my manhood starts to stir to life. "Any objections?"

"Only a request," she pulls away and looks me in the eye. "That after this life, you find me in the next."

"In heaven, in hell, you're mine Maria," I whisper. "Forever."

THREE HOURS LATER

I GRIP her hand tightly in mine, her back is flush against my chest, my free hand grips her slender waist and a wicked smile spreads across my face as she trembles in my arms. My chin rests on her shoulder as I reach both our hands up and trace the knife across his bare flesh. His screams echo through the basement as the metal breaks into his skin, blood trickles slowly from the wound, and a sick grin pulls across my lips. Maria shivers. Her body is tight, rigid in my arms as together we stare down the man in front of us.

She's never been my weakness only my strength. We're stronger together. Always have been. Always will be.

Pressing the blade deeper into his skin, Maria sucks in a breath as blood starts to trickle faster down the shiny metal.

"From this angle," I hiss into her ear, "with one deep horizontal incision, the biggest threat to our families will be disemboweled." She trembles again in my arms but her grip under my hand tightens on the knife. "Gutted," I hiss. "His insides will fall quickly to the floor at our feet. A floor he should've kneeled on and begged for our mercy fucking decades ago."

Maria's hand slowly inches forward as she presses the blade in further. The traitor hanging from the ceiling by his arms and feet above us writhes in pain as she makes a small cut into his slimy skin. He tries to muffle a scream, but it eventually falls from his lips when she twists the blade and pressed it in further.

"Fuck, Maria," I whisper, my mouth brushing against her neck. Her spine straightens as she holds the blade against his chest. "Seeing you like this, just as vengeful as me. I thought you were my obsession before, mi Amore. Now, the way you're making me feel. It's fucking driving me insane."

"You're sick! All of you!" Giovanni hisses out as his life hangs in the balance. Quite fucking literally actually. His naked form is stripped of all he has left in this world, all the lies and deceit he's hidden behind all these years. Betrayal of the worst kind never comes from a stranger. It's always someone you know. Always someone close, trying to steal what you love most. "If only Maria would've died at the hands of her kidnappers like originally planned, none of you..."

"Would what?" My wife hisses, pressing the blade in further, making my eyes widen as she twists it again into his skin. She makes a cut deep enough to cause his disloyal blood to rush down the knife faster as it starts to trickle across my wife's wrist. But it's not deep enough to take his life. Not yet. "Would be alive?"

She tries to take a step forward, but I keep a tight grip on her, wanting to take my time with our consigliere's death. I want to draw out his suffering as he has drawn out Maria's and mine. Declan's tip ended up being correct. Daniella wasn't the only rat. In fact, turns out our families had a pest problem for fucking years. My anger rages as my mind races, tumbling fast over all that Declan told me an hour ago. All the secrets that finally unfolded as both Maria and my hand grips the blade that's bound to take Giovanni's life tonight.

"You went behind my mother's back and worked for Luigi, all those years," my wife begins to slightly cry. "You helped him kidnap her, hold her hostage as he raped her, as she cried for my father and Luigi forced her into a marriage with the Lombardi's that never should've happened. You planned Gia and her lover's death. You forced Leonardo onto the streets. What's more, you worked with Big Jim Costello, Daniella, with Nicoletti, planning to ruin us once and for all. But what you didn't plan on was Alfonso. Declan. Magnolia. Loyal people who found out the truth. Something Leo and I have grown to suspect for a long time now."

I release my hand from Maria's grip on the blade and plant a kiss on her collarbone. Loosening my grip on her frame, I give her hip a squeeze for strength as I take a step back and walk to a table across the room. As I look over my options for torture, I glance back over my shoulder and see Maria take another step forward toward the man that's been behind everything since the very beginning. A man who ruined all our lives and deserves to die a slow painful death. No mercy. No Forgiveness. Only judgment for what he caused in our lives.

"Before I gut you alive," my wife seethes, and my cock fucking twitches in my slacks.

Fuck, Dec was right. Watching my woman work has just become my fucking kryptonite.

"Tell me, Consigliere, just one fucking thing. Why?"

He hangs mute. A deep scowl on his face and defiance staring back in his eyes. When he still doesn't respond after a moment, Maria slowly pulls the blade down his chest. His teeth clench together but he doesn't scream. Just stares back in her eyes telling her silently to go to hell.

Funny, because that's exactly where we plan to send him tonight.

The cut is deep, but not deep enough to gut a man. Although I think my wife knows as I watch her enjoying his pain and I stand by, getting off on seeing her inflict a slow evil torture. She smiles, wanting to only take more suffering from a man we trusted for years. Picking up the machete knife on the table, I hold it between my teeth as I walk back towards them, rolling up my shirt sleeves as I go.

Blood drips down from Giovanni's body onto Maria's dress. She twists the knife deeper and he finally screams out but doesn't offer up the answer she seeks. Her frustration shows as she presses the blade in further, more blood gushing out on the floor at her feet.

"You know," I taunt with a grin as I make my way back to her side. Removing the blade from my teeth, I take a step forward into our man. "There are three penalties for treason where I come from."

Maria steps back, and I turn her way, stopping her with my hand on her wrist. She stares up at me and I smile, wiping

Giovanni's blood from her cheek with my thumb. Darkness fills her eyes in a way that I have never seen before. It's a look I recognize all too well from the fire that normally rages through my veins. The darkness that once filled my heart. Until she came along. It's one that looks more breathtaking on her than any I've ever seen before.

Vengeance. It's fucking sweet. And it's all ours for the taking.

"They're big into hanging," I continue, turning back to our man still hanging himself, naked, from the ceiling. His hands tied up in front of him. His feet are tied up and hanging at his back. "Drawing, quartering," I shrug, "should I let you take your pick?"

He attempts to spit in my face, but it falls at my feet. I look down and shake my head.

"Fuck you, Moretti," Giovanni seethes. "I swore allegiance to the Lombardi family before you were even born. I worked undercover for years for him, infiltrating the De Luca Family. Getting close to Sofia. Making her trust me more than anyone else. You took the same oath. An oath you broke for a fucking woman. A fucking woman. My own mother discarded me as a child. Left me for dead until the Lombardi's took me in. I'd die defending them, even after their own demise. Even when you wouldn't!"

"Personally," my nostrils flare, his words cutting deep, as I look back up into Giovanni's eyes. "I much like the way the Scandinavians handle traitors."

He eyes me as if I've gone mad. But hell, madness claimed me years ago, consigliere. If you were any good at your fucking job, you'd know that.

"The blood eagle," I hear my wife whisper behind me.

Turning, I lock eyes with her and smile. Fuck, she was made to walk by my side. And I by hers.

"That's right, mi Amore," I grin, curious as to how she knows. "Shall you do the honors, or should I?"

"Cut him down," she responds instantly.

Her eyes widen, cloud with evil, as blood fueled by the need for retribution rushes through both our veins.

My blade cuts through the rope at his feet and Giovanni starts to plead. He hangs before us now only by his hands, a fool, thinking he has a chance. We watch him with disgust as he babbles. Maria and I take a moment to regard the man that was once held so esteemed in our family's life. Letting him think there might be a way out of the web he's weaved.

Fat fucking chance.

"I'd have more respect for you after your death, Consigliere," Maria hisses, "if you'd shut the fuck up and meet your fate with your dignity still intact. Not begging for a life that you'll never have the chance at walking out that door with."

She gestures over her shoulder at the back door as I cut his hands from the ceiling and he drops to his feet.

"Please," Giovanni begins. He kneels down finally at our feet, doing something he should've done years ago, even though he still would've met the same fate. "I beg of you…"

Grabbing his hair, I pull his head back and look him in the eyes as Maria walks around my side to his back.

"Begging won't get you anywhere in life, Giovanni," I hiss. "I should know. I grew up begging. Searching. Needing to find my way back to what you took away from me." I point my blade at his chest before my eyes raise and catch my wife's over my shoulder. "My fucking lifeline."

"I had my reasons," Giovanni swallows as I hold Maria's stare. "I'm not saying what I did was right, but I had my reasons, and I..."

Maria reaches forward and quickly slices her blade across his throat. I watch as blood gushes out onto the floor in front of his knees, quickly pooling and making him kneel in a lake of his lies. His treason.

He doesn't die right away as his hands quickly go to his neck attempting to stop the inevitable. Her cut wasn't deep enough to end him in a second, but perfectly inflicted to make him die slowly as he kneels at the feet of a power he never had the chance to destroy.

Taking a step back, I look up into Maria's eyes, hand her my machete, and whisper, "finish him."

She takes a deep breath, takes one step forward, and slices into Giovanni's back severing his ribs from his spine. He attempts to scream out but can't with the cut Maria inflicted on his neck and then falls to the floor on his hands and knees. Maria raises the knife again, her hands shaking as she stares down the man that stole everything from us. I take two steps to her side, wrap my hand around hers and help her bring the blade down again through his back, slicing him open as his blood squirts up in a wave, splashing across the front of our clothes.

The machete falls to the floor. Maria takes a step back. But I'm not fucking finished.

As the life finally drains from Giovanni's body, I take a step forward, push him down onto the floor, reach inside the large cut in his back, through his severed ribs, until I reach his lungs. Yanking them from his body through the gap, forming wings that look like eagles, I twist them free and then kick his frame to the ground. To hades. To burn in hell for eternity.

Turning around, I see shock fill Maria's eyes. The darkness that once possessed her before is slightly fading. She looks down at her blood-soaked hands before glancing up at mine. Her hands begin to shake, and her bottom lip trembles as Giovanni takes his last breath. I'm at her side in an instant.

"Maria," I whisper taking her hands in mine.

I pull her into me and wrap my arms around her tightly. I've never been so brutal. Maria has never been by my side when I've unleashed torture. From the looks in her eyes, maybe this pushed her too far.

"Maria..."

"In heaven, and in hell," I hear her finally whisper a moment later. Stepping back, I keep my grip on her waist as I look her deep in the eye. "He deserved to die," she says. "He deserved to die a million more times, each time more brutal, for what he did. For the life he stole from us. For the pain he caused."

My bloodied hand comes up and brushes a tear that's quickly falling from her eye. I lift her in my arms and she wraps her legs around my waist. Walking slowly towards the exit, she nestles her mouth next to my ear.

"I love you, Leonardo Moretti," she breathes causing chills to sweep down my spine.

"I love you, Maria Moretti," she raises off my shoulder and looks me in the eyes. "For fucking eternity, mi Amore. In heaven, in hell..."

"You're mine," she whispers as her lips find mine in a tender kiss. She pulls back and stares me in the eyes and my heart aches.

"Forever."

Blood soaks our clothes, stains our hands, her face, but I swear I've never seen her look more beautiful knowing she loves me like I love her. That she'll fight by my side. In this life. Through our days of heaven, and any days of hell that could come our way. I made a promise to a girl a long time ago. One I'll never break. One I'll forever keep. In this life, and our next.

CHAPTER 27

LEONARDO

ONE YEAR LATER

"Face the wall and raise your skirt," I hiss out as I force Maria to turn around. "Bend over and show me that pretty pussy."

She immediately does as I say and my cock hardens painfully as I step up behind her. She's not wearing any panties. Taking the liberty, I stick two fingers at her clit and run them back slowly, entering her wet cunt and feeling it clench down around me.

"Leo please," she purrs.

But she's been teasing me for hours since we left the house. I wanted to wine and dine my wife. Spend time with her that we don't normally have the luxury to spend together. I wanted to enjoy her. Slowly. But knowing she's been bare underneath her skirt for hours, watching her lick her lips as she ate dessert, and then having her stroke me under the table while she finished has made it damn near impossible.

"I like it when you beg, Maria," I whisper. Her pussy clenches, grows wetter, and I smile. "Tell me what you want," my fingers slip out of her cunt and roll back across her ass, "when you want it."

I drop to my knees and force her legs apart with my palms. Breathing her in, my dick painfully needs a release, but she comes first. Always.

Kissing the inside of her right thigh, I blow against her center, the sexiest moan escaping her lips at the sensation, and then place another kiss on her left inner thigh. Admiring what's mine, my mouth waters as I slowly lick her seam apart before sticking my tongue inside her tight walls.

She lets out a small scream as I pinch her nub with my fingers, rolling it around between them before caressing her up and down, back and forth, matching the rhythm of my tongue in her center.

"Oh God," she groans.

"God's not here, mi Amore," I say, pulling back and running her wetness back across her ass. She squirms as I stick my fingers back in her sex. "Which is good, because what I want to do to your body would keep me out of heaven, send me straight to hell, and I'd never be sorry. Not when I remember the taste of your sweet pussy exploding on my tongue."

Rising to my feet, I instruct her to stand and then pick her up in my arms, carrying her to the bed. She makes quick work of unbuttoning my slacks, slipping my dress shirt off my body, and ridding me of my clothes. I do the same to her. Taking time to run my finger across her hardened nipples as I pull her shirt over her head, trail them inside her dripping center as I pull her skirt from her waist.

I push her back against the bed and climb on top of her, upside down, my cock brushing against her lips as I take her pussy back in my mouth. With greed, she starts to suck me off. Swirling her tongue around the tip. Taking the length all the way down to the back of her throat. Sliding her hand fast up and down my shaft.

"Tell me when to stop," Maria says as she takes a breath right before she takes my cock in her mouth again and sucks the crown like she's working her tight mouth around the tip of a fucking lollipop.

"Fuck, you keep sucking my dick like that, and I won't make you stop."

She gags. *Fucking beautiful.* And I swear I almost blow my load.

"Wider," I demand, bracing myself above her with one arm as she lays upside down beneath me. She complies, her legs and her mouth opening as I thrust inside her hot lips again at the same time that I force two fingers inside her pussy.

She groans around my cock and I hiss out from the sensation. "Maria," I moan, "with your mouth full of dick how the hell will I ever be able to hear what I crave most, mi Amore. The way you fucking scream my name."

My mouth closes over her clit just as I thrust my hips down and my fingers deep inside her again. She cries out around my length, and it only fuels me. Over and over again I take what I want from her. Her hot mouth. Her tight pussy.

When she lifts her hips wanting more, I roll my fingers back over her ass and enter one finger inside her.

She squirts in my mouth seconds later, her screams muffled by my cock in her mouth. Her jaw closes tighter as I thrust in between her lips. She struggles and screams as her orgasm rushes through her, but I don't let up, only fuck her mouth harder as I drink up every last drop of her cum.

When her screams turn to muffled moans, I pull my finger out of her ass and lick her slit tenderly. She squirms and I fucking smile. Pulling my cock finally from her lips and turning around to cage her in on the bed, she looks up at me with so much desire.

"Fuck, we needed this."

I rub my cock up her slit, still swollen and tender from her orgasm as I take her tit in my mouth. I mumble my agreement because I'm too busy enjoying my wife to stop and respond. Her body is mine to do with as I like for the next forty-eight hours - uninterrupted. The grandparents have taken the children. I've put my first in command in charge, and I've secretly flown my wife off to Sicily, where we boarded my yacht. The one we spent that first week on a couple of years ago.

My fingers find her sex as she grinds up into my palm. She moans again as I enter one, then two fingers back inside her and curl them deeply, pulling out slowly and rubbing her just how I know she likes it. She mumbles my name just as I capture her lips and kiss her desperately, like a man dying of thirst. A thirst that will never be quenched as I feel the need to taste her pussy once again rise inside of me.

"If you don't fill me full of your cock soon," my wife purrs as I stroke her deep, hard, deliberately with the need to bring her to another orgasm, "I swear I will never let you go down on me first again."

I laugh into the side of her neck, knowing she's so full of shit because she loves the way she feels against my tongue just as much as I love the taste of her there.

"Is this what you want," I whisper, fisting my dick and rubbing it against her clit. She bucks her hips, trying to get me to enter her, but I anticipate it and slightly rub my crown through her folds.

"I want to hear you beg, Mrs. Moretti," I taunt with a slight growl. "Just because you came once, doesn't mean I'll stop torturing you in so many sweet ways." She tries to grab my hips and force me against her, but I pull back and spank her pussy which earns me a scream. "Accept your punishment like a good girl, Maria," I tease, seconds before I lift her, spin her around, and force her down on her stomach against the cool sheets.

Smacking her ass hard, she bucks back against me, but I pin her still and run my finger along her ass cheeks.

"Cheeks blushed and pussy wet, Maria," I groan, dipping lower into her hot folds and feeling her clench around my finger. "You like that, don't you, my dirty little girl," she screams as I pull my fingers back and force three fingers inside her ass, stretching wide.

"How do you think my cock is going to fit in this tight hole if you can't take three fingers?"

"I've taken your dick before," she tosses back over her shoulder which earns her another smack across the ass.

"Not for a while, mi Amore," I kiss down her back,

removing my hand and spreading her cheeks wide. "Fuck I can't resist your juicy cunt."

Like a fiend, I stick my tongue deep inside her. She spreads her legs wider, granting me access to do as I please and God, I take all I want and more.

Her second orgasm approaches quickly, too quickly, and I pull away from her before I've had enough. I'm completely unsatisfied with having to stop so soon. Smacking her across her red cheeks, I grip her hair in my hand and pull her back towards me.

"You don't cum again until I say so."

"I can't stop myself," she whines. "I need... I want..." she grinds herself back against me and I get lost in the feeling of her slick ass wanting more, needing more from me.

"You want to cum?" I tease, my fingers dancing across her hip, dipping lower until they meet her clit. "You need to cum, Maria?"

"Please, Oh God, please, Sir."

"I'll let you come, mi Amore," I whisper in her ear. "After you ride my fucking face. I want you cuming down the back of my throat, Maria. And I don't want you to stop until I've had enough."

I climb further onto the bed and she does the same, straddling me until she reaches the headboard and her pussy sits right above my face.

Tracing a finger through her folds, she shivers and I glance up to meet her eye. "Don't. Fucking. Look. Away." My lips close over her clit and she obeys perfectly. Sucking down slowly, deeply, her mouth falling open as she screams slightly.

Releasing her pussy, I hiss, "Good girl. Now, ride my fucking tongue until I tell you to stop."

"How will you tell me..."

I smack her across the ass and she complies immediately, my mouth devouring her wet center. My tongue slips between her folds as my hands roam around to her ass. I grab her tighter against me, the friction giving her just what she needs as she grips the headboard above me and continues to stare into my eyes. When she's close, I slide my finger in her ass and feel both her holes clench down around me.

Her second climax is stronger than the first as she tries to pull back and stop it. I pull her tighter against me, and she never looks away from my eyes. She's still coming when I pull my finger from her and slip out from underneath her. Her orgasm is relentless on letting go, and fuck, I wouldn't have it any other way.

Forcing her forward, I thrust inside her tight walls and they clench down harder around me than ever before.

"Fuck," we both grit out in unison.

"How many times do you think we can do this tonight?" she asks breathlessly as I thrust her body down against the sheets.

"How many times do you think your pussy can take it?"

She doesn't respond as we find ourselves lost in the carnal need to just *feel alive* as our bodies slap against each other over and over again. As I thrust up inside her, forever marking her as my own. Her pussy tightens, a warning she's close.

"Not yet, Maria," I warn as I punish her flesh harder, faster, more urgently, bringing us both closer to the edge.

"Please," she pleads.

I pick up my pace, gripping her hips tightly. My balls tighten, my mind clouds, and the last thing I hear is my voice whispering, "now."

Our climax sends us both over the edge at the same time. Becoming one has never felt more fucking perfect as I spill myself inside her and her wetness pools, her tight cunt tightens, and she releases around me.

I collapse on top of her a moment later, too spent to pull myself from inside her tight walls. Kissing down her back, I think back to that girl I met all those years ago and the one thing she told me that brought me hope when I had none. Something she said that brought me life when I didn't believe I deserved it.

"*La vita e' bella*," I hear her sigh, almost as if she could read my mind. Amazed, I pull out and roll to my side, gathering her in my arms.

"Sei bello, amore," I whisper. "Our life is beautiful, as long as you're by my side."

"You and me," she sighs, placing her hand against my heart and looking deep into my eyes.

"You and me, Maria. I made a promise to you a long time ago. I love you," I say, staring deep into her eyes. "And I'll die doing what I have to. To protect you and our family, always. And never stop."

EIGHTEEN YEARS LATER

"I KNOW what I have to do," Luca grits out. "Stop treating me like a fucking child and maybe, *according to you*, I won't act like one."

"This is your first job on your own, Son," I hiss back. "I just want to make sure you don't get in over your head."

"Yeah right," he snaps. "Guarantee, if it were Massimo, you wouldn't be thinking twice." His anger rages as he talks about his younger brother. The fire builds to a feverish high in his eyes, reminding me of myself at his age. "You trust him with everything, yet you're always on me like I'm going to fuck everything up."

"I don't play favorites."

"Tell that to *Madre*, she knows..."

"More than anyone," I cut him off, " your mother knows that I would never put one of my children before the other.

It's your hot head and quick fucking temper that'll always get you into trouble. Get you killed, Luca."

He levels me with an icy stare as Maria and Francesca walk into the room. The presence of my wife softens me. Maybe I have always been a little too protective of my first-born. Maybe I have always looked out for him a little more because of his disabilities as a child.

But that doesn't mean that I don't trust him with a job.

That doesn't mean he isn't first in command when I'm not around.

And that also doesn't mean I am not stepping down at the end of the year and handing my empire over to him, regardless of the fact that it feels like Luca and his younger brother have been fighting for the title of Don ever since Massimo was born.

In the past, I believed differently, that only Maria and my own son could take my empire. But he has her blood running through his veins too. More than that, he's *our* son. We love him the same as we love our other two children. He will take my place. And I will make sure he's more than ready to do so before I ever hand over my fucking kingdom.

"Be honest," my son seethes. "You wish it were him, and not your bastard son who's still disabled in more ways than one."

"Hey," I shout a little too loud, causing my wife and daughter to flinch from their spot across the room. I glance their way before stepping into Luca and whispering under my breath. "What I do with our family's legacy is *my* choice. *My children are all equal.* You were born first before I met your mother. But regardless, you are your mother and I's child. Period. I don't ever want to hear you refer to yourself as a bastard again. And I don't ever want to hear you give your weakness any strength. You are not your disabilities."

His jaw sets in stone as he stares angrily into my eyes. "My past will always define me."

"Only if you let it," I snap.

His jaw ticks. His nostrils flare. Shouldering past me, he says, "Hard to ignore it when it's always staring back in my fucking face. Do you think I can't do the job? Call your backup, Massimo. We both know you always have him ready on speed dial. He's the real prince of this fucking family. I'm just the joker, a fool to ever think I could fill his shoes."

He storms out of the room as my eyes lift and catch Maria's. She studies me, searching my eyes, wondering if we should go after him. I give her a slight shake of my head telling her, no, and her stance softens, worry filling her eyes a moment later as she walks closer to me and her gaze drops to the floor.

It's no use going after him when he is like this. Through the years we've learned sometimes Luca is better off being left alone. He takes more time than I ever did to cool his temper. The only way to avoid a fight is to let him have all the time he needs to settle down. Bring the fire that always storms inside down to a simmer. No need in pushing him, because I know the bitterness he wrestles with well. I've also seen a side of him that rivals my darkest past. For that, I'll give him all the time he needs before he ends up doing something he might one day regret.

It's hard enough to walk through this life as it is. He

308 / EVELYN MONTGOMERY

stands to inherit a power this family has never seen before. For that, he needs to be ready. Regrets will only weigh him down.

"No wonder Ella broke up with him," my daughter huffs, as she saunters across the room and flops herself on the couch. "He's always been a moody son-of-a-bitch..."

"Francesca!"

"No offense Mom," she shrugs, "but lately he's been a tyrant."

"When did that happen?" I attempt to enquire covertly as my daughter pulls up her phone and is immediately distracted by something on the screen. I wait her out for a response, a few minutes later, the silence finally registers that she's missed something as Francesca glances up at me over the back of the couch.

"Huh? Oh! Um, last week I think."

I steal a glance at Maria who looks just as worried as I feel and then focus back on our daughter. We both know what happened last week, and we both worried it might push him over the edge.

"Yeah, it was the night we all went out to the new club uptown," my daughter continues. "God, he was *so* in love with her, I don't know what got into him or what happened. The way he was talking earlier that day, it was like she was the one you know? And then wham! He flipped a switch as only Luca can. I don't know all of how it happened. But when I walked out front to see where they both had gone, she was screaming in his face and he was just standing there, motionless. Cold. Turned off. Dead to all she was saying. All she was accusing him of. Kinda weird, right?"

Her attention immediately goes back down to the device in her hand as *my* attention casts on my wife. A second later, Massimo enters the den, looking over his shoulder with animosity. He no doubt had just run into his brother in the hallway.

I give Maria a look, one that says we'll talk about it later. She nods and walks towards me, pausing briefly to grab my hand in hers and give it a little squeeze, a symbol just between the two of us throughout the years for us both to be strong. She continues towards the bar in the far corner of the room and pours us each a drink.

Our life isn't always easy, but walking side by side all these years has made the bad days good, the long nights shorter, and the years full of as much joy and love as possible.

We're stronger together. Always have been. Always will be.

"What's up Cheska," Massimo calls out when his eyes land on his sister.

When he was younger, he never could say her full name, Francesca. Cheska was an easy compromise, and it's stuck throughout the years. They're closer in age than her and Luca, Massimo having been born only one year after our daughter.

Our children are our entire world. We've built our life every day with their future in mind. We planned for a large family, but when complications arose during childbirth with Massimo, we decided we were blessed enough and kept our circle small.

"Hey Mo," Francesca greets him, still not looking up from her phone. He gives her head a gentle push as he sits down on

310 / EVELYN MONTGOMERY

the edge of the couch, and she sticks her tongue out at him in response.

I feel Maria at my side as I take in my children's sibling exchange. Taking the tumbler from her hands as she lifts her glass of wine to her lips, I pull her to my side and tighten my grip on her waist. Maria looks up at me and smiles making my world right again with her tucked closely into my side.

"The south-side job's complete," my son tells me as he stops pestering his sister. "Couple fuckers wanted to make it a little more difficult than necessary. But I took care of it."

Massimo is only seventeen, but he's been taking on jobs for me, helping out the capos in command since he was fifteen. He's a lot older in age mentally than his years. Physically he's tougher than most men I have on payroll. It's always been a sore spot between him and his brother, and another reason why Luca sometimes sees himself as only a weakness to this family instead of the heir Maria and I know him to be.

"I trust there were no..."

"Witnesses?" He rolls his eyes before rolling up his left dress sleeve. "Nah, but those fuckers got a few decent jabs in before I made sure of it."

His arm is bandaged, and he unwraps it gently, revealing a deep cut across his forearm. Maria rushes to his side to mother him. Francesca studies it a moment, and gives a disgusted look the next, returning her attention to her phone.

From where I'm standing, the cut doesn't look deep enough for worry. Not that I would. I have never babied our children, especially our boys, and don't plan on starting now.

Besides, the tattooed sleeves climbing up both of his arms will more than hide most any scar that might happen to him over the years.

"I'll take a guess and say those cunts are no longer breathing?"

Maria gives me a disapproving look over her shoulder as she gently takes his arms in her hand, examining the wounds. She doesn't like me swearing around the kids. Never has. Especially using words like *cunt*.

Words I know she likes whispered in her ear as I fuck her pussy every night like it's the first time.

I usually obey that one house rule. But today, Luca's temper tantrum, Massimo's condition, and a few loose ends I still need to tie up with my business, have me a little on edge.

"There's not a piece of those fucker's left to be found, breathing or not, does that answer your question?"

Massimo hisses out as Maria touches the stitches and then starts to rewrap his arm. Turning his attention back to his sister, he says, "going out to Fourth Street tonight, Cheska. You game?"

"Stella going to be there?" she huffs, attention still on her phone as she rapidly sends off a text.

"Fuck yeah, you know my girl..."

"Pass!"

She rises off the couch and elbows him as she starts to walk out of the room. He taunts her by raising his fist, jaw clenched, ready for a fight. But the smirk that falls across his face a moment later gives him away. Plus, we all know he'd never actually hit a woman. If there is one thing I've made

312 / EVELYN MONTGOMERY

sure of, it was to make sure I raised my sons right. My daughter hurries off in my direction, grabbing me into a hug, kissing my cheek quickly, and then her mother's, before scurrying off towards the door.

"Where are you going?" I shout after her as she saunters out into the night.

"Out!"

"With who?" Maria calls.

"Friends!"

I eye Massimo who sits motionless for a brief second before rolling his eyes and rising.

"Yeah, yeah, I know. Watch her. I got it."

"That involves actually watching," I hiss. "Not getting your cock sucked in the back seat of my Bugatti while she manages to sneak off again."

"Leo!" Maria snaps.

"But the broad had such nice cock-sucking lips," my son shrugs with a mischievous grin as he walks toward us.

"Massimo!"

He laughs. "Love you, Mom," he places a kiss on her cheek. "Dad," he nods, strutting past like he owns the fucking world. A piece of it at least, and I laugh knowing he fucking does. "Don't do anything that I wouldn't do."

Which isn't saying much considering we're both cut from the same cloth. Both my sons are opposites. One resembling the darker side of my youth. The youngest, the man I became.

Turning, I face my wife and raise my glass to my lips. Her eyes dance with mischief as she puts her hands on her hips and smiles. It's the same breathtaking smile that I fell in love with all those years ago and my heart tightens in my chest as I fall more in love with her with each second that ticks by in our life together.

She's older now, as am I. Her hair is slightly graying at the temples, matching my own. There are laugh lines around her eyes when she smiles, only making her more beautiful, and filling me with pride knowing I'm the one who put them there.

I shoot back my bourbon in one drink and wrap my arm around her waist, pulling her into me and quickly setting my glass down on the table next to us.

"La vita e bella, mi amore," I whisper into the curve of her neck. "You've made it beautiful."

"I couldn't have walked through life without you, Leo," she smiles as I pull back and place a tender kiss against her lips. "You're my beginning and my end. Everything I need today, tomorrow, forever."

"You and me, Maria," I breathe, as my lips descend on hers once again. "In this life and our next. Our love knows no boundaries. In heaven and in hell, you're mine, Amore. Forever.

THE END

Read Declan & Magnolia's novella by clicking below.
Buy Now!

Want more from this dark & dominant world?
Who would you like to see next?

Luca, Massimo, Francesca - Collin?

Join my ARC Team and cast your vote by leaving your post/comment in my EM Hipster's group on Facebook.

Join Now!

PROLOGUE

ROSE

ONE. Two. Three.

Breathe.

I will the voices to stop. The ones that haunt me day and night and every second in between. I hear my daughter's cry echoed by my son's laughter in the front room, and I know I need to go out there. I know, as their mother, I need to make sure everything is alright, but damn it if I can't pull myself up off this floor in the tiny closet me and Michael used to call our own.

I look up and see his fatigues. Tears prick the back of my eyes as a burn quickly rises in my chest.

It's not possible.

A little more than 6 months later and I still can't believe

he is never coming back. He's never coming home to me, our son, and will never get the chance to meet his daughter who was born just three short weeks after his passing.

The noises from the front room grow louder, but I'm crippled, paralyzed, by the deafening silence inside me as I softly fall apart on the floor.

I realize it's quiet in my mind for the first time in hours as fear grips my soul knowing the peace can't last forever, but the noises that rage out in the living room have me finally pushing myself up off the carpet and slowly, reluctantly, putting one foot in front of the other. Breathe, Rose, just breathe – I tell myself, but the tremble in my hands as I walk a few steps forward restrains me to the truth. I'm a prisoner, and I doubt I'll ever truly be free. Rounding the corner, the scene that unfolds makes me wish I could turn right back around and continue to hide where I finally found peace, if only for a few seconds.

Worthless.

You have to hide from your own children?

What kind of fucked up mother are you?

Michael would be so ashamed.

I shake my head and try to will the voice to stop. The taunting, haunting monologue that cripples me daily ceases, for just a moment, as I blink back the tears that fill my eyes and make my way over to Olivia in her highchair. She's hanging over the edge, screaming at the top of her lungs, while her little brother, Liam, spins in circles in front of her with his favorite truck making all sorts of loud noises.

Wiping my eyes as a few tears fall free, I pick her up and try and steady my nerves. Quiet. The voices are quiet. But for how long, I wonder, as anxiety kicks in and I walk with my screaming daughter in my arms to sit in Michael's favorite recliner. My tears fall harder as I clutch my daughter to my chest, attempting to soothe her, and swear, I can almost smell him, hear him, feel him in the small house we used to call our home. A small house that has fallen into disrepair as I've lost more than I care to admit since he's been gone, and pray our situation doesn't get worse, for my children's sake. They deserve better. They deserve, a life I'm scared I'll never be able to give them.

After Michael's passing, his life insurance policy went to his mother. A devil of a woman, who took it to support her needs, such as railing blow up her nose any chance she gets. Her grandkids are the furthest thing from her mind.

I didn't need the money. Or, at least, I thought I didn't. Nothing could replace what I lost. But our kids... I shake my head not wanting to think about how losing Michael has made them lose so much more than I ever would have imagined. I look around this small living room, with stained carpet, wallpaper peeling, and a few holes in the drywall, and wonder if this place will ever feel like a home again.

Between the demons that fill my head, the emptiness that crowds these four walls daily, nightly, and the loneliness and load I am forced to carry alone with our two children will never make it a happy home - not ever. Not like it once was.

The walls close in on me. The thoughts get louder. My daughter's relentless cry and my son's piercing laughter meld together until I feel like I can't take anymore.

Maybe you shouldn't take anymore.

Maybe you should end it.

For yourself, your daughter, your son.

Put you all out of your misery.

Come over to where it's finally quiet. In the darkness. Where it won't hurt any longer.

My body shakes. Goosebumps rise up my arms. I look down at my daughter and wonder what the fuck is wrong with me? More importantly, what the fuck is wrong with my head?

Make it stop! Please someone make it stop! I rock back and forth as I silently beg myself to be stronger, to be more powerful than the invisible chains that bind me to insanity. A force I can't shake and worry I never will.

I'm alone, in life, in my mind, with no one to pull me through but myself. A strong realization that hits me harder than it ever has before as my body feels like it's about to be sick. It's a sudden understanding that's more influential than anyone might ever know. On wobbly feet, I sniffle as wipe away more tears and force myself to rise out of the chair. Making my way to the TV stand across the room, I retrieve Olivia's pacifier. With shaky hands, I place it between her lips and sway back and forth hushing her in my arms.

Just a few seconds of quiet, please, I beg of you – I plead with my own mind. Not even registering the fact that it has been quiet, I've just spent so much time dreading the return I haven't even realized it. But as if the sudden recognition flipped a switch, I swear I can feel it crawling like venom out of the darkness right before it steals away my light.

What is wrong?

You can't take being a mother?

You knew when you signed up for this shit what it would take!

I thought all you ever dreamed of was to be a mother?

What a joke!

You can't even stop your daughter from crying!

"Stop it!" I hiss out quietly through heated breath, trying to talk some sense into myself.

I am not going crazy, I am totally fine, I tell myself. It is just the loss, the pregnancy, the realization that I will forever be alone with no one to help me. To stand by me. To be my partner. To pull me through like I need to pull myself together to take care of my children, take care of myself, and my family.

I look at the clock and see the time. Damn it! I have 30 minutes to get myself and the kids ready, get them to daycare that I can't afford, in a shitty neighborhood Michael would roll over in his grave if he ever saw, and somehow get to my new job, and then pretend like the voices are not ruling my damn life. A new job I need like crazy as the bills continue to pile and the only family I have to turn to is a distant Aunt who lives three hours away. I avoided all of our friends after Michael's funeral, and I wouldn't blame them if they never wanted to talk to me ever again. But I don't allow myself to linger on why as the heaviness of my choices weighs on me and I start to walk towards the bedroom to lay Olivia down, then step on one of Liam's Legos in the process.

"Fucking hell!" I yell out in a loud shriek.

"Fucking hell!" Liam echoes.

I turn around quickly and look at my son with wide eyes, totally forgetting about the searing pain in my foot until it begins to throb so hard, I'd swear I punctured through the sole of my foot. Are you kidding me right now? I sternly stare at him, knowing I should reprimand him, tell him he can't say those words, as more tears spill over and I'm momentarily stunned to silence.

"Fucking hell! Fucking hell!" He begins to yell as he runs around the living room with his truck in his hand.

"No, baby, don't..." I try to force the mother out inside me, but my thoughts are cut off as the voices start again.

Pathetic.

You call that being a good mother?

Michael would divorce you so quick for the shitty excuse for a parent you've become.

"I didn't mean to," I cry softly in the space around me, pleading with the voice, as I fall against the wall behind me and drop to the floor. Olivia's pacifier falls out in the process and her loud shrill yell somehow rises above my son shouting the phrase over and over again as he swings his arms around the room.

I look up at the time and see I know have 25 minutes to get my shitty life together and somehow make it to my first day of work.

I won't make it, I tell myself as I close my eyes and feel cursed. I can't. Not today.

Call in sick.

Stay home.

Stay where no one can see the mess you've become.

The fucked-up excuse of a woman you've let yourself be.

You call what you're doing mourning?

You never had what it took to be a wife. A mother. You're just now finding out the truth!

"Stop it," I say a little louder to myself, as my son still spins in circles. "Stop it," I yell louder, but the chills spreading over my skin drag me under with them. The dread the voice will begin again sets in. Fear rises in my chest. Anxiety at an all-time high. "Stop it!" I yell as loud as I can.

Quiet!

I open my eyes in shock to see my son stop abruptly, thinking I am talking to him. Tears fill his eyes. Oh, God! His cry quickly matches Olivia's in my arms as he stands in front of me, his screams getting louder, and I realize the voices are right. I am a fucked-up mother, and I don't deserve them, either of them.

Told you. Pitiful. What a waste of life.

***

JUSTIN

Leaves crunch under my feet as I make my way into the town I now call home. I don't know what's more pathetic, the fact that I can't keep my shit together after deployment to stay around the little family I have left, or the fact that I am now forced to walk to work on this cold, wet, rainy October day because I left everything behind in Knoxville a few months back and promised myself I'd never look back. A desperate attempt to not be reminded of the horror that fills in my past.

They teach you how to fight. They never teach you how to come home.

322 / EVELYN MONTGOMERY

I shake my head and look up at the sky, at the sun peeking through the clouds. I watch, dazed, as it glistens off the puddles the morning rain left on the street below my feet as I make my way towards Ball Ground, Georgia. I feel the air leave my lungs in a heavy sigh as I force my mind to be at peace. The nightmares can't haunt me here. Not if I don't let them.

Pulling my jacket closer around my waist as a harsh wind blows past, I shove my hands deep into my pockets, warding off the chill, and find my mind searching, calculating, trying to stay busy so I don't think of all I left behind as I wonder just how much further it is into downtown where my new office is located. I've walked it a few times before, having only recently taken an editor position at the local newspaper, but damn if it doesn't feel like it's taking forever this morning when the chill outside matches the eerie thoughts that still try to rule my mind.

Glancing up once again at the cloudy sky, I breathe in deep as I try and force myself to continue to master my silence. Having turned off my old cell phone, selling my car for cash, and explaining to my publisher fragments of my past, just enough so he knows I don't want to be found without causing concern, silence is all I know, and in it, I find the most comfort I've had in years. I know all too well what some would give up completely to achieve this kind of peace. Feeling the reality of that all too well as ghosts from my past try to resurface, I force them back, having been forced to come to terms with my own personal demons a long-time ago, at least that is what I keep telling myself. One thing the Navy Seals taught me was the damn 40% rule. The only damn thing that has kept me sane through all life's unfortunate ups and downs.

When your mind is telling you you're done, you're actually only 40% done.

Hell if that ain't the damn truth.

Nearing a bend in the road, I pause to pull my coat tighter as a wind comes up out of the north but come to a complete stop when I hear a loud scream followed by a louder cry coming from the house in front of me. My senses alerted, I train my ear to listen to the sound and finally realize it was a baby's cry. No big deal, right? But just as I'm about to continue on my way, I hear another yell. A woman. A little quiet at first, but the damn words her beautiful voice shouts next ring loud and clear through my ears, calling to a place deep inside me I tried to forget about a long time ago.

"Stop it!"

My feet have a mind of their own as I jump the little fence separating me from the front door of the tiny house and quickly take the stairs two at a time as I climb up the front steps. Powered by a force unknown to me, I don't bother to knock as I plow against the door and it swings wide open, nearly falling off its hinges and banging against the wall behind it. I look frantically to my right and see nothing. A glance to my left and I lock eyes with a woman who has fallen against the wall, clutching her small infant tight. A young boy, a few years old, maybe three or five, stands in front of her with wide eyes and a tear-stained face as he takes me in.

In two short strides, I am at the woman's side. She rises off the floor and flinches when I come near before trying to back away but the all behind her stops her movements as she bumps into it. Raising my hands to show her I mean no harm, her eyes pull me in and for a brief moment, I get the sensation that she is drowning in me just as much as I find myself over-whelmed by her. Gently, I clutch her shoulders in my hands and force myself to speak.

"Ma'am, are you alright?" but she doesn't say a word, just stares at me with those wide, blue, breathtaking eyes, and I swear my heart skips a beat.

It has to be the adrenaline.

I hear a cry behind me and turn to see the little boy scared, stepping back in fear as I release my grip on his moth-er's shoulders. He looks terrified, and it pulls to a place in my past I thought I'd never feel the sting of again.

"Don't worry," I say, turning and kneeling to his level as I force my own fear to subside. "I am not going to hurt you."

His sobs slow to a whimper a little, and I thank God for that because between his crying, the screams of the tiny baby in his mother's arms, and the look in his mother's eyes I don't think I could take much more. Turning back to the woman beside me, I notice a look of concern creep across her face as a shiver breaks out across her skin. Breaking our stare, I glance into the bedroom just beyond where she's standing as rage boils inside me wondering where the bastard is that she must be afraid of.

"Where is he?" I demand harshly on instinct and catch the slightest flinch in her posture out of the corner of my eye as the words leave my mouth.

Glancing back her way, her eyes look confused, and it throws me off slightly, but I continue anyway as I make my way into the bedroom and take a good look around. Peering into the bathroom and closet, I stand in the middle of her bedroom and do a 360 looking for any signs of danger as my mind tells my heart to slow down. I come back to the living room just as the woman clutches her son to her right side, her baby protectively swaddled in her tight grip on her left. She stares at me puzzled before releasing her son only for a moment to put a pacifier back in her daughter's mouth which finally succeeds in making the crying stop. Thank God! Her son burrows his face into her leg, and I watch as he sniffles and tries to hide his tears.

I take long strides across the room to the other side of the house and glance in the only other room this tiny shack has to offer. Boy's toys are thrown everywhere, and I have to side-step my way through the mess to make sure no one is hiding in the kid's closet.

Nothing.

Equally confused, I come back out to the living room and take a look in the small kitchen before finally meeting the eyes of the woman in the corner when I am confident there is no one around. She questions me with those damn eyes that pull to a place inside me I'd rather forget, the place her voice called to minutes ago, but the fear that once filled her blue irises is gone. With her baby clutched to her chest and her son at her side, her posture seems to slowly soften.

Then I see it.

My eyes dart past her to the mantel on the fireplace. The symbol, half the battle I've been running from, stares back at me and pierces my heart like the first time I was forced to accept it. The folded flag. The dog tags. The picture in a frame next to an urn. My eyes dart back to hers quickly, questions hanging between us that are best left unanswered, but it doesn't escape me that she saw where I looked, she knows that I know. She straightens her spine, as only a soldier's wife could, and stands tall.

I nod my head before standing straight, my spine stiff, my eyes downcast to the floor. With tears building, my throat and chest tight with emotion, and confident that she is in no danger, I look up and slowly salute her. I watch as she fights back tears before giving me a sad nod, a silent exchange between the two of us that needs no words. I look to the floor again and swallow over the lump in my throat, unable to meet her eyes once more.

"Thank you for your service," I whisper just as a soft cry escapes her lips.

Turning on my heels, I leave quickly and slam the door behind me, taking the steps down her front porch just as fast as before, propelled by something else entirely to put space between the things I see, know and feel behind me. I know all too well the demons she faces, and hell if I can fight hers after surviving mine.

ALSO BY EVELYN MONTGOMERY

All books in the
Can't Help Falling In Love Series
can be read as standalone novels, with the
exception of Book 1 & Book 2, which should be
read in order.

The Can't Help Falling In Love Series:
Book 1 | Indecision
Buy Now

Book 2 | Devotion
Buy Now

Book 3 | Reckless
Buy Now

Book 4 | Rebellion

Buy Now

Book 5 | Deliverance
Buy Now

Book 6 | Catch
Buy Now

Peaches
A standalone RomCom
Buy Now

The Dominant Love Duet:
Book 1 | Amico
Buy Now

Book 2 | Amante
Buy Now

Atonement | A Novella
Declan & Magnolia's Story
Buy Now

The Love Conquers All Trilogy
Book 1 | Resurrection
Buy Now

Books 2 & 3
are currently being written

and will be released in 2022.

Join my -
Facebook group &
Mailing List
for news on future releases.

Born and raised in California, Evelyn Montgomery now resides in Central Kentucky with her husband and three children. Writing all types of romance, her novels include love stories that revolve around contemporary, suspenseful, thriller, psychological, comedy and much more.
One thing readers can always expect when reading one of her books is a twist somewhere between the pages they'd never see coming. With over 10 novels currently published, her goal is to keep producing a fictional world that isn't forced, but genuine, heartfelt, and desirable.
To keep in contact, follow Evelyn on one of the platforms below.

Website

Facebook

Instagram

TikTok

Twitter

Mailing List
FB Group

Please consider leaving a review.
I LOVE to read reviews from readers!
Both good & bad,
my heart melts with your kind words,
and I use your criticism to improve on my next big idea.
In this world today,
indie authors are nothing
without the reviews you, the reader, give us.
Please consider leaving a review on
any platform you use.
I'd love to read your thoughts!